# FOREST GUARDIAN CHRONICLES
# BLUE'S WAR

## BETH ROOSE

*Blue's War*



Published by Red Penguin Books

Bellerose Village, New York

Library of Congress Control Number: 2021905791

ISBN

Print 978-1-63777-042-9

Digital 978-1-63777-043-6



This is a work of fiction and any resemblance to any person, institution or organization alive or dead is purely coincidental.

Boston Mills
Ski Run
Wheatley Road
Bridal Falls
Blue Heron Rookery
Everett Cover Bridge
ukwudgie Camp
Everett Road
Everett
Szlays Farm
Indigo Lake
Iale Farm
Oak Hill Road
Grissom Farm

Bigfoot Camp
Blue Hen Falls
Oak Hill Road
Everett
Cuyahoga River
Cuyahga Valley Scenic Railroad
an's Lab
Urbank Christmas Tree Farm
Train Depot
Ledges
er Lic Cave
Ice Box Cave

# CONTENTS

## Cleg

The Bigfoot Leader of the Hairy Tribe of the Forest. He is 9 feet tall with black & brown long fur. He was husband to Ja'al and is dad to Bitty. He is full of compassion and the ability to love deeply. Most think he is loyal. He is also a skilled hunter.

## Ja'al

Cleg's late wife and mother to Bitty. She is 8 feet tall with red & black long fur. She had exceptional critical thinking skills. Her skills also included the art of negotiation and the ability to work not only with the tribe but with the Pukwudgie and humans. She felt that it was her responsibility to teach others to be open to new ideas.

## Bitty

Cleg and Ja'al's daughter. She is 4 feet tall with light brown long fur. Bitty inherited Ja'al's critical thinking skills and Cleg's ability to love deeply. Curiosity and discovery is an asset for her when dealing with humans with whom she has bonded. She desperately wants to be a leader like her mom and works hard at making her dad proud.

## Zonga

Leader of the shape-shifting Pukwudgie Tribe. He is 3 feet tall, tan & black, with porcupine quills. As a leader, he is an excellent listener with the foresight to take advice. Most know him as fearless and a risk taker. He is married to KiKi.

## Elle

A Meadow Sprite. She is 5 feet tall, light blue, with white hair and green eyes. She is not often seen as most sprites are hidden among the flowers in the meadow. While not shapeshifters, they are excellent at camouflage. She is known for her kindness and brave heart.

## Freda

A Great Blue Heron. She is 6 feet tall with grey, white, and blue feathers. She loves mothering others. She plans ahead by thinking things all the way through; and while she is a critical thinker, she is also a planner. She has a deep love for Bitty and Bev.

## Tiny

A Baby Turtle. He is 4 inches tall and black with an etched heart on his back that his friend Bitty put there. Most say he is an accomplished prankster.

## Bev

A Human. She is 5 feet tall white with red hair and blue eyes. Highly intelligent and loves to take on projects. Most know that she will jump in and help without a second thought. She loves Bitty as if she were her own child. She has a deep love for the tribe. Marsha is her best friend and Morgan is her go-to person to help solve problems or to at least tell her if she is on the right track. She is married to Dr. Jim Mottice and is mother to El, Dallas, Finch and John Grissom Mottice.

## Princess Celia

An Olympian Titan. She is 5.5 feet tall, light brown, with brown/blonde hair and brown eyes. Daughter of Zeus, she is kind and brave. She has the special skill of light voice translation. She is a skilled negotiator. Most think she is over 3,000 years old. If you ever need a friend to talk to you, she is your gal.

## KiKi

Zonga's wife. She is 3 feet tall, tan & black, with porcupine quills. Most go to her for help with their problems. She has keen listening skills. While she is married to a leader, she is more of a follower. Very skilled at building and food storage.

## Hybrid Hornet Queen

A mixture of Human and Hornet, she is 5 feet tall with a human top and a black hornet bottom. An abomination. Evil would be one description. There is not one ounce of kindness in her human half. She allows the emotions of anger and hate to take over every aspect of her being. She was created by Morgan King.

## Morgan King

A Human. He is 6 feet 4 inches tall, white, with white hair and blue eyes. While highly intelligent, he is known for being a comic. He also secretly loves Bev but believes he is too big of a nerd for Bev to ever notice him. He has a special love for predicting the weather. His respect runs deep for Cleg. He grew up in the Cuyahoga Valley and plans to remain there.

## Marsha King

A Human. She is 5 feet 8 inches tall with light brown hair and brown eyes. Marsha is Philip Garman's daughter and Morgan King's wife. She is mother to seven children, Morgan-Barkley, Dorothy-Alice, Zoey, Liam, Caci, Wyatt, and Tig. Marsha is best friends with Bev. She finds herself to be medically compromised. She is a spitfire and take-no-nonsense person who works through issues with her own process.

## Philip Garman

A Human and Marsha's dad. He is 6 feet 1 inches tall with dark hair, brown eyes, and silver glasses. The community loves this man. He is known for his kindness to children. He helps children and adults alike to volunteer and become part of the community by helping others. He also is a critical thinker. Most know he has a love of science, especially the TV show *Star Trek*.

## Myles Masterson

A Human. He is 5 feet 9 inches tall with dark brown hair and brown eyes. He is the descendant of Bat Masterson. Myles loves living in the wilderness. He is more of a loner, unlike his great great great grandfather. He is a helper and a listener. Most know that he reasons things out and is very down to earth and easy to talk to.

**Bat Masterson**

A Human and legend of the old west. He is known for his fast gun and was a lawman with Wyatt Earp. Many knew him as a gambler with high rolling friends like Diamond Jim Brady. He was totally fearless. Due to an injury, he carried a cane that he used as a weapon. Excellent at twirling, it had a magical stone hidden within the tip of the cane. Ancestor of Myles Masterson.

**Emma Masterson**

A Human. She is 5 feet 2 inches tall with brown hair and grey eyes. She is in her late 30's. All characters love her. She knows how to organize and run a household. She can keep everyone on task caring for the babies. She is firm, however, exudes love and kindness.

**Dr. Jim Mottice**

A Human. He is 6 feet one inches tall with dark hair and brown eyes. He is an old friend of Morgan and is acquainted with Philip Garman. Originally from New York, Jim is into research and development of vaccines for humans. Highly intelligent. Most call him a good listener. Others say he is arrogant.

## Elias

Indigo Lake Guardian. He is a 15 foot tall zebra-striped seahorse. Horse to the Ocean Olympian Poseidon. Wise and majestic, he has the ability to give humans a glimpse into the afterlife to see loved ones. He is also a healer.

## Ciril

A Blue Alien. A war hero who shares galactic medical technology. She is selfish, deceptive, and manipulative. She is driven with the desire to save her civilization at the expense of humans.

# Chapter One

# THE UNMITIGATED ATTACK

The pine tree rising off the cliff that overlooked Buttermilk Falls started the whisper orders with the red maple, Paw Paw, and acorn trees. Their root system was exposed and intertwined with each other and could pass the whisper orders along to other tree root systems. The whispers orders passed along quickly as it traveled root to root. Soon, every tree in the forest had heard the whisper orders of the Blue's instruction. It could take about a week to pass along to every tree worldwide. The Curry Tree in India intertwined with the Mango and Arjuna trees. They, in turn, passed the whisper orders root to root of the Kapa Kapa, Lisak, Baobab, and Rainbow trees in the Philippines which then passed it to others in the Pacific Rim. Worldwide, the whisper orders for the planned arrival of the Blues moved swiftly. It appeared the tree guardians in India, the Philippines, and the United States would soon be set. The trees involved had their orders to move to their pre-planned secure location. Once there, they would be able to meet the army of Blues. Each tree would guide the Blues to a designated, out of the way, hiding place. They planned to arrive just after sundown in one week. The trees knew they could walk 12 miles total before sun-up. The landing zones were well within their walking capacity to reach the remote cave systems created by the root balls of trees. Additional trees would move to conceal the tree-created caves. That would give the trees time to move and create bigger caves if needed for the Blues. The Mango trees used their acid excrement to seal rocks within the caves. It made them hard which prevented slides and detection. In the United States, it was the Paw Paw trees that provided the same type of sealing of the caves. In the Philippines and around the Pacific Rim, it was the orange trees. There would be tremendous difficulty concealing the arrival of the Blues. In addition, the Forest Guardians noticing the trees walking by using their roots could cause alarm. They were tuned into Mother Earth. This plan would require cleverness to outsmart any of the Forest Guardians. Any of the Forest Guardians who came against the trees would encounter the use of acid excrement to burn and incinerate them.

Fear and darkness had spread over the Valley. There were rumors of trees walking and shooting poison spores that were killing the livestock as well as wild game. People were keeping their children inside. Many were boarding their windows and barring their doors from these tree-killing machines. Some scientists believed it was due to an outside extraterrestrial force that seeded spores that would create the killer trees. It seemed to only affect citrus-type trees. It possessed the citrus trees and brought them to life with killer thoughts and killer actions. Their citrus fruit buds were turning into acid bombs that the trees could toss at any victim they desired. Many of the trees were growing thorns that were poisonous, and each tree could blow the poison thorns to pierce and saturate victims with fatal dripping poison.

Two of Cleg's tribe met an untimely death by the fatal poisonous thorns that were deliberately blown into the tribe members passing the apple orchard affected by the extraterrestrial spores. The Pukwudgie tribe lost nine of their members in the same manner as Cleg's tribe. Cleg and KiKi thought a council should convene. They had heard that the Dogman in Michigan and the Snallygaster in Pennsylvania each lost three members of their tribes. The Dogman tribe sent word that the Hodag in Wisconsin lost all but four of their tribe. The Flying Folklore fared better than most. They lived high in the mountain caves where no trees lived. Snallygaster was the most vulnerable because most of their prey lived below the treeline. Once it was proven that trees had turned on humans, as well as everything living on planet Earth, the Snallygaster, Gargoyles, Piasa, Mothman, Teratorns, Thunderbirds, Jersey Devil, and the only known dragons stayed hidden deep in the caves. The Flying Mountain Lore Monsters adopted a plan to stay at least a mile north of any tree lines. While prey would be sparse, the alternative was death. The ground-based Lore Monsters retreated to caves high in mountains where the Tree Monsters found it extremely difficult to traverse the terrain. The more rocks and no water, the safer they were. The Sasquatch tribes had already begun working with the Winged Lore Monsters to help augment food when possible.

It was a mass migration of humans and animals to the perceived safety of the mountain tops. Humans, animals, and Lore Monsters of all kinds were now learning to live and work together. There was yet a clear leader to emerge. They were all adrift together, attempting to make it through each night. There was one Sasquatch that seemed to have an ability to work with humans and Lore Monsters. The Sasquatch known as Cleg was the leader of the Hairy Tribe of the Cuyahoga Valley National Park. He had an innate ability to communicate across species. Another emerging leader coming from the scientific realm was Nobel Peace Prize winner Morgan King. There also appeared to be several leaders in the animal kingdom—Nodane the Black Deer not of this planet and Tibu of the African Chimpanzee. The challenge was to get them within proximity of each other for a more expedient dissemination of plans that affected all species of Planet Earth. Individual species and leaders of those species could react quickly as plans changed. Once there was a clear and provable working plan to defeat the trees affected, they would quickly roll it out to individual species as well as continental leaders. A global effort would be a huge task that had never been attempted before. The President of the United States once attempted to bring the world together with a Star Wars-type plan in the event of an alien attack; however, after many years it was discarded and forgotten. Now, all nations on this planet needed a concrete, provable plan that would bring this alien force to its knees in defeat.

A plan to move Tibu to a deep underground bunker in the Rocky Mountains was underway. In addition, they devised an individual plan to move Nodane the Black Deer, Morgan King, and Cleg to the same secure location with many world leaders. Tibu seemed to be in the most hostile region and in the most peril getting to the location. They were using one of the two remaining dragons to bring him to the bunker. At one point in between South Africa and the Falkland Islands, Rama the Dragon had to transfer Tibu into the mouth of a whale to be less conspicuous in this audacious attempt to bring the leaders together. Rama the Dragon was able to fly on with no attempted assassination. He met the whale in the port city of Myrtle Beach. It was a majestic sight watching the elusive dragon flying over and scorching the Earth for two miles to assure a safe transfer from the whale to Rama the Dragon. Rama the Dragon was waiting on the beach as the whale slid ashore as far as he could without grounding itself. Tibu left the mouth of the whale and jumped into a small fast rubber boat that could almost fly in the water yet was inconspicuous as it moved along the beach. As it approached the beach, two men aboard could see trees beginning to move toward the boat and dragon. They needed Tibu and Rama the Dragon to be airborne and heading toward the Rocky Mountain bunker. Both jumped out of the boat with

Tibu. One of the men with a fire weapon ran ahead scorching a row of trees that was making serious headway to reach Tibu and Rama. As the flames were expelled from the weapon, they reached about six feet in height and eight feet in length. He was able to incinerate all but one of the Tree Monsters near the end of what seemed to be a wall of Tree Monsters. He assumed he was far enough away from any of the blowing spores that were targeted to reach him. It was a terrible miscalculation. The tree blew its thorns, and the man was hit with at least one hundred poisonous fatal thorns. It melted him slowly as he screamed. Inch by inch, he melted while screaming in pain. After three minutes he was gone. What remained of him looked like a puddle of red slime with just his eyeballs floating on top. This brave man bought enough time for Rama to take off with Tibu. The entire flight was fraught with peril. Every tree along the way blew venomous thorns skyward in an effort to dispatch both Tibu and Rama. At one location over the Mississippi River, a UFO chased Rama until he circled around and blasted it with heat and flames that penetrated their obvious shields. The chemicals that caused the heat and fire in Rama's built-in defense system started to melt the ship, which caused it to dive back into the water. Tibu thought it an important clue to the possible defeat of the Tree Monsters.

The sky turned dark, full of rain just waiting to burst forth. Tibu wondered what the imminent rain would do to the tree. As they flew along, Tibu asked Rama if he thought the rain would cause the Tree Monsters to multiply. Both agreed it was probable. Rama suggested that if it were snow or ice it might kill them as it did many plants or citrus-bearing trees; however, he explained he was fearful the rain would trigger the Tree Monsters to multiply by thousands.

Rama had the site of the bunker in the Rocky Mountains. The clouds released their rain as Rama and Tibu approached the entrance to the bunker. It was a massive burst of rain with winds up to 60 miles an hour. Tibu was hanging on for dear life as Rama dove straight down toward the entrance. As the rain pelted Rama, his skin felt like it was on fire. Tibu was spared the burning rain as his fur was protecting him. Tibu could see the raindrops sizzle and smoke off of Rama's skin. The odor was that of burning flesh and skunk spray. It was a horrendous stench. He could feel Rama speeding faster and faster. Tibu could see large blisters forming all over his body. He knew Rama had to be in excruciating pain. They were 100 yards from the bunker door. Tibu feared they would crash into it. The doors opened when they approached from 75 yards away. There were trees all around, however, they all stood fast not moving an inch. Rama was able to fly right in through the doors that were only half-open. There was a group of Marines ready for the arrival of Tibu and Rama. Each Marine held a hose that released a foam upon Rama and Tibu once they cleared the doors. They skidded to a stop inside the bunker hall. As soon as that happened, the Marines released the foam which covered Tibu and Rama. It was heaven-sent, though Rama. The foam quenched the pain from the acid rain. Rama laid in the bunker hall with his eyes closed enjoying the coldness of the foam. Tibu jumped down and approached Rama's face. Tibu spoke softly to him as the Marines closed off the foam from the hoses. Tibu thanked Rama for being so brave.

A military man covered with medals approached Tibu. He had a black bag which he set down beside Rama's face. He knelt beside Tibu and asked if he needed medical attention. Tibu told the military man no, but his companion Rama was in an unbelievably bad way. He then asked his name. He responded, "I am Dr. Hoffman, a veterinarian. That is a doctor for animals." Tibu stepped back to give Dr. Hoffman room to work on Rama. Tibu heard a commotion and was incredibly surprised to see a Sasquatch approaching him with another military man. Tibu backed up against the cold steel wall. He only knew that

Sasquatch was a creature to be feared by humans and creatures alike. Cleg could sense Tibu's fear and stopped about 30 feet from him. The military man looked over at Cleg and nodded to him to stay where was, then proceeded to approach Tibu. Tibu was clearly frightened. His teeth were chattering, and he was almost curled in a standing ball. The military man knelt to Tibu and introduced himself as Captain David Gerlinger. He was assigned to Tibu and Cleg, the leaders of the Lore Monster team. Tibu looked the captain square in the eyes and asked if he and that thing over there were to be the leaders. "Yes, Tibu. Oh, may I call you Tibu?"

"Yes," he said as he slid up the steel wall. That was when Tibu looked closely at the hallway they were in and noticed they were 20-foot walls, and the hall was 40 feet wide. He said to the Captain, "What do you have that you would need a hallway this tall and this wide?"

"You just never know," the Captain explained. "They can and do use it for a variety of things." He directed Tibu to follow him to meet Cleg.

They approached Cleg and Tibu stayed behind the captain as he stopped in front of Cleg. The captain was a strategic yet diplomatic thinker. He turned sideways while still positioning himself between Cleg and Tibu. Cleg told Tibu it was his good fortune to meet him and a privilege to work with him. Tibu took a deep breath in and let it out again in full relief. Tibu returned the compliment and added that he had always feared Sasquatch in Africa. Their species had fierce and violent legends involving the Tribes of Sasquatch.

Cleg nodded and agreed that there were tribes that were violent, but he believed all were now working to save the planet. He told Tibu that he hoped all species, big and small, could work together more closely after this trial of humanity was over. The captain interrupted the conversation and asked that they follow him, there was a teleconference about to start that they needed to attend.

Tibu turned around to see Dr. Hoffman and three others still tending to Rama's injuries from the acid rain. Tibu shook his head and said to the captain and Cleg, "Rama looks awful. I hope he makes it." The captain reassured Tibu that Dr. Hoffman was incredibly good at veterinary medicine and he was in the best hands possible. It was at that point Tibu stopped and looked at the captain and asked how he was able to understand what everyone was saying and how they understood him. The captain apologized and advised him that they had voice translation technology that permeated every room in the bunker. So no matter where you were in the complex the translator would be available to interpret. Tibu scrunched his shoulder upward and said, "Wow, who knew?"

They began walking down the long hallway. He noticed a glass box off to his left side. The captain told Cleg and Tibu they would be taking the elevator down six levels to the War Room. He signaled for them to walk into the glass box elevator. Tibu was leary of this device. Cleg had already been in it so was not as unsettled as Tibu. All three were finally inside the glass elevator, as the captain said out loud, "Level 6." The elevator jerked and Tibu fell backward. Cleg extended his hand to help him up. Tibu sat for a minute while the captain remained facing forward in the elevator. Tibu reached for Cleg's hand just in time to exit the elevator on Level 6.

This level looked completely different from the one where they first arrived. This level was steel from the floor to about 12 feet high. Above the steel was smooth concrete. The door was a strange glass with lights all around the door frame. It scanned everyone as they walked through and identified each one out loud. At that point, an inner glass door opened to enter the room. Each one came through the door. As Tibu looked around the room, there were rounded screens all along the back wall. The screens had all sorts of information lighting up the panels. Tibu asked what all the shiny moving images on the glass panels were. The captain explained that each of them were electronic panels. They heard a noise and Tibu and Cleg both turned toward the door. With three rapid swooshes, three military personnel entered the room. They immediately went to panels and activated them. There was much activity that bewildered both Tibu and Cleg. The captain escorted Cleg and Tibu to the center console. From the center console activation, they could see four parts of the world and their leaders—China with Leader Sze, Europe with Leader Sopher, Africa with President Brown, and the United Kingdom with Prime Minister Churchill.

An additional six swooshes came through the scanner door. All heads turned and the captain yelled, "Attention!" All turned and stood in salute attention. The six made their way to the center console. Nine chairs rose from the floor. They were a beautiful blue acrylic compound. The captain gave the at-ease command. All turned to their tasks. The captain escorted and directed Tibu and Cleg to have a seat.

President Kennedy from The United States Of America addressed the group. "Welcome Leaders of Humanity and Lore Leaders. Perhaps the first thing all of us should consider is to stop making assumptions on our issue and start listening to solutions." Each leader explained in a summary format their ideas for the obliteration of the killer trees and their leader they called The Blue. President Kennedy asked Cleg, the Lore Leader, his thoughts.

Cleg responded, "We are intrepidly connected in our efforts to eliminate a formative enemy. With the future at stake of every living thing, humanity and lore struggle to stay connected with government, work, family, and friends. It is difficult to feel that connection from which we draw our strength and ideals. As I reflected from this perspective, it occurred to me that what Blue brought with her was an evil symbiotic life form that has taken hold of citrus-bearing fruit trees. In the symbioses with these specific trees, they can communicate with each other through their root system. They have also developed their own internal bioweaponry. It is unclear how the symbiosis is delivered to infect the trees worldwide. Currently, each nation is attempting to solve this mystery. I believe we could accomplish more together with Morgan King, the scientific leader. Our estimated loss on the Lore side is currently in the hundreds of thousands. Humanity is experiencing the same degree of losses." Cleg thanked Madam President for the opportunity to address the leaders of many nations. Cleg reminded the leaders that runners would need the information from this conference to disseminate to the Lore leaders in each nation. President Brown wanted to advise the group of a discovery their scientists had stumbled upon with acacia plants against pathogens. The nectar and the hollow thorns were used as nests for ants. The Dalai Lama interjected that his scientist also found a symbiosis between the long corolla tube plant and the long-tongued fly in the Himalayas. President Kennedy asked if any of the other nations stumbled upon anything similar. All said they had not. President Kennedy asked if either nation had tried to capture a tree to experiment upon. Neither had been successful in their attempts to procure an infected tree. President Zarfonzo from Mexico, who was a biologist by trade, said this triggered something else to address—a bacterial leaf nodule symbiosis in flowering plants. Many scientists had made progress and achieved a molecular phylogenetic analysis and also genomic data of the bacteria. They believed there was a way to plot genomic sequences that would show the symbiotic bacteria that may serve as a defense roll. Maybe combining the research will produce something we can use against the symbiotic trees that are infected. President Kennedy asked the group if they could reconvene in three days after a discussion with Morgan King. All agreed that they would encourage their scientific communities to continue their research as expeditiously as possible. She thanked the conference group for their efforts and told them should any significant discovery happen they would reconvene earlier than the three days. The captain stood and disconnected the line.

President Kennedy approached Cleg, a bit apprehensive as she looked up at his sheer size and bulk. She started by saying she never dreamed of having the privilege of meeting a Sasquatch. She said she had read many reports of help and assistance from many of the Sasquatch tribes. The reports came from Rangers at most of the National Parks. Cleg made eye contact with President Kennedy. He considered her to be very sturdy and had a powerful aura. He sensed total honesty and sincerity with her. He wished his friend Bev were here to meet her.

Cleg knew that Bev and her baby El were safe with the tribe in the hidden cave behind Brandywine Falls. It was a deep cave surrounded by giant granite rocks. He knew there was no way the trees could penetrate that waterfall. In the event of an attempted attack, they could roll a giant stone that was inside the entrance of the cave. It would make it impenetrable. They had stored plenty of food and firewood for light, warmth, and cooking. Morgan's wife Marsha and their twins, Bev's husband Dr. Jim Mottice, and Ranger Kopchek also joined them in the cave for shelter. Marsha brought a shortwave radio and plenty of toys, formula, clothing, and diapers. Ranger Kopchek brought a first aid kit, a tool kit, and her weapon. She also brought ten cots with sleeping bags so the humans could be comfortable. Additionally, Jim brought nine teepee-style lodging for the tribe and nine family-style pop-up tents for the humans. Everyone was expecting at least a six-week stay in the cave and felt that was probably optimistic. Ranger Kopchek knew, as did Bev and Marsha, that this was a war of all wars and totally unpredictable. It would depend on how fast Morgan and other scientists could come up with a viable solution that would win the war against the Tree Monsters and their alien leader, Blue.

Ranger Kopchek, after hearing many reports, decided the best solution for surviving this war would be to roll the giant stone in front of the mouth of the cave. There would be nothing able to penetrate the stronghold barrier to the cave. Virg, Boc, Aggie, and Kron pushed the stone with ease to seal everyone inside the cave and anything attempting entry would be denied. Ranger Kopchek thought that two gaps should also be filled so that no thorns could be blown into the cave. Virg stacked two large rocks that wedged into the gap nicely. Once they were wedged in, Virg decided to mud them in for a more complete seal. They had everything they needed inside the cave to sit out a four-month siege. Marsha was afraid there would be few survivors left if the siege lasted longer than eight weeks. Ranger Kopchek wanted the water pools labeled so everyone knew the first one was for drinking water, the second was for bathing, and the third was the bathroom. The third pool was at the farthest point back in the cave, and she knew that would be clear to understand; however, she asked Virg if there was a way to put a blanket up as a reminder of what this pool was to be used for. Virg chipped away deep crevasse within the rock above. The crevasse was a good four feet from the water pool. It took him a good portion of the day. After that task was complete, however, the final task of mudding and hanging the blankets would wait until the next day. He would need Kron to assist him. None of the others in the tribe or humans was tall enough to reach the height of the cave at 16 feet. Bev was happy she brought plenty of paint. It was so dreary looking in the cave. It appeared to be mostly grey and she thought it was depressing. After Virg and Kron completed the bathroom water pool task, she would ask them all to paint whatever they desired on the walls, ceiling, or themselves. She did not care what they painted, this was a multi-purpose task to form a tighter community, one that would not let isolation diminish community love for one another.

Morgan and his three assistants as well as four virtual scientists each took different approaches to expedite a hypothesis in finding the cure. Once a person hit a dead end with their investigation, they would then begin to assist the study with another scientist. Morgan had kicked off the approach stating, "Reach for the best in yourself and each other." Morgan knew this would be long and difficult. It would be up to him to keep them all motivated in the research and discovery process. The one fact that was unassailable was saving lives past, present, and future no matter how long it took and no matter the cost. It was a heavy burden to carry the responsibility for every living creature on planet Earth, all waiting with the expectations that a solution would be found quickly. The bunker lab was like none he had ever witnessed before. Most labs were assembled on an excruciatingly low to no budget. It reminded Morgan of Madame Curie's lab. Housed in a shed in the rear of the Sorbonne in Paris, they were subjected to the extremes of the weather. Through cold, rain, and heat, it was almost an unbearable location. There was no help or assistance, so all the backbreaking manual labor was up to them. It was the passion of both her and her husband Pierre to persevere for this new element called radium that they believed could help save mankind. He knew that most of the virtual scientists, more than likely, had labs similar to that of Madame Curie's. Morgan stood looking at the immensity of this lab and the limitless tools available to him and the others working with him in the bunker. He knew they all were invincibly eager to find this cure. He also knew it could be like capturing stars with your fingertips. Their journey would be one fraught with many obstacles; however, they would meet each one head-on. Morgan considered this a three-point perspective moment, like the beginning of the Renaissance. It seemed people, for the first time, began to look up during that period of Earth's history. At that time, they had just endured wars, pestilence, and plague. It was certainly a rebirth of mankind. He deemed this could be considered year Zero, a new beginning and a date to equate to the new beginning for all mankind. He looked forward to the human race feeling safe in the homes they hold dear. With all the struggles of this period, it would mark what he knew all would somehow feel, a connection through ideals in extraordinary new ways.

It was while he was contemplating Madame Curie's discovery that he recalled it was within a rock called pitchblende that radium was discovered. The rays it gave off led Madame Curie to pursue its potential. Perhaps he should explore the properties of pitchblende more fully. These rocks found in the middle of the earth have never seen the sun, yet they give off some type of rays. He sometimes doubted himself and questioned his own hypotheses, and perhaps other scientists would think him foolish to continue to pursue his conjecture of the possibility of pitchblende being the solution to this worldwide catastrophe. He wondered if it was perhaps beyond him. Do we dare think that there could be a matter that was dynamic, not inert? Maybe a crystallization process. An active element. It may enable us to investigate the secret of this unknown element and use it to alter the living and destructive elements of the Tree Monsters. Maybe it was Madame Curie who left the gate ajar long ago for this moment in time. Morgan shook his head and thanked his Heavenly Father for bringing that thought to the forefront of his mind.

A military liaison approached Morgan in his vast, yet unexplored lab. He notified him that President Kennedy needed to speak with him as soon as possible. Morgan asked if he meant now, and the liaison responded, "Yes, sir. Follow me please." Morgan took a last glance at the electronic glass panel displaying a globe image with dots that were swirling and flashing different colors.

He looked back at the liaison and followed him out of the lab. As he walked down the hall to the glass elevator, they passed the president of Mexico as well as the president of Chile. Both were deep in thought and, frankly, never noticed them. The liaison pressed the down button on the elevator and signaled for him to enter the elevator. He told Morgan someone would meet him on Level 12. He shut the door before Morgan could ask what was on that level. Morgan was looking up as the elevator descended in the concrete tunnel. He felt the jerk of it reaching Level 12 and caused his gaze to look straight ahead as the door opened. Morgan was stunned at what was greeting him at the door. It was a 7-foot robot. It greeted him as Dr. King. Morgan stepped out of the elevator and stood in front of a giant and red number 12.

"Dr. King, I am called Suri and it is a pleasure to be assigned to you as your number one assistant." Morgan was having difficulty taking in what he was saying. He was still focused on looking at him in all his "Darth Vader" gear. "Dr. King, right this way, please." Morgan followed Suri who he fully intended to call Vader. He noticed this level to be darker and more mysterious than Level 6. It was still concrete and steel but felt ominous. About halfway down the hall, Suri stood in front of a door that was illuminated and marked as President C. Kennedy. They entered with the same light scan and swoosh. President Kennedy was watching a glass screen of the globe. It appeared there were certain satellites marked around the globe along with the International Space Station. She appeared to be studying it intensely. She waved her hand over a control panel in front of her, and it turned the screen off. She turned as both Suri and Morgan stood silently awaiting her attention. She turned and addressed them. Morgan was feeling the weight and responsibility of solidifying a plan of action in writing for her. To his surprise, she asked them to both be seated. She pointed to the sofa, and she sat in a chair that faced them. She was polite and attentive, however, very matter of fact in the discussion. She started with a statement that will forever be seared into Morgan's brain.

"The torch of knowledge builds a path for the future. Your torch of knowledge will light this unknown road. No one can carry this torch by himself. While some candles darken and dim, even in that darkness, each of your scientist's love of humanity and the coming together of all species will illuminate this unknown road. It will be filled with divine wonder and will never fail." She wanted to inspire both A.I. and Humans. In the days and weeks ahead, there would be failure and success. The key was to keep the torch of knowledge and hope at the forefront of this pursuit for a viable solution. Morgan and Suri stood as she stood and both thanked her for her kindness and inspiration. The door swooshed behind them as they left the private quarters of President Kennedy.

Neither spoke during the walk back to Morgan's lab. He was silently running things through his brain. He thought about how nothing in the universe lets anything go to waste in chemical reactions. Mass was neither created nor destroyed. Everything organic would have mitochondrial DNA. Could these thorns be something that breaks down lipids and proteins? He wondered if there was a vibration pattern before they blew their thorns. Why would they want to destroy all sentient lifeforms? So many questions. Morgan had to organize his thoughts after he met with his team.

They entered the lab where his assistants had already pulled up Marsha on the screen via FaceTime. Morgan's eye grew to the size of silver dollars. He ran to the console. He was able to see the twins being held by Bitty. He greeted Marsha by putting his hand on the screen and her hand placed onto his on the screen. Marsha began to cry, and Morgan told her how much he loved her and missed her and the twins. He asked if Bitty would be taking the night feeding and changing the diapers. Both laughed. Morgan did not notice anyone else in the lab, including the Darth Vader look-alike, Suri. Morgan asked how everything was in the Cuyahoga Valley. Marsha told him that the Tree Monsters wreaked most of the destruction at night; and in the mornings, they could see that they were ravaging the environment. Ranger Kopchek stepped into the picture and described not only the thorns but what appeared to be a multidimensional fungus-type of parasite that was devastating plants and attaching to trees that could be what was infecting the citrus trees. Morgan asked if she could transmit that information to him via text message. She nodded yes. Morgan refocused again on his family. He wanted to see how they sealed the cave. Marsha moved her phone camera around the cave and showed him the sealing of the door. She then walked to the back of the cave to show him what Virg had done to separate their bathroom from the two other water pools. She explained the other two were for bathing and drinking. She also showed him the cots with sleeping bags and the large tool kit, first aid kit, and the food storage area. Morgan thought it looked good with the shelving for the canned goods, baskets, and dried meat. He voiced concern about the fire area for warmth and cooking. He told Marsha he would feel better if there was a way to create a barrier around it so that the young of the tribe would not accidentally be burned. He suggested moving it to a corner so that two sides would be protected and there would just be one side to tend to. Virg pointed out there were plenty of loose larger rocks in the back of the cave that he could bring up to the fire pit, stack them, and then mud them in place. Virg hoped there was enough for a 3-foot rock fence. He also suggested the iron bar used for cooking be secured by drilling a hole on each side of the two walls that they could slide the bar into. Therefore, it would secure a cooking pot in place yet could still be removed for washing.

Morgan asked Virg a question that neither he nor Ranger Kopchek could answer; however, they promised to investigate. They were sure there was no way the Tree Monsters could come up through the water pools to attack them. They would make sure of it. Marsha wanted Morgan's assurance that he had everything he needed to find the answer to this disaster. He told her the lab was unbelievable and that there was no other on this Earth that could ever compare in size and equipment. He also told her they had functioning A.I.

Morgan had Suri come forward to meet Marsha and the group. He addressed them, "I realize that I am not your biological family; however, I consider you as such. Words cannot express the great balance that is to be reset across species. Please, I humbly ask to be part of your family of sentient life." Marsha, Bev, Dr. Jim, and Ranger Kopchek all warmly responded with a heartfelt yes. Virg, Kron, and Bitty stepped forward with an eager yes, nodded, and extended hands of welcome. Morgan turned and took Suri's hand in both of his and said, "Welcome, only if I can call you Darth Vader or just the nickname Vader." Suri agreed to change his name over to Vader.

Marsha told Morgan that she would call him each day around this time. Morgan looked puzzled. "How are you guys charging your phone batteries?" Ranger Kopchek leaned into the screen and explained that she had attached battery chargers to the rocks above and on the side of the falls. They were secured down with mountain-climbing pegs. She said she strengthened the cable in four well-hidden places and weaved them down through the rocks and into the caves. She told Morgan that Virg hand-mudded them and sealed any holes. There were a total of nine charging stations funneled into the cave for a generator that could charge lighting and cell phones. Morgan asked if they had plenty of batteries in the cave for lighting. Marsha assured him that there was enough for an entire year. Ranger Kopchek leaned in and told him she had brought at least a six-month supply, as well.

Dr. Jim added that they would also be setting up individual pop-up tents for each family. He assured Morgan the cave was very wide and had enough room for 10 families with plenty of distance between each and that they would take pictures when they were assembled and in place tomorrow. He added that the tribe members had teepee-style tents. They all had doors of some sort. This would assure everyone's semblance of privacy. Virg made a family table that seated 14 comfortably and was sturdy enough to accommodate the weight requirements. He also made the cutest round chairs for each of the babies. The ladies brought baby carriers, as well.

"All the comforts of home, Morgan. We are just missing you," Jim explained.

Morgan told everyone how proud he was of each of them for pulling this shelter together. He felt it was rock solid and knew that they would all work together as a family and that he looked forward to the daily visits and updates on what happened each day.

Jim asked Morgan to stay on the screen for a second. Everyone dispersed while they stayed on to discuss what was on Jim's mind. Jim looked behind him and to either side of himself. He leaned into the display and told Morgan that Kron was pregnant and quite far along and that he was concerned because of their obvious predicament. He revealed, as well, that Bev was also pregnant but still in her first trimester. He then asked Morgan to sit down. Morgan took his advice and sat, bracing himself for dreadful news of some germ or mite or something. Jim then confessed that Marsha was also pregnant and in her second trimester and that he was in a hormone-crazed den with three prego's. Morgan was overjoyed by the news, but his expression suddenly changed, fearing he might not be there for the birth.

Vader was not sure how to take that reaction. "Did you hear me, Morgan? You are going to have a baby in about five months." Morgan laughed with trepidation and said, "Get to training Bitty to be your assistant, my good doctor." Morgan told him he had to move along and meet his team. They both agreed to talk and share notes of each responsibility they had been assigned. Vader signed Morgan off the teleconference.

Marsha looked worried. Bev came to comfort her while Kron looked after El. Bitty was busy with the twins, which allowed a private discussion between them. Marsha broke the news to Bev that she had just started her second trimester. Bev was so excited for her but knew this would almost be like having triplets, with just 10 months separating the twins from this baby. Marsha told her they had interviewed several potential nannies, but then this horrible event had happened. Bev then told her she had a secret and confessed that she was in her first trimester and was overjoyed to have a new baby coming. Marsha was excited for Bev then revealed that there were three pregnant in the shelter. Bev looked puzzled and then looked over at Kron. Bev shook her head and told Marsha she knew it had to be Kron. Both women looked back at her with the twins and turned to each other laughing. They knew she would be a perfect mother. Bev pointed out that Jim will have a blessed time delivering all these infants and a first time for him delivering a Sasquatch baby. Bev wondered if they had the same type of unbearable pain in childbirth as human women. Marsha had never given it any thought. She agreed with Bev that they would all find out soon enough. Jim came over and sat down with Bev and Marsha. He wanted to know what the busybodies were talking about. Bev told him they were discussing all the pregnant people that were entrusted to his care during this vacation away from home.

He laughed and then went to meet up with Virg, Kron, Boc, and Aggie. They decided to pitch all the tents. Jim showed the tribe how to assemble the tepees. Jim was surprised at how fast they all caught on. It took just under an hour to assemble all the teepees. Then they turned their focus to the pop-up tents which took around 30 minutes to erect. Everyone now had their own quarters to share their private moments. Bitty was so happy to have her very own teepee. She felt so grown up. Once in their teepees, none of the tribe members came back out. They all shut their doors. You could hear soft talk through the soft walls of their temporary homes. All of the humans decided they would do the same and get settled in their pop-ups. Bev put El in the pack-and-play. It worked beautifully. She laid out her sleeping bag on the cot. She was happy that she had grabbed the foldable picnic table. She used the metal cart to store all the baby diapers and clothing. She had her baby bathtub and used that to hold powder, lotion, shampoo, and soap. She left all remaining items of hers in the suitcase. Tomorrow she would fill her water bottles for use while in the tent for the evening. She wondered if she should lay out Jim's items. She decided that she would fix his cot and then place his suitcase on the cot to sort what he needed daily in a collapsible canvas bin she had slid into her suitcase. The tent had a built-in battery-operated light, as well as hooks to hang clothing from. She assumed she would eventually have to use the cloth diapers she had been utilizing as burp cloths as a replacement for the disposable diapers that would eventually run out. The hooks would come in handy for air-drying them after she hand washed them.

Jim made his rounds to all the humans for any last-minute help they needed in the final setup of things. Everyone seemed organized with their personal belongings. It seemed Ranger Kopchek brought a vast supply of dish detergent, laundry soap, and bath soap. Jim figured she just had a thing for cleanliness. She also had one entire locker of protein bars. She had excellent ranger skills for planning a siege. Jim showed each person how to plug in their generators and at the same time charge their phones. Most were equipped with crank radios, so they were able to pick up news reports. That fact concerned Jim greatly. Bev brought a laptop with 12 DVDs to watch on movie night. Most would use the generator for coffee, tea, hot cereal, or soup. Jim unpacked and put everyday needs into the canvas bin and left the remainder in his suitcase. He had covered the entire bottom of his suitcase with Bev's favorite maple brown sugar cream of wheat packets. When Bev saw that, she cried at such a thoughtful gesture.

Jim moved his cot next to Bev's. She asked why he didn't think of a queen size cot. They both laughed. She asked Jim if he had any concerns with the cave and the setup. He told Bev he was still not sure if the arrangement of the tents and teepees provided everyone with optimal privacy. "Gottcha," she giggled. He asked her why she was laughing. She responded with a question. "How can a bigfoot be quiet during sex?" Jim looked at her and told her to go to sleep. She rolled over still smiling.

Suddenly, there was a loud scream that echoed throughout the cave. Everyone jumped up from their slumber and rushed out to see who it was and what was the problem. Marsha had awoken and had stumbled half-asleep to the bathroom water pool. She was terrified to find a snake coiled on the lip of the pool and out of the water. Aggie was the first to reach Marsha. She grabbed the snake and ripped its head off. She looked at Marsha and said, "I caught breakfast and will share with you." Marsha just stood there with her mouth hanging open and unable to speak. The others of the tribe were giving Aggie a pat on the back. They were happy to see a food source.

Jim and Bev put their arms around Marsha and helped her back to her tent. She had composed herself on the way and kept saying over and over, "I am zipping my tent and not leaving it." Bev spoke softly to her and told her she should keep calm so as not to upset the twins or the baby that was currently residing within her womb. Ranger Kopchek came to the tent and told Jim, Bev, and Marsha that she thought perhaps there was a way for water snakes to make their way into the cave. She threw three fine screen nets on the ground. She asked Jim if he was up to installing these tonight. He, of course, was on board with that and suggested they stop at Virg's teepee to ask him to come along for assistance. Ranger Kopchek was concerned the tribe would not take kindly to this solution because it removed an easy food source. She felt that she could present this preventive solution to keep snakes out of the cave in a compelling way to protect the babies and the pregnant mommies.

Marsha had calmed down and went back to bed but not before she zipped her tent up. Her pack-and-play had a top that zipped, as well, and she made sure the babies were protected. Jim and Bev did the same when they returned to their tent. Bev told Jim she knew it was nonvenomous but she was still not taking any chances that something would hurt her baby El. As they laid down on their cots, Bev looked at Jim with a smile and asked if he supposed it would taste like chicken. Both laughed and then kissed. Jim brushed Bev's hair back and stroked her face. She smiled warmly and invitingly at Jim. He rolled on top of her and they had another passionate and loving kiss, as they rolled onto the ground, turning out the light.

Everyone in the cave could hear Marsha's twins crying to be fed. Jim looked at his watch as Bev held onto him and whispered, "Day 1, giving it a 10." Baby El awoke when she heard the noise and Bev's voice and expressed herself by crying, as well. Bev slipped on a pair of leggings and a tee-shirt and began making her bottle while Jim changed her diaper. They could hear that one of Marsha's babies was still crying. Jim suggested that she go and help Marsha and he would feed El. He no sooner said that when the other baby stopped crying. Bev said she would still see if she needed an extra hand. Marsha's pop-up door was open, and Bev found Bitty was feeding the other baby. She asked if she could come in and help. Marsha told Bev she woke up the entire camp.

Bev was impressed by Bitty's natural ability as he handled the babies and told her how well she was doing. It appeared Bitty's depth of humility was shallow by her surprising three-word answer, "I know it." She told Bitty they would work on humbleness but did give her praise by telling her she was impressed with her kindness and helpfulness. Bitty thanked Bev and then shifted her focus back to Morgan Barkley, while Marsha tended to Dorothy-Alice. She asked Bev if she could put some coffee on for them. She plugged it into the generator without any glitches. She was happy it worked perfectly because she needed some caffeine. As they sat having their coffee, Bitty told Marsha she was going to ask Virg to make a rocking chair like Bev had at her house for baby El. Marsha looked at Bitty and told her that was a wonderful and thoughtful idea; however, they would need the wood to carry them through for cooking and for warmth.

Bitty then looked at Bev and asked what she was going to name her son. Bev put her head down and shook it. "Not shocked," she told Marsha. She looked at Bitty and said, "Thank you for my painless scan to tell me the gender of the baby." Bitty gave a big smile like she had done something great.

Marsha asked Bitty, "Well, what about me? What am I having?" Bitty smiled and with much excitement told her it was twins, a boy and a girl. Marsha was clearly stunned and began to cry. Bitty did not know what she had said wrong. Bev jumped up and kneeled beside her. She did not have to be told what was so upsetting—four babies to care for by herself and just ten months apart. Bev knew that would be overwhelming for even the most organized person. Bev tried to explain to Bitty why Marsha was upset.

Bitty looked at Marsha and said, "The tribe always helps raise the young. Every member of the tribe is responsible for that." She told her that Kron was having a boy, as well. Bitty told Marsha she would have lots of help. "The newborn of the tribe needs little care. It holds onto the mother by itself from day one and only cuddles when it is feeding time. Most females are up and hunting within an hour of birth."

Bev laughed and replied, "It sucks to be them." Bitty had no idea what that meant and asked why humans did not do that. Bev shook her head and threw her arms in the air, shrugged her shoulders, and added that she didn't know as she looked over to Marsha who was holding back her laugh.

Aggie came to the door and asked if she could make breakfast for the women. Bev looked at her and told her she was amazing and would love it, then she remembered the snake. Aggie turned to go make breakfast when Bev asked them, "What do you think snake tastes like? Maybe I can add it to my maple brown sugar oatmeal." Marsha and Bev were mortified at the thought of eating a snake for breakfast. Aggie was back in what seemed like a remarkably fast turnaround. She had four mugs in her hand. Bev and Marsha glanced at each other and then up at Aggie. Both smiled as Marsha laid Dorothy-Alice down and Bitty laid Morgan Barkley down. Bitty took one cup at a time and served the first one to Marsha and the second one to Bev. Aggie nodded and Bitty took hers. Bev was impressed at how structured and respectful the exchange was between Aggie and Bitty.

Bitty said immediately, "You will love this, and don't worry, this is not a snake. We already ate when the tribe rose for breakfast." It appeared the inhabitants of the cave were each carving out their own niche in this small community. Bev thought that Virg was the master builder. Aggie was the cook, Ranger Kopchek was safety patrol, and Jim was a babysitter and physician. She was unsure about Boc and Kron. Marsha was focused on two babies and Bev assumed the role of diplomat, wife, and mommy to baby El. Bev asked Aggie what the broth was made from. She said it was deer jerky soaked to make broth and herbs added like coriander, parsley, and thyme. They had plenty of nourishing herbs that would be high in minerals for Kron, Marsha, and Bev's babies. Aggie told Marsha and Bev that she understood the difference in the cooking approach between the tribe and the humans. She felt with her knowledge of herbs and blends that she would be a natural to cook for the camp. She told Bev that Kron was a cleaning enthusiast and would be great at tidying up after cooking and eating. She added it pleasured Kron to think that she could contribute to the community with something she loved to do. Marsha and Bev told Aggie they had been talking between themselves about how the camp would be set up.

Aggie told them that the tribe always did things as a tight-knit community, each taking a crucial task to make the community run efficiently and to support anyone who had additional needs. "Bitty is brilliant at babysitting duties as well as games and all-around fun."

Marsha looked at Bev and said, "Bitty is the Cruise Director." Both laughed.

Bev looked at Aggie and told her she would love to continue her role with the tribe as mediator and diplomat. Aggie sat silent for a moment and said she was, well, a nurse and planner. Bev looked surprised, smiled, and said, "Yes, of course. That is perfect."

Marsha sat there awaiting her assignment. Aggie smiled and looked at Marsha and then over to the babies. "How would you feel about childcare and a friend to all?" Marsha felt a rush of hormones overtake her very being as she cried, shaking her head up and down signaling yes, she agreed. Aggie put her hand on Marsha's knee and told her, "No worries, these emotions will calm and subside when you are busy with your hands taking care of everyone's babies." Marsha somehow managed to thank Aggie for the faith and trust she was delegating to her in caring for everyone's babies while they were busy performing other community tasks. Bev looked at Aggie and asked what task they may give Ranger Kopchek. Her response was to check the cave for its safety, including taking water readings with her special-looking device (Bev knew she meant microscope) and to also through the special-looking device make sure the food was safe to eat and free of bacteria or fungus. Bev and Marsha agreed she would be perfect for that. Bev asked about Boc. Aggie put her head down and explained that Boc was taking this confinement difficult, and he needed adjustment time as well as time to discover what role in the community he will take. Aggie told Bev and Marsha that Bitty would stay with the babies while they washed their bodies for the day ahead. Both laughed and agreed. She asked them to have Ranger Kopchek, the safety officer, stand on the other side of the curtain to keep the sacred washing private. Bev thought that was a unique way of putting things.

After lunch, Boc asked to talk to the community. He was shy to begin with, and Bev knew it was a big step for Boc in asking for community time. He started with a quite simple thank you for allowing him to talk and then began, "I envy those who believe there is a greater hand in writing their story. Those who choose a certain word to keep chaos at bay. Those who have a connection of joy, love, and resurrection. With these words, there is always a path that becomes clear but for a moment and then disappears. I have a path I am still searching for. How I will find my way, I believe, is by choosing to walk forward together as a community. And if there is a greater hand, it can, and I suspect it will, lead us into uncertain futures; and I can only hope it guides all of us well. I am your humble servant to our community." Bev and Marsha both had tears running down their faces. Bitty was sitting between them and told them their eyes were leaking and they needed Dr. Jim. That snapped them right out of it with a hardy laugh. Bev felt both surprised and relieved that Boc was taking a servant role in the community. She felt that he really found his role and was embracing it with the community. She believed that, in this, Boc was attempting to be the best he could be in offering advice or assistance in whatever tasks the community needed to be done.

Ranger Kopchek asked them all to call her by her first name, Karen. She set up a schedule of what she would be doing each day. She wanted to make sure everyone knew that her day started at 5:00 a.m. with a walk around the perimeter of the cave looking for holes that needed to be filled or any loose rocks that needed to be secured and to look for vermin that may have found a way into the cave. Her next task was to take samples of the water. Once she had the results, she would then take scrapings from various foods that planned to use that day and look at them under the microscope for nasty critters, as she called them. Jim would also help with this task. After lunch, she would take another perimeter run to look for vermin holes she missed. In the watering hole, she had brought a fishing pole and fishing net that she would use to see if she could catch any fish or snakes. After people were in their tent or teepee for the night, Boc would make rounds throughout the night hours while everyone slept. He was the community night watchman.

Aggie was busy grinding wheat that Bev had brought. Bev had Marsha and Bitty watching El, Morgan Barkley, and Dorothy-Alice while she went to show Aggie how to make tortillas. She had her add a small bit of butter and water to the ground wheat. There blew a flat rock she used to flatten out three tortillas. She then put a heated flat rock on top of it for a few minutes. When she lifted the rock, there were the tortillas. She told Aggie it was very filling for humans and would be for the tribe, as well. Aggie was surprised at how easy they were to make as well as how fast they cooked. Bev told her to make sure she used potholders on each side of the rock before she heated the top rock to prevent burning her hands. Aggie nodded in agreement.

The first week everything ran smoothly and without too many hiccups. Every night they looked forward to talking with Morgan and his A.I., Vader. After the conversation with Morgan, they would gather together facing the cooking wall. Karen had been able to rig her laptop to project movies she was able to pull down from YouTube. The community had a nice rhythm going, and it was working well for everyone. After the movie, Karen would put her laptop away and would take a stroll around the perimeter with Boc. Yesterday, they had found a hole that mice could easily slip through. Virg fixed it today. Karen enjoyed her walks with Boc each night. You could clearly see a bond and friendship forming. Bev was happy for them. They had the same issue going into this siege. Both were shy, and both were looking for their path; however, Karen was a lot further along down her path. Still, it was amazing to watch a true friendship blossom.

Jim and Bev walked the cave perimeter as El slept. Hand in hand, they walked. Bev told him how her day was and Jim talked endlessly about the herbs and other wild vegetation the tribe used. As they sat at the drinking water pool filling up their 10 water bottles, he told Bev that he believed Kron was due any time and that Bitty thought it would be tomorrow. Bev jokingly asked if Bitty used her Ouija Board to consult for a delivery date. Jim laughed and looked at Bev's eyes sparkling with delight at delivering her witty response. He laughed and agreed she had an uncanny ability to determine things. He told her that he was overly concerned because he had obviously never delivered a Sasquatch, nor did he understand their anatomy and physiology. Bev told Jim, "Perhaps their delivery is not like a human. It could be very easy. Stop worrying about stuff you can't change or have control over. You will make the best decision when the time comes. You ALWAYS do, you silly doctor." Jim smiled and kept filling the last bottle. Bev looked into his face and eyes and told him that she was sure she had not convinced him of his superior doctoring skills. He looked back up at her and then back at the bottle. She scooted close to him and whispered in his ear, "This naughty doctor knows how to fix what ales you. Wanna come try out my skills?" Jim's eyes became as large as silver dollars. His big grin might blind Bev if she stared long enough at his brilliant toothy smile. She picked up her bottles and ran for the tent with Jim running right behind her. Bev put down the bottles, unzipped the door, and leaned on the tent with her arms above her head, eyes closed and her lips slightly apart. Jim put down his bottles and grabbed her by the waist, pulling her to him, and gave her a deep passionate slow kiss. Bev pulled back, smiled, and took Jim's hand, then pulled him into the tent, zipping it closed. Jim sat on the cot waiting for her. She removed her tee-shirt in a slow and seductive way, followed by her leggings. Only her panties and socks remained. Jim continued to kiss her and moved his hands down to her panties and slid them down to her ankles. Bev kicked them off as Jim rolled her to the floor of the tent.

# Chapter Two

# A NEW LIFE

Jim awoke with the smell of bay leaf, clove, and thyme cooking. It smelled like Thanksgiving. He then heard a knock on the tent. He knew it was Karen. She said, "It's Kron time. You should come now." Jim told her he would be over to her teepee shortly. Bev heard the conversation. She stood as Jim dressed and worked hard to reassure him all would be fine. She reminded him about the hot tub they had created in the washing water pool. She hurriedly got dressed so she could prepare the tub. They both left the pop-up at the same time. She headed for the warming stones first. Jim had yelled back to her that she should not move heavy rocks; he would send Boc to carry them for her. That was when Bev could smell the herbs cooking. It did smell like Thanksgiving dinner. Bev stood waiting for Boc and decided she would go find him to assist with the rock carrying.

Jim arrived at Kron and Virg's teepee. There was a thick log in the middle of the room that Kron had her arms wrapped around. He asked her if she was doing okay, and she nodded her head yes. "Good. How far apart are the pains?" She did not answer so he looked to Virg. "Remember, I told you it was important to know how far apart the pains are." Virg pulled out the stopwatch Jim had provided him and handed it to Jim. He could see they were three minutes apart. This was Kron's first child so it could take a while. Aggie came into the teepee with a broth. It was the broth that smelled like Thanksgiving. Jim asked Aggie what was in the mixture. She advised him that it was a drink that accelerated birth with little to no pain. Jim laughed. She explained that it was bay leaves, nutmeg, cloves, and thyme. Jim laughed and told her they were the herbs used when roasting a turkey. That seemed to shock and annoy Aggie.

Jim advised Kron that he wanted to examine her and listen to the baby. Kron laid on the special table Virg had built for birthing. Jim took out his stethoscope and asked Kron to lay quiet. It was a strong heartbeat. Then he listened to Kron. It sounded like a murmur in her heart. He had not heard that last week when he listened. He turned to Aggie once again and asked if that broth worked. She said that it did most of the time. Jim's eyebrow went up. He thought this must be as painless and stress-free as possible. He turned and Marsha had just arrived to begin laying out the instruments. She had worked in the mission field and helped in many deliveries. She knew where and what order to lay each instrument for the procedure of childbirth by Cesarean section. He asked Marsha to go into his tent and find the copper-colored suitcase. It contained a bottle of bourbon. He wanted it right away. And he told Marsha to not run but be expeditious. He could feel Kron's contraction which was like steel. All he could think about was the pain and how she endured it without even a whimper. Marsha returned quickly with the bottle of St. Lucy bourbon from Prichard's Distillery in Tennessee. He asked her to open it and mix it with the broth. He added to that request to make it half and half. Marsha did what Jim requested and handed it to Aggie to have Kron drink. Jim was sure this would dull any pain for sure. After her contraction, he asked Kron if he could examine her like they talked about so he could feel for the baby. Virg left to help Bev and Boc with the warming water. Jim put on a glove and asked her to bring her knees up to her chest. Kron did as asked. Jim could feel the hairy head of the baby. He told her to relax. He felt like it was time to push or if she wanted to give birth in the water, now was the time to head over. She wanted the water, however, when she sat up she almost fell off the table if Aggie had not been there to catch her. Jim told everyone she was staying on the table. He wished he knew what her blood pressure should be. That was when he knew Morgan was in just the right place to know that answer. He was sure the government had a few of this species. He had time and asked Marsha to find Karen right away and have her bring her phone so they could connect to Morgan.

Marsha and Karen returned to the birthing tent in a matter of a couple of minutes. He told Karen to reach Morgan. Vader answered. Jim turned to the phone so Vader could clearly see what was going on and told him to go immediately to get Morgan, as this was life or death. Vader acknowledged the request and sent an assistant to wake Morgan and get him down to the lab. Morgan ran in, putting his bathrobe on over his pajamas. He could see from the giant panel screen what was happening. He could see Marsha laying out more instruments and asked what they needed. Jim ran the scenario down and told Morgan, "You and I both know that the government captured this species after the Mount St. Helen eruption, and they would know what the normal vital signs are." Morgan turned to Vader and told him to search the computer system and give him an answer. Surprisingly, he located it rapidly and told him the blood pressure should be 190 over 120. Morgan watched as he put the cuff on Kron and pumped it up. He looked at Morgan with a troubled expression and told him she was 248 over 174. He asked if he had mixed an IV solution and had enough pain medication in case there was an emergency C-section. Jim looked back at the phone and said yes, he had plenty. He told him he could feel the baby's head but could not see it. Morgan turned to Vader and asked how they should proceed knowing this information. Vader stood still as he searched data banks. What Vader had to say was not a good scenario or outcome. He said the baby was apparently stuck in the birth canal at which point the common thing was to leave mother and baby to die. Jim turned around and looked into the phone at Morgan and said, "No person or tribe member of this community will be left behind to die. I need the best scenario without cutting her open." Vader tabulated and informed Jim that if that baby did not come down the birth canal and out in the next five minutes, he would lose both patients.

Morgan told Jim to grab the forceps and pull the baby down the canal. He did not have time to sedate her by starting an IV. Morgan said, "It is too late, this baby will be here in seconds." Jim asked Marsha for the forceps. He told Aggie to have her drink without stopping the bourbon. Kron gulped it and was moving back and forth on the table. Jim yelled for her to stop moving and be still. Aggie dropped the bottle and laid on top of Kron. She pushed on her abdomen while she held her down with her body. She told Kron to hang on tight because this baby was coming out one way or another. Aggie kept pushing, making it easier for Jim to pull. He finally had hold of the head and turned the baby on its side, as Morgan told him the head was too big. Turning the baby sideways helped with pulling the baby down the canal. He followed further instruction from Vader to do an episiotomy the same way he would on a human female. He made the cut but this time Kron let out a roar that felt as though the roof would collapse. It took three minutes from the start of Morgan's instruction to the birth of baby boy Sasquatch. He told Kron he had to suture this cut once the afterbirth was delivered, and it would be painful to suture. She was not listening because she had her baby laying on her chest. *He's making the sweetest sounds*, Marsha thought.

Jim asked Marsha to take her blood pressure again. It was 290 over 181. Morgan gasped when Marsha gave him the numbers. Jim looked to Aggie, "What do you do to stop bleeding in your species?" She came running back with yarrow powder and told Kron to take the entire bunch of it. Jim had no idea what it was but if it had an effect, he was all for it. The afterbirth delivered, and Jim looked concerned when he saw it. He looked at Aggie and told her there was another baby. Aggie looked shocked. Kron heard him say that and tried to sit up. Marsha and Aggie had her lay back down.

Jim walked to the head of the table so he could talk to Kron. He told her there was another baby to deliver and it would be exceedingly difficult. He would need her decision if it came down to it, "Do I save you or the baby." The room was so quiet you could hear a pin drop. Kron looked into Jim's eyes and then to Aggie. She told Aggie that should she not make it, she would have to raise the babies. Aggie shook her head. She had her answer. This was her path for the future and uncharted territory. She could not sacrifice her baby yet to have this path defined. Kron felt the massive contraction and Jim, Marsha, and Aggie screamed at her to push as hard as she could and not stop. Jim also yelled, "DO NOT HOLD YOUR BREATH!" It took just one giant push and the baby was out. It was extremely small. Morgan, still watching on the screen, could see how tiny it was. Jim did not look at Morgan. He took the warmed blanket and told Marsha to take warm stones and place them around the baby and to make a small tent out of one of her baby's quilts. It would be helpful for her to put the baby in this makeshift heat-tent incubator. Marsha ran with the baby. The baby made funny noises like the other, so they knew there was a fighting chance. Jim asked if Aggie noticed if it was a boy or girl, but she had not looked at anything except its breathing. Kron lay motionless and unconscious. Jim came around the table and took her blood pressure. It was down to 200 over 112. He hoped she would sleep until her blood pressure was somewhat stable. He asked Morgan for other ideas for the tiny one. Vader already had a solution that was a totally herbal remedy to give both babies. Morgan told Jim to get a blood sample of each infant and send it to him for analysis.

Karen put the phone down and donned gloves to clean the wound and shave the hair around the suture to prevent infection. Jim asked Aggie what they used, and she told him cabbage leaves. Jim said, "Oh no, we will give her a shot of antibiotics. Is that right, Morgan?" he yelled.

Vader answered for him. "Yes, they are remarkably like humans when it comes to infections and how to clear them up." Jim removed his gloves, as did Karen. Jim looked down and saw all the glass from the broken bourbon bottle. He shook his head and was saddened that he lost a half bottle of his prime stash of St. Lucy. He walked over to the phone to express his appreciation to Morgan for helping him through this emergency.

Morgan replied, "We would not have saved Kron or the babies without the help of Vader." Jim thanked Vader. He told Morgan to go back to bed and he would call if any other issues arose.

Kron awoke as Aggie cleaned up the room. Jim was sitting beside her holding her hand and had covered the new baby with a blanket. Kron asked where the other baby was. He told her that Marsha was caring for her and that her baby girl was being kept warm surrounded by warming rocks and Marsha's babies, Morgan and Dorothy. She asked if the baby would live. Jim nodded his head and told her he was sure she would. Aggie grabbed her other hand. With fierce determination, Kron said, "There is no word for the agony of uncertainty. While I do not yet know the fate of my little girl, I refuse to lose hope. I want to believe she is a survivor; a fighter, and it is possible for her to live. I want to have that faith. But in its absence, I know she is resilient and has the unshakable virtue of this tribe. She is to be fierce. She was willing to sacrifice herself for her brother to live. I choose life for my daughter. She and the memories of this birth will shine like a constellation of stars. She will share every memory of what she saw, did, and remembered. She is a fierce and noble warrior." She and Aggie roared, and Jim yelled as loud as he could in unity with them.

Jim told Aggie that they needed to move Kron and the baby to her teepee and have Boc place warming stones around the perimeter to keep it warm. He also gave Aggie a package of absorbent pads so that the blood could be contained and would not soak into the ground. He instructed her how to slide them under Kron once she laid down with the baby. Kron settled in with her son and Virg was with them. He was so attentive to her and his son. Jim and Aggie knew they would be in wonderful hands with Virg.

Boc was already cleaning the room with disinfectant when Jim walked back in to get his instruments to sterilize. Jim thanked him for all the work he put forth. It was difficult for them all. Boc's response was incredible. "This birth put a trillion particles in space that have been forever changed simply because of the willingness of this baby girl to sacrifice herself for her brother. Now, we get to be the best of ourselves; but most importantly, we should reach for each other. What a pivotal moment for this tribe. I am proud to be a member. We will sing remembrance songs of this pure and unequivocal love and self-sacrifice for her brother. What a fierce and mighty warrior she will be."

Jim had wrapped all his instruments and headed back to his tent. Most were still asleep. He stopped at Marsha's tent and could see the light on. He said, "Knock knock. It's your favorite repairman. Is it safe?" She laughed and told him to come in.

Upon entering, he remarked that it was like living in Houston, it was so hot. He told her to back off of the heat a touch. He said warmly, "Not so hot that you could cook eggs on a sidewalk." He walked over to the pack-and-play and saw that the babies were asleep. "Now isn't this sweet, triplets. You go, girl!"

She laughed. "I took a picture and sent it to Morgan and told him it was a girl and what could any man want more than triplets. Of course, I am waiting to hear his response." He looked at Marsha's face. She looked pale and tired. He sat down next to her and asked to take her blood pressure. It was 180/80. He told Marsha that she would need to be on complete bed rest for the next two weeks. She could go with someone to the bathroom and then back to bed. He was going to go get Bitty to stay with her and care for the babies. "If Kron's little one continues to do fine, we will take her to Kron in the morning. I am going to drop off my bag and instruments, then go retrieve Bitty." He told her that when he returned he had better find her in her PJ's and lying down on that cot. Marsha looked at him and nodded, acknowledging that she understood.

Jim was concerned for Marsha as well as Kron and her baby daughter. It was a rough time for all. He unzipped the door to his tent. Bev was waiting inside for him. She stood up and told him she was proud of the heroic effort he and Morgan put forth to save Kron and both babies. He thanked her as he put everything on the table. He took one look at Bev and could see she was pale and looked tired. He told her to sit down and that he wanted to take her blood pressure. Sure enough, hers was extremely high as well. He told her to get in bed immediately. This was not a good thing. He was running through his mind what in the cave could be causing high blood pressure. When everyone was awake, they would have a debriefing on the birth and figure out how to be more efficient and what they could do differently. In addition, he would be taking everyone's blood pressure and having Karen log blood pressures of everyone twice a day for the next three days. For now, he would sleep until around 9:00 and then get up and bathe. It was nice of Virg to make a shower out of wood and bamboo.

He felt so much better after the shower. He went back to the tent and took off his robe and changed into jeans, a tee-shirt, and tennis shoes. He knew everyone had to be curious why a meeting was called. He told Bev and Marsha to stay in bed. They did not need to come to the meeting. It was just a debriefing. Karen sat at the table with a chair across from her and the blood pressure cuff. Jim stood in the middle of the room with the table and chairs beside him. Everyone had trickled in and were waiting for Jim to tell them how Kron and her babies were doing. Jim started by thanking the community for coming together. "Kron is doing fine this morning and both of her babies are with her. She will be doing a naming ceremony later this week. It was a difficult birth for mom and the babies. I want to thank Aggie for being the calming force for Kron and for being brave enough to jump on top of her and physically help to push the baby down the canal. Had that not happened, I would have had a much different outcome." Jim looked at Aggie and told her she could be his assistant anytime. She nodded and gave a soft whoop in thanks for his appreciation. After going through what each person did during the delivery, he had a better idea of how to revise the plan for efficiency during delivery and pre-planning prior to delivery.

He then advised them of something new that had popped up. For the next three days, he would be taking everyone's blood pressure twice per day. It was to rule some things out.

# Chapter Three

# A WORLD AT WAR

Watching the news was frightening and depressing. It looked like what the news media was putting out was nothing but failure of the human spirit to fight back against this onslaught of multidimensional fungal parasites that had infected citrus-bearing trees. It appeared to be a symbiotic attack on the core of the tree. It could communicate through the root systems and walk at night to reposition for optimal killing of organic matter. Many of the scientists appeared to be focused on the dripping venomous thorns. There was also a study of the crashed spacecraft of the Blue Alien. They found seeds that were in ionized gas that somehow transformed them into the parasite. The gas was an unknown element that was extraterrestrial. They could tell little else about the Blue from the ship. Many compartments were locked and inaccessible. The military scientists had it in their hangar in Nevada to determine how to open those locked compartments. To many, the inside of the ship reminded them of the seed vault in Norway. Their approach to come up with a solution was experiencing fragmentation at the highest levels. Many leaders kept shifting the research rather than letting the scientists finish a thorough evaluation of the problem. There was not a uniform approach to unite the discovery effort for a solution.

Morgan was sure one of the approaches was a quantum transfer of the multidimensional fungal parasite that attached itself by a symbiosis of sorts. That was the approach to pursue along with the black pitch with radium, uranium, and barium. He felt that could potentially be a gas otherwise unknown. Perhaps that was how the parasite was empowered with a quantum transfer technique. He had his team looking at this approach and working with Area 51 on ideas of how to open the compartments in the ship. None of the military or NSA could locate The Blue. Homeland Security thought the alien would stay close and look for an opportunity to retake the ship. There appeared to be the largest saturation of Tree Nightcrawlers (a name dubbed them by the media) around Area 51. For an unknown reason, they had not discovered Area 52 in Utah. In addition, Skinwalker Ranch was extremely active with paranormal activity. They had found a cow that had been pummeled with thorns. The thorns embedded in the cow were now growing trees that when four inches tall would jump from the cow and run through the field implanting itself in a freshly-tilled field. It only took one night for them to grow to five feet in height. When anyone on Skinwalker Ranch attempted to dig up the saplings, there was an immediate adverse effect. The ranch manager and his wife both began bleeding in the eye and a large lump appeared on the top of their heads. One thing they discovered on the saplings was that they contained not one venomous thorn. That was a particularly important finding. Morgan's team could not fathom how the cow acted as a host to produce over 100 saplings that could not only walk but run. They stayed grouped together so their roots touched each other. It gave them the ability to communicate, as many had stated.

Morgan presented a question to scientists worldwide as to why Skinwalker Ranch was the only place in the world that had this vampire-like activity between a cow and the saplings. This seemed to be the test area for The Blue and her Tree Nightcrawlers. Morgan assigned two scientists out of Bangalore, India to try growing thorns with cattle as hosts to determine the connection and how it worked. Morgan assigned the scientist in Antarctica to work on phasing and identifying magnetic radiation hit by bright lights of CMEs (Coronal Mass Ejection) from the sun.

He asked the scientific groups of Scandinavia to isolate the proteins in the venomous poison in the thorns. Morgan knew their specialized labs were well equipped to handle this task. Morgan's lab was working on polarization of the magnetic field around the Tree NightCrawler and the vibrations detected before they began to move. He knew there had to be something in common that linked all of this together. Privately, Morgan was working on the black pitch and its properties and considering how each would interact and if it could possibly counteract the poison thorns and kill off the walking Tree Nightcrawlers. If it did work, what type of delivery mechanism would be needed to vaporize mass Tree Nightcrawlers rather than one or two at a time?

Vader told Morgan he had a video call waiting. It was Dr. Lin Lo from a lab in Hong Kong. Morgan quickly walked to the communications lab. It was an encrypted call, which was unusual. "Morgan, this is Dr. Lo. I came across something that I think you may want to pursue. When I looked at crystals and the reaction with supernovas and their tachyon radiation on mitochondrial DNA, I detected a strange signature of a gravitational binding element. I think I found a way to track The Blue. We have discovered, after careful video study of the ship you have in custody, that attached to the top of the hull are over 300 smaller ships that are armed with a destruction device that could decimate the population of a country. There appears to also be a delivery system that sprays a crystal mist on the vegetation that affects just citrus which, of course, is acid-based. We would like you to attempt to disrupt their compartments with an electromagnetic pulse. We strongly believe it will dislodge the magnetic bond securing the lock on each compartment."

Morgan told him his A.I. Vader would make the necessary contacts with the military at Area 51 and 52. "Do you have a guess at tracking The Blue, Dr. Lo?" Morgan asked.

"We believe she has a high component composition of crystal. The crystal has a definite signature and emits a unique data wave. We have traced that unique wave to a high cliff with a deep and long cave system that runs under, as well as adjoining, Skinwalker Ranch." He also advised Morgan that a large formation of the Tree Nightcrawlers was forming in Arizona along Crystal Cave. Morgan knew that could not be a coincidence. *They were tied in some way. I only wish I knew how.* Morgan thanked Dr. Lo for giving him his findings and would make sure the information was passed along. Dr. Lo told him that Dr. Kay Vanni was in Winslow and a leader in the research of crystals and data. He advised Morgan to recruit her to investigate things at Crystal Cave. Morgan agreed and disconnected the call.

Morgan asked Vader to reach Dr. Vanni and to let him know when she was on the viewer. Morgan thought since he was on the phone, he would give Marsha a quick call and see how the new family was doing. She picked up on the second ring. Morgan was smiling and didn't wait for the formal hello. He jumped right in with, "I love you and I miss you." She threw him a kiss and he made a goofy face to see her laugh. He told her he missed that infectious laugh. He wanted to know how the twins were acclimating. She told him that Bitty and Boc were spoiling them. They were always being held and in someone's arms. She told him that Boc, while shy and quiet, was a genius in philosophy. He told Marsha he had a call waiting and needed to run. Morgan made sure to tell her that they were making progress, and he knew they were on track to figure this out. Marsha knew he missed the community and that he felt they were all his family. He told her to stay strong, and they both blew kisses to each other. Morgan disconnected the call.

Vader hooked Morgan and Dr. Vanni together in a video conference call. Morgan briefed her on the conversation with Dr. Lo. She advised Morgan that she'd already had a conversation with him and felt The Blue could be after data. She felt that the Crystal Cave held all Earth's information from past, present, and, most likely, future planning for the planet. The Blue obviously needed it desperately to come up with a plan to turn our citrus trees into Killer Nightcrawlers. Morgan told her that conclusion made sense; however, could she prove any hypothesis she had? She told him crystals had a distinct energy signature and that she had arranged for her and a contingent of military to do a helicopter drop at the cave to pursue this avenue of research. She told him that a fleet of helicopters would be firing flames to torch the Tree Nightcrawlers if they came close to the cave.

Morgan went back to his lab to work with Vader and his assistants. They had achieved a few successful experiments with the black pitch. Devin explained to Morgan that she'd had a mishap working with the separation of the barium of the black pitch. She started with Newton's Law that for every action there was an equal and opposite reaction. "With that said, I believe I may have stumbled upon a genetic replication because it was exposed to tachyon radiation which caused a toxic, if you will, affixation of all but one of the minerals within the black pitch. The uranium caused the toxic affixation. It holds great promise, and we should have the first look at this affixation soon.

Morgan walked over to his own experiment. He was working on a time displacement theory with crystals and perhaps using The Blue's ship spray disperser against her. One thing he knew for sure was there were several promising solutions in various stages of development. He found it amazing that almost all the labs had focused on something similar. He was not sure if that was good or bad, but what he did know was that it was a fact. He shook his head. He now knew and felt that same passion and push as Madame Curie.

Then Morgan thought for a second about anti-matter and dark matter and the detonation of that matter in a small, controlled environment. He asked Vader to call Dr. Wells at Wright Patterson Airforce Base in Dayton. "Would you ask him to do some research on this in relation to the Tree Nightcrawlers as a possible solution or, at the very least, as a piece of the puzzle combined with another approach?"

Morgan sat in his chair and turned on a news channel. He could not stand to look at the destruction and lives lost up to this point. He felt like hope had been ripped from him. He had not realized that Vader was beside him and could detect the feeling of hopelessness that Morgan felt. He told Morgan that his strength and resolve reminded him of Marco Polo, the great adventurer and warrior, who was fighting to save humanity through knowledge and determination and who would never allow nor accept a catastrophic failure while searching for this solution. This point in time was pre-ordained to be the exact time for Morgan. Morgan looked up at Vader and said, "Every moment I grow more sure-footed in this, and I am more certain of who I am becoming. The universe is under no obligation to make sense of this for me; however, I believe that we will be successful, and I choose to believe it with all my being. I might not be the most logical thinker, but I am proud to bear this mantle. Every sentient creature on this planet will see a future, a clear path. We will make it so!" Vader was an A.I. with few words. He did not waste anything, including words. Morgan reminded him that words made us who we were—they defined us. Like man, woman, champion, basketball player, astronaut, scientist. Do not ever be afraid of being wasteful with words.

Morgan had a meeting scheduled at the military lab in an hour. They had been working on an approach with a protein inhibitor that may counteract the venom from the thorn on the Tree Nightcrawlers. He was extremely interested in this, especially combined with dark matter possibilities. After this meeting, Morgan convened with all the Forest Guardian leaders to update them and to ask for their suggestions and ideas. He also wanted to check on Rama. Morgan wished that Princess Celia and her Titan relatives could help; however, they were not to interfere. It was against their overall directives in that it could alter the future of the planet Earth. Princess Celia could direct peace talks and look after the sick or injured. They may have to call on her. He hoped that she would answer KiKi's arrows. He hoped the rest of the tribe would be safe, taking refuge with the Mammoth Cave tribe, and that they would be able to ride out the siege together. The cave splintered into unknown caves that could be blocked off like Marsha's group. He knew Cleg would be worried about his tribe being divided.

Vader interrupted Morgan, who was deep in thought. He told Morgan he had blood work from Jim's cave. He advised Morgan that he took the liberty to run the blood work and he should review it. Morgan shook his head and asked if he could transfer it to the screen here at his console. Vader did not answer. Morgan blinked his eyes and there in front of him on the panel were the test results. It did not make sense. All the male blood work looked fine. The women's blood was perplexing. He wondered if there was an extreme amount of a certain mineral. Perhaps it was lacking vitamin D and, if so, how would they fix it, especially with three of them pregnant? He thought he may have a task for Princess Celia as a courier of meds for the various tribes that have taken in humans into their cave system. He would have to notify Jim, but he had to prepare for his meeting with the tribes. He asked Vader to call and ask Jim what he brought with him for vitamin D deficiency. If he did not have that in his stock, to let him know that Princess Celia could act as a courier for delivery of vitamin D to the tribes.

Vader advised Morgan his files were loaded into the conference room and were ready for his use. He also advised that the room was full and some were standing. He added that there appeared to be about 30 military personnel of all ranks and that the presidents of the United States, Mexico, Canada, and Chili would also be in physical attendance with four other leaders joining via teleconference. Vader told Morgan he could not count accurately the number of Forest Guardians; however, his best guess would be around 28. He also advised Morgan the Black Deer alien and his mate were there and currently engaged in discussion with General DeSalle and President Kennedy. Vader told Morgan he was happy to see Rama in attendance and he had healed nicely from his burn wounds. In addition, he had around his neck a Presidential Medal Of Freedom for his heroic and meritorious contribution to the security and safe delivery of Tibu's delivery to the bunker. Morgan was impressed and told Vader it was well deserved.

Morgan gathered his notes and told Vader he was ready to head over to the large conference room, but he had forgotten how to get there. Vader said in an interesting vocal tone to follow him. They left the lab and headed down the steel and concrete hall to the glass elevator. They exited at Level 6 and took a left turn at the end of a hall that was covered in copper with a sign that read Train. They waited on the platform. It took only moments and the train was easy to spot. It was a brilliant yellow color with bright orange and white flashing lights. Morgan noticed it was up off the platform and rails. He asked Vader if it was magnetic. Vader told him in simplistic terms, "Yes, it is magnetic with other properties and elements to give the train the ability to move over 600 miles an hour through an unground highway that would be taking them to Area 51. We will arrive in about 13 minutes." Morgan looked shocked. He questioned why this technology had not been declassified and released for public use. Vader responded, "It is classified and top-secret only, sir." The door swooshed open. Morgan and Vader entered the two-seat train. It had beautiful black leather seats of which two could sit and there was a rail for two additional guests to stand. The doors swooshed shut and Morgan heard a seal pop closed. He turned to Vader and asked if it was not only air sealed as well as hermetically sealed. Vader replied, "Top secret, sir." Morgan sat silently for the remainder of the trip which gave him the opportunity to look out the window. The tunnel was smooth concrete with the ceiling being titanium. He assumed the ground was also titanium. He could smell something unique and was unsure of its origin. He turned again to Vader and before he could ask, he answered, "Top secret, sir."

Morgan was annoyed, just enough to be sarcastic, when he said, "Nice to see my tax dollars spent on such an extravagant black ops project."

Vader answered, "I would not know, sir."

Morgan laughed and told Vader it was okay—he understood, top secret. In fact, he had plenty of top-secret projects himself pertaining to his work that had a designation of "Eyes Only," meaning his, of course. Vader sat silently for the remainder of the trip. Morgan now wished he had never said that to Vader. The ride of the train was smooth. There were no bumps or swaying of the vehicle. He had heard they'd developed this technology; however, he felt more like they back reversed engineered this technology, along with at least a dozen other technologies, like microchips. He could not wait to see what was at Area 51. He did not know what to expect. Morgan imagined he would hear a lot of the same type of words as Vader.

Vader finally spoke, "Arrival in three minutes. Please have your ID out and visible for inspection." Morgan looked at him and thought that was strange. He removed his wallet with his driver's license and Government ID card. Vader spoke again and told him to remove any metal and to be prepared to drop it into the container provided, including his cell phone. Morgan's growing suspicion of Vader was now on high alert. He thanked him but said nothing else. The train stopped; however, it was dark. They were clearly still underground. The lights must have been on sensors as they now illuminated the train platform with a Giant number 3 and the words Exit and Wait facing the camera. Morgan thought this was creepy. Vader looked at Morgan and said, "Just a security precaution." Morgan did a brain-block technique of thinking about a brick wall. He focused and concentrated on that wall with all his being. Vader asked if he was nervous about this presentation or if he needed him to set anything up. While Morgan heard him, he stayed focused and never answered.

A military man appeared. He was in dress uniform from the Army. Addressing him as Dr. King, he introduced himself as Major Danny Landenberger. He was assigned to him as his personal liaison and assistant. He focused his mind on introductions to block out Vader's mind-reading talent. He hoped that he was successful in this attempt to block him. He repeated Major Landenburger's name over and over and viewed it written on the brick wall. The major asked for them to follow him to the security point. Their entry point was grey, dull, and uneventful. Once they arrived at security, it was bright to the point of needing sunglasses. Cameras were everywhere. He was asked to empty all pockets, and to take off his belts and shoes. He was then asked to hand his briefcase to the sergeant sitting at a dual scanner-type machine. He was then asked to go through the x-ray scanner and, once clear, to proceed to the chair situated in front of the eye scanner and fingerprint machine. It took about half an hour to clear security. Vader was nowhere around. He was curious about that, however, he was glad he was gone. Then he thought about Vader's capabilities and decided it was probably a reverse-engineered technology that came from here. Best to be focused, with no mind wandering in awe of everything he was seeing. He had learned this focus technique when he was in med school at Stanford.

The hall they walked down was a lot like the bunker—steel and concrete. Certainly not easy to penetrate with drone eyes or overhead spy satellites. They stopped at a large hangar that was filled with Forest Guardians and humans; and in the front of the hangar, sitting behind the podium, was Princess Celia, President Kennedy, and Secretary of the Army, General Campbell. He felt butterflies and immediately implemented his focus technique. The major walked him to the head of the room and introduced him to the Secretary of the Army, and he said his hellos to Princess Celia and President Kennedy. He looked up as he heard someone approaching. It was Nodane the Black Deer. He nodded to them all and stood off to the side of the chairs closest to General Campbell. Major Landenberger asked all to be seated. He introduced the first speaker—Nodane from the Polaris Star System. He stepped up to the microphone in all his majesty and elegance and turned and thanked all the speakers behind him. He then turned back to his audience.

"Strength and resolve. These are the virtues we need to display in order to save the world from this dire threat. What happened in the past no longer exists. What will happen next has not yet been written. We have only NOW. My friends in this room are our greatest advantage. What we do, here in this moment, matters now and has the ability to determine the future. Instinct and logic together, that is how we will defeat The Blue in this battle to come. We will find a way. All of Earth's future can change with our next move. The solution is ours to make happen. Please let us not form a cocoon around ourselves for protection. No, that will not prevent a catastrophic event. We are looking to our scientists to guide us through this war. They will give us the path to victory. I know I am to be part of this effort by the mere fact that if I were meant for a different future, I would not be standing here with you. Just know that whatever your path is, you can handle it. One of your people in the Cuyahoga Valley National park found me. She saved me. The human race is my balance. You always have been. I am afraid I will not find this balance again if we do not work together to overcome this challenge. Just know there is an entire galaxy full of humanity that will reach out for each of you to succeed. I need you to find that person in your life who seems furthest from you right now and reach for them. Reach out and let them guide you and have them do the same. This is about togetherness. There are many people in the Cuyahoga Valley not here with us today, but I feel them. I am certain of who I am becoming because of the people with whom I have bonded in the Valley. Every night I look to the stars and my planet of Polaris. I choose to believe that I was sent here at this moment in time to stand with you. It may not be logical to some of you; nonetheless, I choose to believe that the only gift I have left to give you is my belief in what the future holds—success. I would like to quote a wise man of your planet, 'Earth provides enough to satisfy man's needs but not for every man's greed.' I promise to fulfill my responsibility towards your, and now my, planet. We are all global citizens and we must and will resolve this unique challenge for our future generations. I choose to believe success is ours."

Nodane turned to stand next to Secretary Campbell. The room had erupted in applause and soft whoops. President Kennedy walked over and put her forehead to his as she stroked his neck. He closed his eyes to send a message to President Kennedy, a message of love for this planet and all its sentient life. She lifted her head as he opened his eyes and thanked him by calling him friend. One by one, all of the Forest Guardians in the room did exactly what President Kennedy had done.

The last to follow in everyone's footsteps was Morgan. He told Nodane that he was honored to know him and work with him. Nodane quietly advised him to focus on High Energy Gamma Rays as well as gravitational waves that were consistent with quantum singularities. "There lies a solution with the black pitch by adding bismuth, magnesium, zinc, and aluminum."

Morgan raised his head and said, "You violated your planet's Prime Directive."

He corrected Morgan and said, "My former planet," and smiled. Morgan thanked him again.

It was Morgan's turn to speak. He started with, "Well, I always get the toughest act to follow." The room laughed. It took a minute or so as Morgan decided to let them laugh. He continued, "The deadly toxin of The Blue's Nightcrawlers is the greatest challenge this planet has ever had put before its people. We have many scientists working on this problem. We thought the most promising countermeasure was the use of thermodynamic energy which can change stability stasis. However, that is looking less likely as we move along. We have been at this for five days now. Each day that we are delayed, thousands of human lives are lost. We are not the only sentient life on this planet. Hundreds of millions of animals, birds, amphibians, insects, reptiles, and all others have been lost. Two species have been destroyed and are now extinct. Now we are focused on a possible solution with the help of Nodane. We should have our first look at it tomorrow. We will be using tachyon radiation to affect the mitochondrial DNA of the infected citrus trees. The crashed disk of The Blue is here at Area 51. Her craft has a type of aerial spraying device that is 1,000 times more effective than our aerial spray technology. I plan to look at it with permission from General Campbell." He looked back at him and he nodded in agreement. "We are also looking at crystal from the Crystal Caves in Arizona that could amplify an EMP. We must pursue that with caution because that solution, as tempting as it is, could take out our own infrastructure. I have used Marie Curie as inspiration many times. She and her husband Pierre were ridiculed and put into an old leaking shed to work. They never gave up and ultimately discovered a new element—radium. We should fare much better because our labs, one might say, are out of this world." Everyone laughed. "We are working 24 hours a day until this solution is proven. Thank God we have many brave military men and women willing to put their lives in peril to capture these NightCrawler Trees. And rest assured, the intelligence agencies across the globe are tracking down The Blue Alien. Uh oh, I think I am stealing the president's thunder." Morgan turned to the president and then walked over and shook her hand. Everyone stood and gave the president a thunderous applause.

"I am grateful for the opportunity to meet each of you. I have to admit I was sheltered as a small girl, sheltered from life's more unsavory things. My mother told me to keep my guard up and my head down and to keep my distance from the world. As I grew older and went off to college to begin to make my mark, I grew bolder; but there was still a great deal I was keeping in reserve. It was easy to ignore the spark of darkness and the shadows in the corner of brighter days. It was a learning time for me. Time to learn about trust, love, kindness, courage, and strength—all things I find I now need to lead this nation forward and to bring hope, trust, kindness, love, courage, and strength to all our communities in the United States of America. One Nation Under God! I see this nation as more beautiful and perfect as we make our way through this crisis. When this is over, we as a nation will mourn our losses; but their stories will never end. They will serve to light our paths more brightly as we carry on and keep their memory always in our hearts. Their stories will show all of us that there are no versions of love, just LOVE itself. It is worth searching for even if it takes a lifetime. It is worth every memory to share and to cherish. We, together, are a blessed nation. We care for all as we struggle together. We rise to meet this challenge together. We carry our candle of light into the darkness to pave our new path with divine wonder and the knowledge to build a better future. Let us stand together, no one by themselves, holding tight to trust, kindness, love, courage, strength, and the hope for a bright new day with no shadows overtaking the light. I have abiding trust in the people of the world. We are all looking for answers to save the world. Today, we rise to this challenge. I also choose to believe Nodane. I believe you are all my family, and I choose to walk forward through this crisis together with all of you. I know we will find our way to a better future. Thank you for coming and thank you for choosing to believe. I am grateful for this family we call a nation." President Kennedy returned to her seat.

A small contingent of the Army band, as well as flag bearers, marched into the hall playing "God Bless America." Everyone stood. It was a day Morgan would carry in his memory forever. He wished that everyone sequestered in their hiding places could have heard this inspirational talk. Everyone present was more determined than ever to seek a solution to this crisis. He looked for Vader who was nowhere to be found. Morgan found that odd. He made his way back to the train and boarded it with Cleg. They both shared their thoughts. Morgan suggested that Cleg come back to his lab so that he could call the tribe and see Bitty. He knew they needed each other right now. A video call would be just the prescription. Cleg was in awe of the panels that had streaming information. *It's a lot to sort through*, he thought. Morgan walked Cleg to a panel that had nothing streaming on it. He punched in the phone number to Karen.

Cleg could hear a phone ringing and Karen finally answered. As she said hello, she saw Cleg and was surprised. She told them both that she hoped they were getting closer to finding a solution to this crisis. Morgan told her they had several approaches he hoped held the answers. Karen told Morgan and Cleg that she was putting down the phone to bring everyone together. It took about five minutes. Soon, all were gathered around. Karen told Cleg she wanted him to meet the newest addition to the tribe. Kron stepped closer to the camera and showed him her strong son and she told him about her fierce and courageous daughter. She told Cleg the naming ceremony would be held when the tribe was together again. Cleg nodded.

Bitty pushed her way to the front to say hello to her dad. She was like a little chatterbox telling him everything that was happening, how she helped with the babies, and how she had been painting the walls of the cave just like he and Ja'al did in their special place. Cleg smiled. She told him on her back was a handprint in blue paint of everyone in the cave. She turned around for Cleg and Morgan to see. She turned back around and told him that Bev called her a walking billboard like the ones in New York. "I carry these handprints as a banner for our community," she solemnly stated. He was so proud of her, as was Morgan. Virg took the lead in letting him know what was set up and how the schedule appeared to be working. Jim took a turn talking through the rough delivery and that without Aggie's help it would have been a different outcome.

On the human side of things, Morgan was advised that they had a problem. He leaned in, his forehead furled with worry. Cleg could feel the anxiety coming from Morgan. He placed his hand on Morgan as Jim told him the women had a complete breakdown of vitamin D, but none of the female Sasquatch had issues from what he could tell. Unless they found a solution, he would run out of vitamins to give the women in four weeks. He explained the food that was brought to the shelter would not supply the boost of vitamin D they needed. Jim added he had no idea what was depleting it from their systems. He told Morgan that Karen and he had been running tests on everything looking for a hint as to the cause. Cleg asked if he could speak. He told Jim that he had seen this one other time with the women of his tribe. There was a specific mold that grew in the sand that when mixed with water grew spores that somehow depleted necessary minerals in their women. Jim looked at Virg and then Virg told Cleg about how he was plugging holes by mudding them with sand from the sandstone. Karen stepped in and asked Cleg how they mitigated the problem. Cleg informed her that the tribe moved to a new location. Jim and Karen looked worried, knowing that was not feasible. She asked Morgan about covering the walls with the extra sheets to block the spores from spreading within the cave air. Morgan and Jim both thought that was an excellent idea. Aggie said she would be willing to cut her fur and put it over the mud to also keep the spores from circulating. Morgan liked that idea, as well; however, he asked what the loss of her fur as insulation would do to her body temperature. She did not know.

Morgan asked if it was affecting their blood pressure. Jim looked down and said, "Only Marsha and Bev. It must be the pregnancy. Both are on complete bed rest." Morgan was upset, and a tear ran down his face. Jim said, "I'm on top of this, Morgan. You do what you do best. Cleg, you do what you do best. Is there a way for a drone flyover that could survey the landscape to rule out any Tree Nightcrawlers around the cave? If it's clear; the drone could drop meds on a flyover." They had no way to determine for themselves if there were any around the cave. Morgan told Jim that would happen in the next few hours and he would call him with the results. Cleg asked if Virg and Boc could push back the stone and grab the meds from the drone drop. Virg told him that would not be an issue.

"Jim, what meds should we send?"

He asked for Lisinopril and vitamin D. "In addition, figure out something light beside the sheets for the walls, like tarps." Morgan assured him that he would have the needed meds and tarps before sundown and instructed Jim to take inventory for other medical items he may need in case the siege went on longer than a couple of weeks. He then disconnected the call in order to organize the drop for him.

Morgan reluctantly called for Vader, who asked how he could help. He told him he needed a satellite look at Brandywine Falls to see if there were ant Tree Nightcrawlers within a five-mile radius. He continued his mind trick with focus by putting his words in front of a brick wall. He was not going to give away why he was interested in the Falls. Morgan tried to keep his focus by thinking about herbs. Vader told him there was nothing close to the Falls, so Morgan asked if it would be clear for a ranger to pick up herbs he needed for his research. Vader continued to expand his scanning of the area for the Tree Nightcrawlers. He looked for 10 miles and it was still clear. Vader told him the closest pocket he found was in Geneva. There was a concentration of them in the grape vineyards. Now was the time to get the herbs. He thanked Vader and sent him on a wild goose chase of retrieving skin scrapings of both the Snallygaster and Rama the dragon and the melon heads would need blood draws. He knew that would be challenging to say the least and would keep him busy for the rest of the day.

As soon as Vader left, he could relax. He called and spoke with Karen and advised her to radio the Park Ranger station to have them drop the tarps. He would call in meds to be picked up and dropped, as well. The drop had to happen that afternoon. Karen asked for extra blankets, a few cot pads, and more towels. She also mentioned that it would be nice to have a couple of cases of Oreo cookies for the pregnant ladies. "Oh, and the last request is for more paint to keep Bitty busy."

Karen heard from Ranger Long that he had gathered blankets, tarps, towels, soap, shampoo, Clorox wipes, and a queen-size cot with a built-in pillow, as well as nine new prescriptions and additional herbs. He contacted Karen on the radio when he was outside the Falls entrance to the cave with the much-needed supplies. He heard the rock being pushed aside; and Jim, Aggie, Boc, and Virg emerged and helped Ranger Long unload the truck as expeditiously as possible. They were about half done when they saw a UFO off in the distance. Karen told Ranger Long to pull the truck into the cave immediately. Ranger Long backed it into the cave. As soon as it cleared the mouth of the cave, Boc and Virg rolled the stone back into place. Ranger Long thought it could not be coincidental that a UFO showed up at this location. That UFO had the entire planet to fly over. Why here in the Park? No one had ever reported seeing a UFO within the Cuyahoga Valley National Park. It was remarkable they were able to get the truck in before she could locate them. Karen thought they should report this to Morgan. First, they tackled unloading the truck and organizing the supplies in the storage section. Virg and Boc then started hanging the tarps while Jim worked on organizing the medical supplies. He knew Bev would like the queen-size cot and had Karen deliver it to Bev and help her make up the bed with new sheets.

Morgan was glad that he ordered tarps with a lead paint imprinted on both sides so they would not be able to obtain heat signatures. Virg, Boc, Aggie, Ranger Long, and Jim temporarily hung all the tarps with sticky tape. They wanted to wait until there would be no possibility of anyone or anything detecting a hammering sound. They also decided to cover the ceiling and floors. It was now sealed completely. They decided to not move the truck for fear someone would hear the engine start. Ranger Long liked the canvas truck and decided that he would make this his home. He took Bev's old cot and made it up with a sheet and a sleeping bag. The truck had a jump seat in the back and a crate for a table. Aggie gave him a light for the back of the truck, as well as two water bottles. She also put him on the schedule rotation for bathing at the water pool. Aggie suggested that Ranger Kopchek and Ranger Long alternate security perimeter patrols. They would also be assigned to assist Virg with repairs and, when time, hanging the tarps in the proper way. For now, they would secure any of the tape that lifted off the rocks and tarps. They would also work on filling in the gaps again using wedged tight rocks. They would still have to mud; however, they would mix the mud in a sealed tent. That would prevent the spores from being stirred up in the air. They used every precaution to keep the girl safe. They sealed their tents for the next two days and limited going in and out in an attempt to keep as many spores out of their tents as possible. Jim gave Marsha and Bev the first dose of blood pressure medicine, as well as vitamin D drops. He prescribed complete bed rest for the rest of the week. By then, the medication and vitamin D would help to keep their blood pressure under control. He felt much better about their situation. In the back of his mind, however, he still thought about the UFO and if it saw them. It concerned him.

Jim went by Kron's teepee to check on her and the babies. He had his black bag with him. When he entered, she was laying on a wool blanket and the babies were on her shoulder. He asked her how she was feeling. She laid there and said nothing. Jim looked concerned and kneeled next to her. He opened his bag, pulled out his stethoscope, and asked her if she was okay with him listening to her and the babies. She turned her head away from him. He hesitated for a moment then decided to listen to the babies. The little boy was active and had bright eyes. The little girl looked like she may be losing weight, which was not good. She lay listlessly as he listened. It sounded to

Jim like her lungs were congested. Then it dawned on him that perhaps Kron thought she would lose her little girl. He listened to Kron and she, too, had congestion. Jim put his hand on Kron and asked her if she felt sick and if she had muscle pain. She still did not answer. He then asked her if her female area hurt from the delivery. Again, she said nothing. He asked her if the baby girl had been coughing and this time she nodded her head yes. He wondered what a normal temperature would be for them. He picked up the baby and took her temperature. It was alarming at 104 degrees. He asked Kron if she had been nursing, and she shook her head no. This was now serious. He did not want to take the baby to Bev or Marsha since he did not know what type of virus this baby had. He told Kron he needed to take the baby for treatment. She continued to look away. He went immediately to Aggie and advised her that he did not know what the virus was; however, he was sure it was probably an upper respiratory infection. The baby was not eating or drinking. Without that, this baby would not last the night. He told Aggie that he needed to insert an IV in her arm to provide fluid as well as an antibiotic and that she would have to protect it so it did not dislodge. They took the baby into the medical niche and laid the baby on the table. Jim decided to shave her arm so the tape would stick better once the catheter was inserted. It was his lucky day. He hit her vein on the first try. He opened the drip so the fluid would infuse faster and decided to piggyback the antibiotic. He let Aggie hold the baby to provide comfort. They stayed with her for an hour, and it appeared she was stable. He told Aggie he wanted to check on Kron as it appeared she also had the virus. He went to her and set up the IV with the fluids and the antibiotic. He asked her again if she was experiencing any pain in the stitches in her birth area, but once more she did not answer. He asked if he could look. She did not answer so he decided to take a chance. She did not fight back. Sure enough, it was infected, and he had a suspicion that she was septic. He drew blood with no objection and then ran to look at it under the microscope.

Jim knew this was serious. She had a bacterial infection known as pseudomonas in her bloodstream. It was imperative that the stitches be pulled immediately and the area thoroughly cleaned. He needed to find Virg to tell him what was happening. Jim located him repairing a portion of a tarp that had pulled away from the tape. He explained that Kron and his daughter were both extremely ill and that they would have to be on bed rest for the foreseeable future since they were being treated intravenously. Jim instructed Virg that he would need to clean the wound in Kron's birth area three times a day. First, though, he needed to remove the infected sutures. He advised Virg that it would be extremely painful; but once they were out, she would feel better. Jim asked if he would allow her to be given pain medicine that would make her sleep. That would mean he would have to take on the "mommy" duties for the next few days. He replied, "All of the tribe takes turns caring for the sick members. They will make their special bark tea for Kron and baby girl." He assured Jim that they all knew how to make the tea. In addition, they would show Ranger Long how to prepare it. He would also assign Ranger Karen and Ranger Long to cooking and clean-up duty for the next couple of days. They now had a plan.

As Jim expected, removing the sutures was painful; however, Kron bravely struggled not to cry out. After the first suture was removed, he pushed the pain medicine and she drifted off to sleep. He was able to remove the remainder of the sutures quickly and clean the entire area. He told Virg to get the clipper and shave the area as it would be easier to keep clean. Virg complied and as Kron slept, he was able to accomplish everything necessary to fight this infection. Jim told Virg to stay with her while he checked on the baby girl.

Aggie was tending to her while he worked on Kron. When Jim came back in, he could see an improvement in the baby. She had her eyes open and was looking at Aggie while she stroked her fur. Jim asked Aggie how she was doing. Aggie told him she was much better and was now responding. She told him there was no way this baby had been nursed for a day. She wanted to feed her and Jim told her he would get a bottle of warm water for now. "We will evaluate after she drinks a bottle and if she can keep it down." Aggie agreed but asked if he would put a leaf of green tea in the water. He hesitated and then decided it would be okay. He told Aggie that she could take her back to her teepee and that he would bring the bottle as soon as it was ready. Jim went to the makeshift kitchen and heated water. He was extremely glad he had these small bottles. The water seemed the correct temperature, so he dropped in a green tea leaf, and tightened down the nipple. Aggie was surprised that he was back so soon. He handed her the bottle and Aggie tenderly touched the baby's lips with her finger. She immediately tried to latch on. Aggie slipped the bottle nipple into her mouth and she took the water and fell asleep as she drank. Aggie told Jim that the baby would be fine and that she and Boc would look after her that night. Jim told her he would be back early in the morning to start another IV bag and antibiotic. He told her to make sure that she protected the IV site. She nodded to Jim while she looked down at the baby and stroked her head. Jim stood for a second and watched Aggie display such love and caring for this baby. He smiled as he turned to check on Kron. Virg was sitting beside her trying to hold onto the baby boy crawling all over him. He took out his stethoscope and listened. Her breathing was not as labored, however, she felt hot. He told Virg he would be back in the morning to give her another bag of IV fluids and another round of antibiotics. He told him to come and get him if he thought she was getting worse or was in pain. Virg never looked up at Jim; he was stroking her arm while she slept and juggling the baby with his other arm. Jim left quietly.

Jim returned to his tent and unzipped it. He entered and zipped it back up, trying to be as quiet as possible so as not to wake Bev. He sanitized his hands again and decided to lie on the extra camping cot rather than waking Bev by joining her in the queen-size cot. He was tired and no sooner had he laid down and covered up than he was fast asleep. He could not believe it when his watch alarm went off. He quickly turned it off. He looked over at Bev who was sitting up in bed smiling at him.

"Well, my wayward husband was out late last night."

He sat up and swung his legs to the side of the cot, putting on his shoes. He told Bev about Kron and the baby girl. "Kron has a serious infection and the baby has an upper respiratory infection. Both serious." He told Bev not to get up yet and that she may NOT be around either of them right now and the same went for Marsha.

"Uh, before you go could I please have one of your prescriptions for a kiss?" He laughed and told her before he went to see them, he would go grab her a cup of coffee. She thanked him and told him to bring her four Oreo cookies to dunk. He laughed and told her he would be back with her special request. PREGO. They both laughed. Jim returned with two mugs of coffee and an entire pack of Oreos. He had two and she had four.

"Okay, dear, I have rounds to make. Bitty will be by, I am sure, any moment. She can't stand not being with El, Morgan-Barkley, and Dorothy. Oh, and tell her to not go around Kron or her babies. If she does, she can't be around Marsha or our babies."

Bev was concerned. "Sounds serious. Will they pull through?"

Jim thought about it and he shook his head, unsure. He looked down and told her it was too soon to tell. Bev knew that Jim was stressed about this. First, the difficult birth and now this. Bev asked if they got all the tarps hung. He nodded his head yes. She could hardly watch as Jim struggled. She asked him to come sit by her even if it was just for a second. Their eyes locked. She smiled at him and held out her arms to him. He smiled back and then walked over and sat on the cot next to her. He asked her how she liked the roomy cot. She thought for a moment and smiled again, informing him it would be much more comfortable with him beside her. They embraced each other and Jim enjoyed her warmth and the tenderness of her hug. He kissed her and thanked her for such wonderful understanding and support. He pushed back and gave her a kiss and asked her if she wanted another cup of coffee or, better yet, dandelion tea. She responded, "Perfect."

He told her he would be right back. He decided he would stop off with a cup of tea for Marsha and see how her blood pressure was this morning. He yelled, "Knock knock," and Bitty came to the door holding both babies. Jim walked in and said, "This community could not function with you, Bitty." She smiled and told Jim she loved the babies, but Dorthy was her favorite. He laughed and said, "A good mommy does not have a favorite."

Bitty snapped back, "Yes, they do; but a good mommy never admits it."

"Well, a philosopher today," Marsha added, "and a great help to me." Jim handed her the cup of tea and told her he wanted to take her blood pressure. He noticed that her color looked better. He sat down next to her, wrapped the cuff around her arm, put his stethoscope in his ears, and pumped it up. As it released, he removed his stethoscope and told her it was much better this morning. Marsha wanted to know how much longer she had to stay in bed. Jim asked why she would want to get up with the most wonderful helper in the world, the beautiful and effervescent Bitty the Brave.

At that moment, the ceiling started to shake and they heard a loud noise. Everyone ran for the very back of the cave close to the water pool. The rangers told everyone to be quiet and sit down. Jim was grateful the babies were quiet. Then he noticed that Kron was by herself. He signaled for Virg to go to her and keep her calm. Both rangers turned their radios off so there would be no traceable sound wave. They could hear the pulsing of something above them. Then there was a fierce roar and vibration again. And then it was silent. They all wondered if it was the alien who somehow discovered that they were around this area.

Boc stood as did Jim. Boc said, "We are safe and undiscovered thanks to these special tarps." Boc told the community how proud he was of their courage to remain calm and to stay quiet to not give away their hiding place. He told them they needed to be vigilant and attentive to being as quiet as possible. He knew it would be difficult with the babies. "It will take Bitty and Aggie who know how to interpret the babies' communication and meet their needs right away. Most tribe members are experts at this because it was always imperative to stay hidden from humans. That meant no crying babies."

Jim, Marsha, and Bev knew there must be a leak in Morgan's lab. Someone was a spy and feeding information to The Blue. Jim had a feeling it was a spacecraft that landed above them searching for them. Thank God Ranger Kopchek thought to requisition those tarps. "Let's have Aggie come to our tent, Bev. Marsha, you come over, too. We need to rethink the schedule and reallocate jobs. I believe we should talk to Morgan about a turncoat in his lab.

It took Aggie no time to reassign tasks. From this point on, Bitty was to take care of the human babies. She would carry them most of the time to sense what they needed before they cried out. Aggie would take both of Kron's babies for the time being. She thought Virg could probably handle the babies but was not totally convinced of it since they were both first-time parents. To prevent the smell of cooking food from giving away their hiding place, only dry goods were to be used. That included no coffee or tea. Water only. Bev interjected that she had brought several packs of Crystal Light iced tea and lemonade. Marsha said she had fruit punch and lemonade. Ranger Long said he requisitioned two cases of Gatorade. Aggie spoke up and told everyone that the tribe would drink water; however, she knew that Kron would need green tea and a bark tea mixture to help her through the infection. Aggie said she had several ways to do it that would create minimum odor and would not be cave-wide, just localized to the kitchen area. There would be no way for detection as it smelled like grass or pine tree bark. Everyone felt like they had a good plan locked down and that it should be effective against noise, vibration, and odors.

Morgan was having his morning coffee when his panel for a video conference came on. He stood and pressed the accept button. It was Jim and Ranger Kopchek. He immediately became concerned and asked Jim how Marsha's blood pressure was. Jim told him it checked out close to perfect that morning. Jim thanked him for sending supplies and then explained that they had a new guest in their community with a truck that was parked in the shelter. He explained a UFO flew low like it was looking for them. They were able to get the truck backed into the cave and the stone rolled back in front of the mouth of the cave. He told Morgan they immediately installed the tarps that prevented EMP and heat signatures. Morgan was happy with the report up until Jim went on to tell him of the incident that just occurred. He felt it was the spaceship's landing thrusters that shook the entire cave. They all stayed in the back of the cave and were totally silent, including the babies. He told Morgan it had to have been The Blue and that he must have a foreign agent or spy in his office that was feeding him information. Morgan told Jim he thought it was his A.I. Vader which, by the way, was a perfect name for the double-crossing piece of walking junk. He then informed Jim that this communication line had been encrypted moments earlier by a military man he trusted. It was on a line that was not within the military data banks, so Vader was locked out of it. He confided that he read an email broadcast that two bunker locations that were not nearly as deep were discovered by The Blue and that the Nightcrawlers found a way in and all perished. The same scenario had happened where they heard the craft land and the next day they were under attack. Morgan told him he did not want to look via satellite because that could easily be traced. However, he had a friend who had a connection to a satellite flyover from the ISS that would snap pictures and send them to a new encrypted non-agency email. In the interim, he would have military recon convene in the Cuyahoga Valley and assign a battalion to stand ready. They hung up and Jim did not feel any better about this situation. Morgan was uneasy about the precarious situation for everyone in the cave.

# Chapter Four

# THE BLUE CONNECTION

She was sure they would never find her in the depths of the Great Lakes. She only ventured out if absolutely necessary. She couldn't believe the luck of her escape pod landing right on top of her teams' craft. She knew that it would not take the military long to open the compartments in her crashed ship. She was sure, too, that the military thought she crashed here alone. She wished there were a way to communicate that this issue was not with Earth's sentient beings. It was another alien life that was microbic, and they needed the spores to terminate the microbial life before it caused a catastrophic disaster that would result in an extinction-level event. She didn't know if she could control the Nightcrawlers any longer. They seemed to inflict destruction upon all life forms. She was working in her lab onboard her new spacecraft to reverse some of the toxicity of the spores that built up in the thorns of the Nightcrawlers. She wished there were a way to contact her other team members. She was on radio silence while the Earthlings were scanning for communication waves that were not terrestrial-based. With the communication blackout, it was as if the other teams were working for the evil demise of life on planet Earth and not adhering to the Prime Directive. There had to be a way to eliminate the spores. She had decided to focus on areas in the Americas that currently had no spores and determine the reason.

Currently, she was working on soil and rocks she obtained in the Cuyahoga Valley National Park and Yellowstone National Park. Today she would be collecting soil and rock samples from Machu Picchu in Peru and Patagonia in Argentina. Her plan for tomorrow was to obtain sample collections from Lake Louise, Sachs Harbor, and Sable Island in Canada. Her samples from the Cuyahoga Valley National Park and Big Bend National Park looked promising for a certain mineral that seemed to repel the Nightcrawlers. She also determined that the abundance of snow and ice in the remote location of Nome, Alaska, was a natural deterrent to the existence of the Nightcrawlers and alien microbial forms. That appeared to be the best hope for Earth, a deep winter freeze. She put her samples in their compartments to work on later and readied the ship for departure to her Canadian stops. She planned to take off with no lights so as not to attract attention to her ship, as she knew the military was looking for her. She also engaged the cloaking ability of the ship. It was midnight in Northeastern Ohio, and these precautions, along with the dark of night, proved to be the perfect solution for not being detected. Her first stop would be Machu Picchu. From there it would be off to Patagonia. She hoped she had time to make an unplanned stop in Tiwanaku, Bolivia. That appeared to be the first reported sighting of the Nightcrawlers, so perhaps that was where the microbial aliens first landed. They were known for hitchhiking on meteors. She at least would have a baseline for that area because it was there where their species first made contact over 12,000 years ago. She hoped that her counterpart was doing the same thing in Nan Madol in Micronesia, where the first contact was made 15,000 years ago. It was perfect for a baseline because they already had the soil samples. In fact, they helped build the basalt seaport for the people of the area.

Blue had picked up her samples from Peru and Argentina and was completing her mission in Tiwanaku when fighter jets appeared in the area. When she left the ship to pick up samples, she'd had to uncloak. She had to quickly enable the cloaking device or they would surely fire upon her. She knew she stuck out like a sore thumb. All aliens on the planet had grounded their ships both on land and underwater, so she was easy to spot. She sprinted up the ramp of the ship and ran to the control room where the navigational panel was located. It did not take her long to engage the cloaking mechanism. She needed to leave and fast because the jets would soon discover her location and would most likely begin engaging with her. She placed her samples in the bin beside her and engaged the thrusters. She noticed that her magnetic propulsion was reacting slowly; however, she was able to rise above the jets as they dipped low to see where her ship had been prior to her lift-off. She thought she may have to postpone the Canadian location except for Sable Island. That was extremely remote and had just received significant snow with freezing temperatures. She would need to study the location in extreme detail; but her landing, gathering of samples, and re-cloaking could be done in less than five minutes. For now, she would return to the Great Lakes and arrive before dawn. She intended to sleep for several hours and then begin her testing of the samples. She remained hopeful that she would confirm her findings from her samples from the Cuyahoga Valley National Park.

Blue awoke to an alarm sounding throughout the ship. She jumped up and ran to the security console to determine why the alarm went off. It appeared an aircraft was using radar to scan the Great Lakes. She would need to keep her cloaking device on at all times. The waters of the Great Lakes would not be adequate to protect her from discovery. She decided to have her meal and then begin testing in the lab. She intended to begin with Tiwanaku samples first. Her hopes were that they would yield what she was looking for.

Blue had figured out how to tap into the communication link between the Nightcrawlers purely by accident. It was a Rainbow Eucalyptus tree in the Philippines at the big volcano in Mayon. She had heard chatter on a terahertz frequency. There were electromagnetic waves within the ITU designated band frequencies from 0.3 to 3 terahertz. Somehow the tree roots of the Rainbow tree discovered that this technology could be accessed through their roots systems. Blue could also tap into this bioelectrical field with a predictive interface and the cloaking system of her ship. She thought to herself, *This is like an old soul...the God of biological communication.* Blue took it a step further and mused, *This should be the standard for all communication in all universes and planets. It contains the magic of storing whispers through infinity. Humanity had so much to learn; however, it was against the Prime Directive for them to know the level of intelligence of all biological beings and their own quests to save this planet. If they only could understand that the process of voice-activated communication through any method that would be novel to all biological living organisms would give organic matter the ability to communicate, translate, and securely deliver messages through any organic substance.* Blue, at one point yesterday, listened to a conversation between the Rainbow Eucalyptus Tree and the Baobab Tree which had been brought to this planet millions of years ago by the advanced civilization, Regulus, in the Leo star system. The tree had been planted in Africa, where much of early civilization began. Baobab communications were transmitted to all universes and chronicled the development of humanity, its potential for the greater good, and the probability of mankind's ability to contribute to the universe. It also detailed their advancement on all levels.

Her ability to tap into this communication system allowed Blue to effectively know where the closest Nightcrawlers were at all times. It enabled her to develop a potential solution to eliminate the microbial aliens that were now parasitic killers destroying the citrus trees. To date, her potential solutions for the elimination of the microbial aliens had not proven successful. Blue thought that perhaps today her research would add additional insight. She also considered attempting contact with the Rainbow Eucalyptus Tree; however, she did not want to give away her location or reveal her ability to tap in and communicate. She felt she had time before she attempted this solution.

The soil samples from Tiwanaku seemed different from the baseline she had as a reference and revealed traces of many alien DNA strains. Blue told herself, *Of course, it was a spaceport for over 9,000 years.* However, she was not able to find microbial alien signatures. She found a DNA trace of unknown origin that was recent, within the last 10 days. The library on board her spaceship could not identify the signature. She could not imagine what species was now inhabiting Earth adding more chaos, if not destruction, to this potential extinction event. She searched all 780 galaxy databases for a DNA match. It still came up as unknown. She moved onto looking into chemical and plant-based analysis of this sample. But the unknown DNA kept reappearing. She felt that this unknown DNA was a potential clue she could not overlook. She decided to run a spectral light analysis on it to see if there was a match in that area. This was going to take some time, so she set up the next experiment on this sample. After a failure to unravel the unknown DNA, she hit a wall. Nothing on the spectral side jumped out, nothing on the chemical side looked out of place. Yet this was still an unknown. Nothing on the planet at this time should be an unknown. She began to wonder about the time jumpers and if they had left behind trace elements of something. She knew that plenty of space tourist elitists made time jumps to see a planet at this stage of discovery. Mothman, familiar to humans as merely a folklore tale, was a time jumper that allowed space tourists to view disasters as they happened. She never understood why this was a tourist attraction. It made her think. Perhaps one of the time jumpers had accidentally left behind something from primordial times that was not in her database. This gave her a new approach to target her research. She would need a core sample at an untouched area such as the Sable Island in Canada. She planned to head there as soon as it was dark so that she could fly undercover. She would not need to even leave the ship; thus she could remain cloaked. She could pull a core using the rock drilling tool she could deploy from the control panel. She hoped the other teams were on to something, too. It felt like the solution to this whole catastrophe was resting on her shoulders. Each day that went by caused more death and destruction. The sands of the hourglass were emptying at an exponentially fast rate. As Blue waited for darkness, she decided to listen in again on the Rainbow and Baobab Trees. Perhaps they would talk about something that could help her understand what to look for or if they potentially knew a solution to this issue that was verifiable.

Blue listened intently to the conversation, only this time there was a third old soul, the Corkscrew Tree, which twisted in so many directions, as did life. She was also planted millions of years ago by the Arcturus in the Boötes star system. Their conversation was interesting. As they spoke, she had the data recorder going, extracting millions of years of information for the Corkscrew Tree. After this was completed, she would extract from the Baobab Tree. This was a treasure trove of detailed information on this planet. Blue continued to let that run as she listened to the tree talk about the Nightcrawlers and how the citrus trees were trying to find a way to protect themselves from the deadly spores. Citrus trees always helped mankind with food and nourishment. Now, mankind was fearful and wished death upon all citrus. They, too, were kind and benevolent souls, and she felt sad that they had been taken against their will to become killers. The Baobab Tree asked the Rainbow Tree if it was nearly time to shed her bark which would expose her beautiful rainbow of colors. She said, "In about three days," and then added, "I wish it were sooner to help humanity."

That caught Blue's attention. She sat up straight and turned the volume up to hear clearly what she had to say. The Rainbow Tree said when her bark was shed it contained a chemical that would destroy the spore parasite. Blue thought, *This can't be.* The Baobab asked if they had a parasite similar to this on Regulus. She explained that Earth experienced the spore parasites before; however, it was before there was life on this planet. When the explorers from Regulus arrived, they found the parasites and decided to plant Rainbow Trees to control the parasite from taking hold. They wanted the seeds of life to erupt on this planet and expand to its greatest potential. Up until this time, the spores had not been able to make their way to this planet. Now, they had the potential once again to end all life on this planet, including us. The Corkscrew Tree told them that he had been in contact with his planet and they were sending an expedition that could spray the entire planet in one day and be done with it. They would also spray all satellites and the International Space Station. This would add a layer of protection by spraying anything falling or entering Earth's atmosphere.

"Wouldn't they disclose themselves to the humans? That certainly is against the Prime Directive," the Rainbow Tree asked.

"So is purposely allowing the death of a planet that is due to an alien invasion. It is their job to protect any lifeform that is experiencing potential extinction by an alien force," replied the Corkscrew Tree.

"How long before they get here?"

"Twelve Earth days."

He asked Rainbow Tree if she had made contact with Regulus. She affirmed that contact had been made. It would also take about 11 days to get here, which by their estimate would decimate this planet, leaving less than 33% of life. "My leader explained that they planned to extinguish the spores without prejudice…kill them all!" The Corkscrew Tree could only think of one word—catastrophic. Rainbow Tree also added that they immediately dispatched a ship to bring help for the survival of the sentient lifeforce on this planet.

Blue had to contact the humans, but she needed a strategy on a grand scale to protect herself from being killed as she attempted to communicate a viable solution of obliterating the microbial spore killers without killing all citrus trees. She knew this would take extensive research and assistance from human scientists. She had heard on the military channel of a scientist holed up in a cave in the Cuyahoga Valley National Park. When she was there, she landed at the coordinates but could not find any trace so she assumed they had escaped to a new location. She thought she should perhaps take another look. You never know what may be waiting in the darkness of a cave. On the other hand, there could be a light that saves the world. She reminded herself of everything good that could come from this meeting. The work they could do to save all life forms on the planet would be worth every risk she encountered. She intended to go tonight. As soon as she had secured the scientist, she planned to reach out to the Rainbow Tree to discuss how to collect the chemical content needed to create the effective spray against the microbial alien parasite. She sat in her recliner chair with her pad for a visual free-floating screen. From this, she could formulate a comprehensive plan to interact with those in the cave and yet still stay cloaked.

Her first step was to attempt to hack into the park ranger's handheld radio. Once contact was made, she would attempt to explain that the microbial alien was a parasite whose spores infected citrus trees. It caused them to form thorns dripping with poison which were then unleashed, intent on destroying the ecosystem. She would try to explain how they communicated and planned their attacks through their root system but that there was a chemical on this planet that could obliterate the parasite without killing the citrus trees. Blue hoped that the ranger would listen and then forward her information to validate that what she said was true.

The radio squawked. "Ranger Kopchek."

There was a moment of hesitation, and a female voice asked if it was Ranger Kopchek. She quickly told the caller she was, in fact, Ranger Kopchek. She was with Ranger Long and Jim having a cup of coffee. Jim's radar went up, as did Ranger Long's.

"This is Blue. I believe you desire to speak with me." Ranger Kopchek immediately put her on speakerphone.

"How do I know this truly is Blue, the Alien," she asked. All three looked at each other.

"My spacecraft crashed after I took my escape pod. You have custody of my ship at a place you call Area 51. I am sure you are attempting to learn the secret of how to open the compartments within the ship." She advised Ranger Kopchek that she knew they were holed up in a cave within The Cuyahoga Valley National Park. She explained she knew there was a knowledgeable scientist with her. She stated very clearly that her mission was to help humanity, not harm them. "There are microbial alien parasites that have infected your citrus trees. They can transform the citrus trees into killing machines by blowing their poison-filled thorns at whatever sentient lifeform is in front of them. These parasites are hitchhikers that stole rides on meteorites that traveled through space to your planet. I have been looking for a way to eradicate them yet save the citrus trees that are infected. Ranger Kopchek, are you listening?"

She answered, "Of course. What is it you want from me?"

"I have the answer of how to eradicate all the microbial alien parasites planet-wide. I will need your help to make this happen. We need to trust each other. If you are going to just turn me over to your military, then we can just end the conversation now."

Ranger Kopchek assured her that she wanted to continue the conversation but thought the scientist should join in on the conversation, too. That would take some time. She asked to reconvene in an hour. Blue agreed to the terms and disconnected the call.

The three sat silently looking at each other. Jim finally spoke. "That was a lot to take in. I am not certain she knows where we are. If she did, she would have just shown up." Jim was fearful she was attempting to play our hand. *While her story is compelling, why is she giving us this information?* Jim thought. He added, "We should call Morgan now. Maybe he can evacuate us."

Ranger Long stated the obvious. "If we leave with helicopters and such, she may shoot us down with her ship. This could be an attempt to target you, Jim. She may be afraid that you have something that could stop this killing. As much as she talks of wanting to help, I'm still not convinced of her sincerity. Maybe I just have a trust issue. Just voicing that I still have some concerns. On the other hand, she could be the answer to the prayers of humanity," Ranger Kopchek explained.

Jim thought they should contact Morgan immediately and called him using the new phone number Morgan had provided that the military was not aware he possessed. Morgan answered and asked him to wait for a moment while he moved to an area with more privacy. He walked to just behind the elevator. The electromagnetics for the elevator would prevent them from tracing or listening in on the call. Jim related the recent events.

"We had first contact with Blue. She called on Ranger Kopchek's handheld radio and told us she was only here to stop the microbial alien parasite. That is what is infecting the citrus trees and turning them into killers. She said she has something that can obliterate the microbial alien and that wants to work with us. I hope it's true, however, I'm skeptical. She said she knew we were in the Park; however, why wouldn't she come in person? So I feel like she is attempting to draw us out. I do not trust the Blue. You need to come up with a plan because she is calling back in 45 minutes."

Morgan listened to what he described and told him he understood. "Under no circumstances are you to leave that secure location. It is obvious she has no idea where you are, and turn off those radios. They are traceable. That will buy me more time. It is daylight so, rest assured, she will not reveal herself. She will remain hidden during the day. She will only come out at night. You must stay quiet, so limit sound in the location." Jim told Morgan he would make that happen. "One other item you need to know. The Killer Trees have converged on sites with nuclear reactors that have sustained accidents. Fukushima has over 1,000 that are camped out and absorbing radiation. They are growing exponentially. The same goes for Three Mile Island, Davis-Besse, and two in Texas, one in Nevada, and one in Russia. There is no telling what they will morph into or how. We do know they will be carrying significant radiation wherever they go. There is a good chance that they will be walking EMFs causing our communication system to fail. Well, for that matter, everything electrical will no longer function, throwing us back to the Stone Age." Jim was shocked and then asked what they were telling the public. "The public thinks it is a swarm of earthquakes wreaking havoc on the world. Tsunami alerts are up in Hawaii, the Philippines, and the entire West Coast." Jim was speechless, and Morgan had to ask if he was still there. Jim quietly replied that he understood and would wait for further instruction. Morgan again reiterated that they stay put and do everything possible to stay hidden. They both hung up. Jim was stunned and needed to take a moment to absorb and process what he was just told.

He went to the kitchen and made a big pot of coffee as well as a pot of green tea and bark. He called everyone to the gathering location and served the coffee and tea. Even Kron was up and came to the gathering with both babies hanging onto her shoulders. When she sat, she pulled the little girl baby down and cradled her. Both still had IV access which Jim thought, as he passed them the tea, he should leave intact. Bitty stayed with the human babies. He would speak with her after the meeting and explain that it was essential to maintain quiet so as not to give away their hiding spot. He would depend on her to know what the babies needed to keep them from crying.

Morgan still suspected that Vader was a leak to the Blue and did not want him to be aware of any of this information. Morgan asked to speak with President Kennedy and was granted access to her on Level 12. He hurried down the hall to the glass elevator. As he exited on Level 12, emergency green lights came on. He knew the dam and nuclear waste plant were not far from Area 51. They must have put the base on high alert. He ran to the president's suite and rang the bell. She released the door lock and Morgan cleared the airlock and then through her door.

He thanked the president for seeing him. She invited him to sit as she came around the coffee table and settled on the sofa. She poured him a cup of coffee as well as one for herself. "Madam President," he began, but before continuing asked if her suit had been scanned for listening devices. She assured him that all security protocols were in place. He told her he was certain that there was a major breach in security regarding the Blue. She looked surprised and asked Morgan if this information had been verified. He told her about Vader and then explained that after two separate phone calls with Dr. Mottice, the bunker experienced attempted breaches. "Whoever programmed him must be responsible." President Kennedy assured him she would take care of any leak regarding the Blue. He then briefed her on Jim's situation in the cave and the phone call from Blue claiming to be their ally and that she knew how to obliterate the microbial spore parasites. He asked her if she was aware of the congregation around the nuclear sites and that Three Mile Island and Fukashima were surrounded by thousands of the killer Nightcrawlers who were absorbing pure radiation and growing more lethal. "It has been confirmed that they now can blow a stream of blue radiation. They will destroy the world with this type of capability." She advised Jim that she had not been briefed on any of this, in fact, none of the leaders were aware of this potentially devastating information.

President Kennedy advised Morgan that she would conduct a private briefing with all senior leaders that afternoon. "In addition, Jim, the people inside that cave, including your wife and children, will be safe." President Kennedy wished a plan to secure Jim's talent to sort through fact vs. fiction could be arranged, but she concluded that there was no way in the current environment that could happen. This was due to the capabilities of the Blue. It was certain they had the technology to listen in on radio waves and conversations. She guaranteed everyone's safety, and Morgan held onto the hope that Marsha and the babies would be secure in their location. The president promised to get back to him on what the next steps would be.

Morgan went back to his lab to wait for President Kennedy's call. He had to get rid of Vader. As he walked to the elevator, he tried to come up with a ruse he could use that would throw him off and take time to track down. When he walked into the lab, Vader greeted him and asked what he was working on so he could set everything up for the day. Morgan told Vader that he needed a patent researched, Number 62/444373. "I also need to know if there are any other patents close to this technology. The technology is owned and created by Faith McGary and Rich Sepcic. No hurry on this. I want it researched thoroughly and then put into a summary report that President Kennedy and other senior leaders can understand. I expect to have this completed by tomorrow afternoon, please." He told Vader he would set up a briefing with President Kennedy first then work with the entire senior level group. He thought there were pieces of this technology that may lead to a clue. He wished him luck and told him they would reconvene after lunch the following day and he would then brief the president. Vader stopped Morgan and told him that he needed to know completely how this data would be deployed, as well as other logistical information. Morgan was not surprised by his request and told Vader that until he knew more about the technology, he could not speak to it just yet. He would need a working understanding of the technology. Morgan asked Vader if he could complete the assignment or if he felt the task was above his capabilities. Vader told him that he would have the report, as requested, and then left the room. Morgan silently celebrated his deception. He laughed and told himself he should have been in the movies as that was an Academy Award-winning performance. He decided he should take a bow.

Morgan then realized it had been about an hour and he should call Jim to apprise him of the situation. He stepped out of his lab looking both ways and then walked to the side of the elevator shaft. He dialed the number and Jim answered. "Okay, I will make it fast. I met with President Kennedy and advised her of our conversation. She will be speaking with the other senior leaders this afternoon. She reinforced that your group will be safe. She promised nothing would happen to you. However, you have to keep it as silent as a library. If you have more tarps, reinforce the ceilings and the door." Morgan told him he would know more later that afternoon and would call back with additional information. He planned to spend the night at a hotel in town, as did most employees. They all took a special flight on the red and white planes called the "Janet flight." He told him to keep up hope that this would soon be over.

Jim told him his job was hard and that he can run computations from his location. "If the matter of DNA comes up, there is no one better," he said.

Morgan laughed and asked, "What about me?"

Jim laughed. "Sorry, but you are one step behind me." He hung up and said to himself, *Second fiddle, not digging it.*

The president walked down to Morgan's lab and entered. Morgan heard the swoosh of the door and turned around in hopes that it was not Vader. She approached Morgan and asked how the experiments were progressing. He told her it was steady but painstakingly slow. She asked if his assistant was of any help and if he could be re-assigned to one of the other research scientists for a short period. Morgan knew what she meant. He agreed that would be acceptable until he reached the DNA splicing piece, then he would need Vader back at his lab. Morgan asked if the lab director would inform him that, effective immediately, he was to start working with Dr. Armbruster on his research of certain components found in the alien parasites that emit a protein that assists in the spread of the microbe. He thanked her for coming to tell him personally. Morgan understood all the underlying messages she was conveying. He would wait for the president to conduct her private conference in a secure location. She would also have it swept for listening devices. It was difficult to believe there was a spy that had somehow slipped through the system undetected.

This person was divulging top secret information to a hostile alien force that was attempting to cause a catastrophic extermination event. He wished he knew who it was who embraced technology espionage. He would be jubilant to see this person charged with espionage and hung from the highest gallows. Traitors to not only humans but all life on this planet. Yep, that was treasonous and execution should be his punishment.

Morgan decided he needed to be productive while he awaited the president's meeting. He focused on the DNA component of the microbial alien parasite. He found anomalies that could not be explained. So many unexpected twists and turns. He felt like he was chasing his tail and going round and round in circles. He found that black pitch was reactive and stopped the ability to travel when an inhibitor was added to it. He hoped that by channeling Madam Curie and Pierre Curie, he would have advanced his efforts to find and understand this parasite. It troubled him that most of the trees were now arriving at a nuclear plant and somehow circling it and draining its power, causing accelerated growth. It also caused an increase in the amount of poison in its thorns and root system. They found that it also contained an acid that was deadly if it came in contact with human skin. Another team member was researching the blue light they developed. They discovered that the streaming blue light was radioactive and caused the immediate incineration of anything it touched. They received images from various surveillance cameras of the Nightcrawlers encircling the Fukushima plant. It appeared that several of the trees had almost see-through areas on their trunks that contained what appeared to be red glowing spores. None of the scientists could determine the purpose of the see-through area. They assumed the glowing red dots were connected to the absorption of massive amounts of radiation and pure uranium. The growth rate was astounding. In one day they had doubled their size. The new characteristics that the Nightcrawlers developed were concerning, to say the least. The ability to cause destruction and annihilation was something the modern world had never seen.

Morgan thought about the arrogance of human beings and the belief that mankind was at the top of the food chain, in total control, and not the other way around. This was a wake-up call for the world. The military's mission was to protect our great nation. He thought that maybe God would spare man, bestowing upon us wisdom, strength, and the courage to overcome.

Morgan was testing the black pitch by removing the barium. It was just missing the right chemical to make it totally effective in destroying the spore. Suddenly, he was called to Dr. Newhart's lab. When he arrived, he found two of the other team members watching the feed from Three Mile Island as the Nightcrawlers were on the move away from the power plant. The lights surrounding the site went out. All communications failed. Measurements taken by local offices showed that a massive Electro-Magnetic Pulse (EMP) took out the entire electrical grid. It was taking the entire population back to the Stone Age period. Mankind had no idea what was about to happen by being thrown into darkness with no electricity or communication. The people of Earth were about to experience pure fear. They had no way to fight back against the Nightcrawlers. The military could not get close due to the spewing stream of radioactivity that caused anything it touched to melt into a puddle of goo right on the spot. Smaller animals were burned to a crisp by the Nightcrawler walking within 40 feet of it. Morgan had to turn away. It was the most awful thing he had ever witnessed. As he looked down trying to process what he just witnessed, he realized that the Nightcrawlers at Fukushima would be migrating away from the plant as they did at Three Mile Island. They could decimate Japan in a matter of days. This could be the start of the cataclysmic event that would obliterate the world.

Newhart called Morgan and the other team members to the viewer. It showed the Nightcrawlers were now over 50 feet tall. They more than tripled their size after the sun went down. It appeared that the night triggered more destructive abilities. Five of the Nightcrawlers were walking into the ocean. The water glowed an eerie green color. They lost the feed, as well as communication. They must be disrupting the EMPs. The undersea cables were directly in the path of the Nightcrawlers. All surveillance in the ocean would be impossible. Were they headed to Hawaii? The destruction there could be total. He wondered if the EMPs would trigger earthquakes or volcanic activity or even a tsunami. Any one of those things could create untold destruction on a level not seen before. Morgan knew all life on this planet could end in as little as three days, and at most, one week. The Earth was in a precarious situation. People needed to be warned to seek protection in a bunker. In the cities, perhaps they could find safety in the subway.

Morgan thought about it as he walked away. It didn't matter if they were in bunkers, the steaming radioactivity would eventually breach the space and all would be lost. The urgency of this dire situation was clear. A discussion with the Blue was necessary. I believe this requires Princess Celia who is the peace treaty expert for humanity, well, at least in the Cuyahoga Valley National Park. How would Bev shoot the arrow to call for the princess? She would have to shoot it in the cave and see if distance did not matter. He knew the princess was also limited because of her Prime Directive; however, this situation was a lot like the one that had recently encountered with the Hornet Queen and the destructive ability of her drones to obliterate every life form on the planet. In that instance, the princess had her father Zeus and her uncle Poseidon to help save humanity. This showed just how fragile life was on planet Earth. He would know even more after he spoke to the president. He was expecting to meet with her at any time. Although he believed she was aware of the urgency, why was she taking so long? It was well after sundown, the most active period for the Nightcrawlers. He decided he would go down to her suite on Level 12 to see what was happening.

It seemed darker than before as Morgan exited the elevator. He was a bit apprehensive as he approached the presidential suite. As he knocked on the door, it swung open. He stood there wondering if he should enter. He decided that something was wrong and she may need help. He entered with his heart pounding and his breathing shallow and increased. He was clearly frightened. He could see her lying on the floor in front of her still-flickering televiewer. He ran to her, calling her name. He checked her pulse which was steady, as was her breathing. He ran to get a cool washcloth. When he returned to her, he put the cloth behind her neck after he wiped her face. He softly called, "President Kennedy." She opened her eyes. Morgan asked her to lie still for a second. She kept saying she was all right and sat up. He helped her over to the sofa.

"What happened, Madam President?" She took his hand and told him to call her Charlotte. He nodded his head. "Tell me what happened." She said that Vader had brought her some coffee as she was meeting with the leaders; and while one of the senior leaders was speaking, she felt dizzy. That was all she remembered until Morgan tended to her. "Where is the cup?" he asked. She pointed to a soft blue cup sitting on the viewing console. It still had coffee in it. He sniffed it and detected a bitter odor. Morgan put it down and told her he would take it with him for analysis, however, it appeared to be a drug that evil men use for date rape. She was shocked. He asked if she had Secret Service protection. She responded that she did; however, everyone here had top security clearance. He pointed out that Vader delivered this. He asked if she had ordered it. She shook her head no. He told her he was curious where the Secret Service agent was now. She told him he had been in the room while she was on the call. Morgan stood and looked in the bedroom and found him on the floor just like the president. He yelled, "He is in here!" Morgan ran for the damp washcloth and tended to the officer. The Secret Service agent came around quickly, just as the president had. He immediately jumped up and ran to the president's side trying to ascertain if she was injured. He urged her to allow him to get a physician to look her over. Morgan advised the agent that he was a doctor and had found her the same way that he was found. Morgan asked if Vader brought him coffee. He confirmed that he had. He inquired if he had ordered it. The agent responded that he had not. Morgan asked where the coffee cup was located. It was also blue and in the bedroom. Morgan retrieved it and found that it, too, had been tampered with. The agent smelled it and agreed. Morgan told him he would analyze it to make sure. He then asked Charlotte if anything was missing. She told him no. Morgan then inquired how far into the meeting she had been. Charlotte was about done. He asked when Vader entered the room. She said he was there for the entire video conference.

The Secret Service agent said, "Madam President, your security has been breached. Anything you discussed is now in the hands of the enemy."

She smiled and told him that he underestimated her ability to play the game. He looked puzzled. "Now, grant it, I did not count on being drugged. I am terribly sorry for not thinking of that. The leaders and I set up Vader. Everything we spoke of was a complete lie. I also had a video of Vader's programmers which recorded the audio of their conversation which was very incriminating. It appears they partnered with two rogue Blues. The plan was to take down the major governments and install a Blue as the leader of the One World Order. The Blue would preside over planet Earth. Vader and his two programmers are now in federal custody with many charges against them. We have also taken into custody the two rogue Blues. They are in the most secure bunker on the planet. They will never cause us harm again. We do have a huge issue with the Nightcrawlers. We believe that the other Blue's claim to help us could be genuine. I am going to have her meet us at our bunker here in Area 51. Troops are being deployed as we speak. Morgan, we need to get your friends on the phone and let them know why we are so late returning their request for help. I do deeply apologize. They must feel alone and terribly frightened. We will call them while Agent Haskell checks the area for our safety. Mr. Haskell, I am requesting additional protection for myself and Morgan, please."

"Jim, I am sorry it took so long to get back to you. I found President Kennedy and her Secret Service agent drugged and lying on the floor. Luckily, they are both fine. Now, I would like to introduce you to the smartest woman I have ever known, President Charlotte Kennedy."

President Kennedy took over the conversation. She started by apologizing for the delay as the entire community in the cave gathered around the table to listen. President Kennedy started to explain but then stopped as she tried to gather her thoughts. She finally spoke and addressed the crowd by saying what a lovely community it was and how much she admired diversity. Jim and "The Community" laughed, including the Sasquatch. Mr. Haskell was standing behind the president, staring at the screen, and was visibly shaken. He stood as still and as expressionless as a statue. President Kennedy told them how she exposed the traitors who perpetrated this extinction-level event upon the world. "Their plan was to install the Blue and themselves as a New World Order with a Blue in control. Of course, they had divided control of the planet. We believe that the Blue who contacted you is not part of this global takeover." The president explained it was for this reason that they wished to speak to Blue and that they had secured radio silence so their privacy would be assured. "When she calls again, give her this number so that we can arrange a meeting to discuss how we can defeat the Nightcrawlers."

Morgan stepped up to let everyone know what a vicarious situation the Earth now faced. "The Nightcrawlers are now radioactive and have the ability to melt everything in their path." He let them know that they had been congregating around nuclear plants, including the Davis-Besse Plant, which was how they became radioactive and had tripled in size. "Not to mention the venomous thorns that are now six inches long." He explained to them about the clear patch on their trunks that was full of potentially radioactive red spores and feared that, like a pregnancy, they would lay them like eggs, so time was of the essence for humanity. "We will await your call or call from the Blue."

President Kennedy took up the conversation again with her disappointment of the enslavement to greed that created the mess. "Life and health are the greatest of God's gifts, but we take them for granted. They sometimes hang like a thread and even the smallest of things like a microbial alien parasite can make that thread snap, which is where we are today. It is because of these brave and brilliant Americans who obviously love this country and this nation of proud citizens that we can hope to succeed in defeating this enemy who is stealing the lives of not only this nation but the world. I ask you to grow bold in your search to end this abomination. Let this dark shadow that has descended upon the world be vanquished by the light of love, hope, and prayer of its people. We put our faith in Morgan and you, Jim, to eradicate the worldwide threat to humanity."

Morgan had seen the killer Nightcrawlers in action and knew that a solution had to be effective and swift against them. He could not express the urgency involved in this nightmare. The president decided they should disconnect so that the Blue could call, and they could arrange the meeting for tomorrow.

# Chapter Five

# A PLAN OF HOPE

The handheld phone rang, and Ranger Kopchek answered. It was the Blue. She expressed her concern about not communicating with them for more than an hour. It, in fact, had been seven hours. Ranger Kopchek explained that she had issues with communication since the occurrence of the EMP situation. She continued that the president of the United States wanted to meet with her and engage her assistance in the destruction of the Nightcrawlers. "She would like me to give you her private number to contact her—President Charlotte Kennedy. I wish you the best as you work with the world's scientists and leaders to find a solution to rid the world of such dark and destructive forces." Blue thanked Ranger Kopchek for her assistance in arranging a way for her to collaborate with those seeking a resolution to this worldwide disaster. Before disconnecting the call, Ranger Kopchek wished her luck and quietly remarked, "Humanity is depending on your success." Jim, Marsha, Bev, Ranger Long, and Virg were at the table listening. They now had hope that a solution would come quickly and that the killing would cease.

Virg asked Jim to check on Kron as she was not moving or talking very much. Jim asked how long it had been going on since she had seemed better the last day. He advised Jim that she had been like this most of the day. Jim went to his tent and grabbed his black medical bag and headed for Virg and Kron's teepee. There was no response when Jim called out to her. Virg then approached the teepee and invited Jim inside. Jim sat down beside Kron and softly asked her how she was doing. He noticed the babies were not with her and asked if Aggie was caring for them. Virg responded that she was as they thought Aggie would be able to keep them quiet. Jim turned back to Kron and asked her if she was having nausea or fever. She turned from her side to her back and replied that her birthplace hurt awfully bad and she felt very tired.

"Okay, let's see what is going on," he told her. He took a stethoscope and listened to her heart, lungs, and abdomen. He then took her blood pressure and found it to be incredibly low. It was possible that she was dehydrated. He asked Kron if she had been drinking enough water. She admitted she was not because it made her sick. Jim then told them that he would like to examine her birth area and inquired if he would be permitted to do so. They nodded their assent and Jim asked Virg to help him by lifting Kron's leg and supporting it while he took a look at what was going on. Virg walked over to the pallet and picked her leg up gently and held it in place. It appeared she had an infection again. He asked if he could tend to the wound and they agreed. While Jim cleansed the area with betadine, Kron began growling. He knew she was holding back a roar. Jim finished up quickly and told them he needed to start another IV for fluids and pain control. She would need to be separated from her babies until she felt better. She nodded that she understood, and he left to get the necessary supplies.

He returned a short time later and asked Virg to prepare a weak dandelion tea. Jim shaved her fur and quickly located a good vein for the IV injection site. He hooked up the bag of fluids and piggybacked Zofran for nausea and then injected the pain meds. She soon became a bit groggy but he wanted her to drink part of the tea before she drifted off to sleep. Virg handed her the mug. "I hope you don't mind, Jim. I also added some honey." Jim told Virg that was a wise choice. They watched her take about five sips and then she handed the mug to Virg. She laid back on the pallet and closed her eyes.

"That's okay, Kron. You sleep now, and I will be back in the morning." Jim closed his medical bag and told Virg to wash his hands before and after each time he touched her. It would keep the infection from spreading.

Jim left the teepee and went to wash up. He stopped and made coffee and took three cups, one to give Marsha, one for Bev, and one for himself. He stopped at Marsha's tent. Bitty was with her and now had a cot to sleep there. Jim thought that was a good idea. He handed Marsha her coffee and asked how she was doing. She gave a half-smile and told Jim she was worried sick about what Morgan was doing. Jim said two-words, "BLOOD PRESSURE!" She understood and shook her head, then thanked Jim for the coffee. Jim looked over at Bitty sleeping on the cot with both baby's tucked under her arm and fur. He told Marsha that was a sight to behold! They both laughed. He then told Marsha to zip the tent and said good night.

He walked over to his tent and unzipped the door. As he stepped in he said, "Special delivery for my sweet." Bev sat up and told him that she loved service with a smile and that coffee was a treat. She then asked how Kron was feeling. He told her that her infection had flared again and that he had her on IV fluids and would start an antibiotic in the morning. "Hopefully, the fluids help her to feel better." Jim worriedly told Bev that if Kron ever got pregnant again it could prove to be fatal for her.

Bev asked, "What do you do for a bigfoot to keep them from getting pregnant again?"

He told her that he could not guess in a million years. "Let's cross that bridge when we get there. I want to get her over this hump first."

Bev assured him he was not only the best husband ever, but he was the best doctor ever! Jim chuckled and said, "Flattery will get you anything."

Bev laughed, "Peek at El so I don't have to get out from under the covers." He checked on her and found that she was asleep. "Just so you know, Jim, I set the alarm to vibrate at 3:30 to keep El from crying so I can get her bottle ready."

"Okay, so how are you feeling?"

"Is that the doctor asking or my charming and caring husband?"

Jim had a great response, "Which would you like it to be?"

"Well, how about we do doctor tonight; and when there is less stress, we will do husband." Jim laughed and waited for her answer.

"I am feeling fine, my good doctor."

Jim asked about her blood pressure. She told him his magic pills were working perfectly. Jim told her she still needed bed rest for two more days which, of course, also included Marsha. He wanted her to know that he was keeping both her and the baby inside her safe. Bev smiled. She laid back down and warned, "3:30 comes early for you, dear."

She asked him to snuggle with her, but he told her that she would have to sleep by herself since was exposed to Kron's infection and did not want the remote possibility of passing it around. He laid down on the cot and covered up. It took him no time to fall asleep. Bev was right, 3:30 did come fast. He got up quietly and went to the kitchen to make El's bottle. As he was standing there waiting on the microwave to heat the bottle, he could hear Kron moaning. The microwave gave a ding that the bottle was ready. He took it back to the tent, woke Bev up, and handed her the bottle. He then reached in and took El in his arms. It felt so good. He handed her to Bev and told her to make sure Bitty gave her a good bath. He explained that he could hear Kron moaning and needed to check her. He grabbed his medical bag; and as he approached the teepee, he could hear her muffled cry. He called to Virg who opened the door and looked as if he was going to cry. "She is not doing well."

Jim came inside and knelt next to Kron. He spoke softly to her and asked her how she was feeling. She told him it was burning and hurt badly. He sat back and told her he was going to get some supplies. He went into the medical cubby and as he was getting the antibiotics, it dawned on him that when Aggie was pushing on her abdominal area to get the baby out, she may have ripped something. How he wished he had a CT scanner or, at the very least, an ultrasound machine. He wouldn't know where to begin on surgery. He walked back quickly, putting it out of his mind for the time being. He administered a stronger pain medicine. She closed her eyes and Jim told Virg to get him when she awakened. He stopped and washed his hands and then went back to his tent to rest for a few hours. He couldn't get the thought out of his mind of having to do surgery on Kron. He wondered if he could Google surgery on grey black apes for what the anatomy looked like. He was sure there would not be anything on YouTube. He would see how she was doing later in the morning, then decisions could be made where to go from there.

He drifted off to sleep and heard Virg's soft whoop outside the tent. He looked and had only been asleep for an hour. Bev sat up as Jim put on his shoes and grabbed his medical bag. Virg walked quickly and Jim had to almost run to keep up with him.

Virg held the door open for Jim. Kron was curled in the fetal position. Jim asked her what was hurting. She was struggling to not make noise. He knew this was serious. She pointed to her abdomen. It was just as he feared. Kron had sustained an internal injury during birth and was probably bleeding inside. He needed Marsha and thought Ranger Long could most likely help as he was a paramedic for the Park. Jim told Virg to step outside after he gave her more pain meds. He told Virg she needed surgery to fix what was torn inside. If he didn't do it, she would die. Jim waited for Virg to process what he had just said. He nodded that he understood and told Jim to fix her.

Jim ran and got Marsha to set up the instruments and then knocked on the outside of Ranger Long's truck. He looked out and Jim explained that Kron needed surgery and he was the only trained medical person there that could help. Ranger Long put on his shoes and ran with Jim to the medical cubby and started to wipe everything down with the bleach. He found a sheet to lay on the table. Marsha was laying out the instruments for them. She wondered who was giving the anesthetic. She shook her head with worry for Kron and Jim. For Jim, this was uncharted territory. He had no idea what anatomy he was dealing with or how would he keep her asleep. Jim came into the room as Ranger Long was finishing up cleaning everything and Marsha had all the instruments laid out for abdominal surgery. Ranger Long asked how they would keep her asleep. He told them he didn't know. He wished he had Princess Celia.

He stopped in the middle of the sentence and took off in a run back to his tent. Bev was still asleep. He yelled for her and she jumped up. He gave her the bow and her quill of arrows. "I need Princess Celia now! Kron took a turn for the worse, and I'm not about to let two babies not have their mother. We must try to save her. She must have surgery to fix a bleed in her belly." He asked her to please get up and call Princess Celia. Bev slid on her slippers and grabbed the silver arrow and bow. She walked out of her tent and aimed for the mouth of the cave just above the truck so if she missed, they could retrieve the arrow and try again. She aimed and pulled back the bowstring and let the silver arrow fly. A blinding light filled the cave. It had no shadow in its corner. Princess Celia walked through looking around at her surroundings. Bev ran to her. She asked what they were doing there. Jim quickly filled her in. Princess Celia took Bev's hand and asked how she could help then started walking back toward Kron's teepee. Jim was attempting to explain the situation, but it was as though she already understood and knew where to go in the cave. She walked into the teepee and went directly to Kron. She knelt on the pallet with Kron and touched her head. The look on Kron's face was intense pain. As the princess touched her head, they could see her facial expression soften and relax. She then ran her hand above her abdomen. She stopped and asked where her babies were. Jim told the princess that Aggie was taking care of them. She stood and looked at Jim and Bev. She took one of each of their hands and told them if she did this, there will be no more children for her, but she would live.

She let go of their hands and went to Virg. "Kron will have no more children if I help her. I know children are important to your species." She explained if she did not intervene, she would die. She turned to Bev and told her to have Aggie bring the babies. She looked at Virg. "We haven't much time. She is near death now. I want her to have the babies in her arms as I attempt to heal her. They will help pull her back from the brink of death." Virg told Princess Celia that she must save her and that it was not even a choice to let her die.

Aggie entered the teepee. Princess Celia took the little boy and laid him down on Kron's chest. She then took the baby girl. She turned to Jim and told him that this one was also extremely sick. She pulled the baby to her chest and a light grew bright as the princess closed her eyes. Then, in the blink of an eye, the light disappeared. Princess Celia opened her eyes and put the baby over Kron's heart. She told them that this baby girl had Kron's heart. The princess knelt back on the pallet with Kron and the babies. She closed her eyes, and a brilliant light came upon Kron's abdomen. It was more brilliant than the one that shone on the baby. She held her hand over Kron for over five minutes. Princess Celia's face changed as if she was taking on Kro's pain. At one point, the light faded and flickered. Then, it once again grew strong before bursting and was gone. Princess Celia slumped down over Kron. Jim laid her down on the floor and instructed Bev to get a cool cloth for her forehead. Upon awakening, Jim helped the princess to sit up. She told him that it was necessary for her to rest. Virg picked her up and carried her to one of the unused tents and laid her on the cot. Jim grabbed a sleeping bag, unzipped it, then laid it on her. She thanked them and closed her eyes. Jim told Bev to stay with her as he ran back to Kron and the babies. Kron's eyes were open; however, she lay motionless. Jim knelt beside her and asked if she was okay. She told him yes but tired. Aggie leaned over and took the babies so Kron could rest. She put the boy on her shoulder and cradled the baby girl as she went back to her teepee. Kron closed her eyes. Jim decided to take her blood pressure. He was surprised it was low but not dangerous. Jim listened with his stethoscope, and everything seemed fine. He asked Virg to hold her leg up so he could see the birthing area. It looked red but so much better. He told Virg to let her sleep, and he would leave in the IV and antibiotics. Marsha and Ranger Long were standing outside the teepee. He told them Kron looked better but they would know more later.

The tribe waited anxiously to see if Kron would survive and if Princess Celia would awaken. It had been several hours since the princess attempted to heal the baby girl and Kron. Jim thought he should go check on the princess. He went to her tent and softly asked if she was awake. She did not answer. He felt he should enter and check on her. He went to her side as she lay in what looked like a deep sleep. He was not sure if he should touch her. After thinking about it, he decided he would take her hand and see if she responded. She did. He told her Kron was doing much better, as was the baby girl. She smiled and told him it was a difficult struggle with death to pull her back and that would need to rest a little longer to recover. He told her to go back to sleep and that he would check on her later. No sooner had he turned around than a dazzling light appeared before him and Zeus emerged. He came to the princess, knelt beside her, and touched her head. She opened her eyes and reached up to hug her father. He took her hand and helped her to stand. They walked past Jim and disappeared in a burst of light.

Jim thought he would be funny by saying that was enlightening. He left the tent and went to check the baby girl. She was perched on Aggie's shoulder. It was obvious she was much better. Jim decided to pull the IV from her arm. The baby girl fought against him as Jim attempted to remove the IV. Aggie whooped sternly at her. The baby looked at Aggie and then at Jim and did not struggle against him. Jim was finally able to remove it successfully.

Marsha approached Jim and asked if he needed help. He responded, "I got this. What are you doing up and out of bed?" He knew that she needed her rest. This last week she had really started to show. He insisted she run along. She called him a worrywart because she felt fine, but he was not giving in. He told her to get going and he would bring her and Bev coffee in a few minutes.

He went and washed his hands and went straight to Kron. He found her sitting on her pallet next to Virg. Jim was surprised and asked how she felt. She assured him she was fine. Virg stood so that Jim could sit next to her. "May I listen and check your blood pressure?" She nodded to signal it was okay. Jim checked her out and she seemed in good condition. He told her she had to stay in bed to rest and to drink plenty of fluids. If she did that all day and kept everything down with no nausea, he would remove the IV. She smiled a big toothy smile. Jim was happy for her and patted her leg. He made one last comment to her, "No babies for two days," but assured her that both babies were doing remarkably well.

---

Morgan and President Kennedy would lead the envoy that would meet Blue in a secure conference room located in a hangar off the side of the entrance to the underground facility. Of course, the area would be protected by a regiment of armed forces. They also intended on having three military specialists there to ask questions about her potential solution. Morgan requested that Dr. Haskell be invited to the meeting as he had vast experience in chemical warfare. The military was currently prepping the room and sweeping for bugs that may have been planted to listen in on the conference call. They also tested the encrypted video conference channel that would be used by Jim and the senior leaders. In turn, all the senior leaders were going through the same security measures. Today held hope for all on this planet—hope that Blue was indeed an ally and would have the solution for the demise of the now morphed Nightcrawlers. Each hour that went by cost the lives of over 100,000 worldwide. The time was slipping away. The World Doomsday clock was ticking toward the end of the world. Churches worldwide were filled or gatherings held in secure areas, most offering intercessory prayers for the world to be saved from this crisis. People sought out refuge and comfort at church locations across every community worldwide. The fate of mankind rested on this meeting with an extraterrestrial.

It was now 10 minutes prior to the meeting. The IT technician connected all the senior leaders worldwide, as well as Jim. Each audio connection and video feed was tested for any anomalies. "General Crosby, everything is tested, connected, and secure. We are ready to go."

The general asked if the bogey had been seen on radar. The tower confirmed that they had her on radar approximately 30 miles from Area 51. He radioed Security to confirm that the birdy was set and ready to fire if needed. They responded, "Yes, sir, General." All was ready and waiting for Blue's arrival. They intended to allow Morgan alone to be up top and planned to keep President Kennedy in a secure bunker. The feelings of tension and apprehension were palpable. General Crosby asked again for the position of the incoming craft.

The tower responded, "Fifteen miles out, sir."

The general told Morgan, "She is being cautious in her approach."

Morgan responded, "As well she should, General."

The tower radioed again and alerted the general that the craft should be visible in seconds and then directed the landing crew to their positions. "She has the coordinates to land, sir." The general thanked the sergeant and told him to continue scanning for any other bogies that may be following her. Everyone could now visibly see the spaceship hovering over the Area 51 runway and slowly descending. She landed the craft close to the hangar where the conference was to be held. The IT military technician tested everything again when she landed to make sure there was nothing buffering his feed nor any EMP's to disable the connection. "Recheck of communications is clear, General. All parties are online and waiting, sir." General Crosby ordered him to stand by in the event there was an issue during the meeting.

"Yes, sir." He saluted then returned to the conference room. Morgan thought to himself, *How they can stand doing all that formal 'Yes, sir, No, sir' and saluting. Jeez.* He was glad, however, there were men and women who loved that type of structure.

The craft landed. Everyone waited for her to disembark. Morgan straightened his lab coat. Looking at the military men and women, he felt woefully underdressed. Nonetheless, here he was. Military dogs patrolled around the perimeter of the craft sniffing for explosives. A military policeman and his dog stood by the ship at attention. The hatch slid up and a ramp descended from the hull of the ship. Blue appeared at the opening. She made her way down the ramp and was greeted by a military liaison in her dress uniform. She extended her hand in welcome. Blue graciously accepted the warm gesture. She escorted Blue over to the group waiting to greet her. Morgan could not help but marvel at the exquisite alien who was approaching. Her skin was blue with swirls; and her spacesuit matched perfectly, giving it the appearance of her skin. It looked as if it was made of some sort of biomechanical fabric. Morgan thought, *Wow, I would love to hold the patent on that spacesuit!*

She went right to Morgan and extended her hand. "You are from Earth, Morgan, correct?"

"Yes," and followed with "do you have a name?"

She smiled and said, "Yes, it's Ciril, or call me Blue." She moved on to greet the general. He extended his hand and told her his name was General Crosby. She asked the general if her craft would be secure. He said, "Affirmative." and Morgan nearly laughed out loud.

All eyes were focused on her craft as the ramp raised into the hull of the ship. She looked the general in the eyes and snapped, "Security! My ship, General, picked up signatures of my original craft at this location. In addition, two of my Blues are being held close to this location and you have their ship. Forgive me for my blunt and distrusting attitude."

Morgan thought to himself, *This is not a way to start off a propitious relationship. It will be an uphill battle to regain her trust.* Morgan stepped forward and told Ciril it was a privilege to work with an advanced civilization such as hers and that it was imperative that they have her help. She relaxed and smiled at Morgan. He was the only one who was not rigid. Morgan then asked if she was still willing to meet with the president of the United States and join a teleconference with world leaders. She nodded and told him she would follow him. As they turned, he felt the prickle of his hair standing on end as she took his arm. He thought, *The general is probably about to have a stroke.*

Ciril turned to him and said, "Yes, I agree." Morgan asked if she was an empath. She answered, "In a way, yes." Morgan thought that would need further follow-up at a later time.

"We are going to go inside this hangar, Ciril; and the conference room is off to our left." As they turned for the conference room, he looked back to see if the group followed.

Ciril replied, "No need to look back. They follow with great distrust and are certainly in the ready position for now."

Morgan looked at her and said, "I see you are more than an empath, you also are a telepath." She just smiled and entered the conference room where the military IT technician stood. He saw the general, stood at attention, and saluted.

Ciril remarked, "What a good little soldier."

Morgan laughed. "Exactly, but what do I know? I am just a nerd boy." Ciril looked quizzically and told him that she had never heard that title before. He laughed and told her it was a self-appointed title.

She tilted her head to understand what he meant. She said, "I believe that is humor." Morgan laughed.

He escorted her to the table facing the screen and would be seated next to Morgan who would be sitting next to President Kennedy. Morgan apologized for just having the word "Blue" written on her identification table card. "Next meeting, it will be Ciril." She looked around the room like it was a warehouse on her planet. Plain, grey, and nondescript. She thought about how antiquated the video conferencing technology was. Not even a picture on the wall. There was a flag she recognized in the corner.

The guard at the door yelled, "Attention!" A woman entered. Ciril assumed it was the president. She turned to greet her. President Kennedy extended her hand warmly. She smiled with gentleness. Ciril reached out and took her hand as the Secret Service Agent almost put himself between them. Morgan thought again, *Jeez, there goes trust. I see it flying out of the hangar.*

"They tell me your name is Ciril. My name is Charlotte Kennedy." Ciril told her it was her honor to be their guest. President Kennedy followed with, "All hope is on this meeting today, Ciril. Hope for a successful meeting and a plan to defeat the microbial alien parasites that are now radioactive with a few about to give birth to hundreds, if not thousands, of radiated spores." It was imperative that they reach a working agreement today. The president was seated, and all followed her lead and sat down at the table. The president opened the day with a proclamation of hope between species for the good of all mankind. "I do not want this to be the last advice I ever offer. We have the ability right now to work with the entire galaxy. It is no longer just Planet Earth. We are part of a whole galaxy full of beings who will reach out to us. We must not have prejudice in our hearts and minds. We must look to the stars now full of wonder and excitement, embracing our new benevolent friends.

I have said this many times. I choose to believe. I choose to put my hope and belief in this new friend named Ciril. We have given her so many reasons for distrust, but she still came. I am proud to know Ciril and look forward to her compassion toward humanity, and I resolve to help defeat our enemy, the Nightcrawlers. I predict while the sentient life on this planet has been decimated, our future looks more certain, the path clearer. Ciril brings with her a plan for us to successfully defeat our common enemy. This touchstone event today will be what connects our world and communities to the stars. Let us all have hope and not despair, love and not hate, togetherness and not isolation. Let's show Ciril that humanity is indeed capable of compassion and love."

All agreed that Ciril was their only hope. Morgan knew trust would still be an issue. He thought, *While the president's speech was inspirational, fluffy, and nice, it had no meat to it. Nothing from which to build trust. "Proof is in the pudding," as some would say. The next part of the conference had to provide Ciril with the trust-building she needed. She would demand an explanation as to why her fellow Blues were being held in confinement. It would need to be straightforward and to the point. Everything the military holds in the highest regard. This part of the conference would have to display the truth and nothing but the truth, no matter how brutal it appeared.* Ciril looked at Morgan. She had obviously heard him telepathically. He nodded to her and smiled.

General Crosby began to speak. "We, of course, are determined to overcome our skepticism of your motive and build a relationship based on trust. We know that takes time. You have no reason to trust us at this point. However, I will paint evidence that will show you how we've gotten to this point. Is this agreeable?" he asked.

She responded with one word, "Mutual."

General Crosby replied, "Fair. Let us continue and paint that picture for you. Agreed?"

Ciril replied again with one word, "Agreed!" Morgan could feel the bristle in the general's voice.

Before the general could continue, President Rameriz from Honduras interrupted. "Excuse me, General. I would like to inject something here. We, the people of South America, have plenty of experience with ancient aliens; and in the distant past, our ancestors left us plenty of information on working with star beings. We want to show respect to Ciril. Her ancestors first came to this planet in its primordial development. They've made their way back on occasion to check our progress as a species. They have a Prime Directive to not interfere with the development of species or planets. To date, they have honored that Prime Directive with the exception of two rogues of her species. Let's face it, General, we all know what it is like to have deceptive rogue regimes that focus on doing us harm in an effort to rule the world. How many times do we need to repeat mistakes? Let us not repeat this mistake with Ciril. She came in good faith. She has no idea why we are holding her rogue Blues and has yet to divulge the level of deception leveled against this planet and all sentient life on it. Our first error was not detecting the actual hitchhiker spores that arrived on this planet via meteors, nor did we examine the meteor itself to determine its properties. Had we done that, sir, we would not be having this conversation, nor would two rouge star beings find an opportunity to attempt a takeover of this planet. It has been verified that Ciril did not have any conversations with the two rogues. They told us they maintained radio silence so their radio waves could not be traced by Ciril nor us. That indicates that they did not trust Ciril to allow their hostile takeover by working with microbial alien parasites; and therefore, it was imperative for them to lock her out of the plan by having no communication. Ciril, I would like to hear from you. What you have been doing since you arrived and is this your first trip to this planet."

Ciril looked straight into the camera and responded. She told President Rameriz that she, in fact, had traveled to this planet many times. Her focus was on the ancient site of Tiwanaku. "At one time in your distant past, this was a spaceport for study of what is now South America. We collected many botanical samples, and many of the tribal people of that day asked to see our world. They had a real desire to join our tribe. So our DNA now contains human DNA. I will give Morgan permission to draw my blood; and he can, of course, verify the DNA that courses through my veins. We are truly together, friends of Earth. We have always been friends with Earthlings. While our Prime Directive prohibits any sharing of technological advancements, which we have always adhered to, we did assist humanity with plagues. We could not, however, divulge our medical technology that cured the diseases. We did promote and teach hygiene and organic solutions to sickness which did not violate our Prime Directive. While at Tiwanaku two days ago, I found a spore from primordial Earth that was brought by time travelers. They also infected those spores with a hefty dose of radiation from a substance called black pitch. The radiation injected into the black pitch was not diluted. That is why they were attacked by nuclear power plants and especially crippled with nuclear elements escaping into the sea and air. The spores have traveled in the wind and spread across the Earth. They are pulled to areas of the power plants because they feed on radiation. This, of course, morphs them into giants that are capable of just about everything, including the destruction of this planet in a matter of three days."

Everyone sat in silence. Absorbing what Ciril said took some time to process. Morgan stepped right in to address Ciril directly. He told her he had been working with black pitch hoping it was part of the solution. "I am happy that I now know that this is what triggered the spores to want more radiation. I have been researching how various chemicals interact with the black pitch in hope that one of them will cause a chain reaction of destruction. I am clearly not there yet, Ciril."

She told Morgan that together they may find that chemical more quickly. She did not feel comfortable in disclosing the ability to tap into communication with the root system of the Rainbow Tree and the Baobab Tree. She knew the Rainbow Tree would begin to shed tomorrow and that they needed every ounce of that bark to make enough spray to effectively eliminate radiated microbial alien spores. She decided that she would hold back that information until she felt the military was not being subversive with deviant objectives. She continued to listen to the military explain the reasons for their mistrust, yet on the other were asking her to turn over the formula to annihilate the parasite that was now far more dangerous. She was waiting for them to recommend working together. The military never uttered those words. That was all Morgan and President Rameriz spoke about. She wondered if she could only work with both humans. She decided she'd heard enough from what she read in their minds. The military personnel wanted to capture her, use invasive mind-reading technology, and study her like an animal in the zoo. She stood and thanked everyone and told them she would be leaving and would make her decision later. Two military men moved forward with weapons.

Morgan stood and yelled, "Whoa, whoa, whoa, what are you doing?"

President Rameriz and President Kennedy stood. Her Secret Service Agent began pulling and then pushing her out of the room. She commanded him to stop immediately. She walked over to Ciril and asked if she would be her guest and stay in her suite. She thanked her but declined. She intended to leave. Morgan stepped forward and proposed he go with her. He would wear a tracking device, but he would go with her and they could begin work. The military MP's took another step toward her.

President Rameriz asked them to stop and think about what they were doing. It was the total opposite of what they had discussed in this meeting. He called out to Ciril, "You know you can trust us. You are part of our people. We want to work with you, especially since it was close to this location that the spores originated. Please, you and Morgan come here. We have labs for your use."

Morgan said, "I will do whatever Ciril wants."

President Kennedy felt the same way. She looked at General Crosby. "This is a direct order for you to cease this attack; she could be the savior of mankind. Stand down and stand aside." He saluted her and all the military left the room. All senior leaders stayed online. President Kennedy said, "We will find a way that works for you and that is safe from the killer Nightcrawlers." Ciril could read her mind and it was pure hope and commitment to saving humanity. She felt a strong connection with President Rameriz, as well. The other leader was not malevolent. This was the first time during this meeting she felt secure. She could relax. Ciril told the leaders she would work with Morgan on eradicating the killer microbial alien parasites. She could not give the technology for part of the formula as that would be against the Prime Directive; however, there were quantifiable workarounds to any solution. Under no circumstance would she agree to stay at this location to work. She knew by reading the minds of the military that they had nefarious intentions.

Morgan turned to face her. "Tell me what you need. I am here to help. I am at your service. I cannot lie, I would love to travel in that ship." She knew he was genuine and was telling the truth.

She looked at President Kennedy. "Charlotte, may I call you Charlotte?" she asked.

"Of course, Ciril."

"I trust you, Morgan, and President Rameriz. I believe I could work at Morgan's lab in the Cuyahoga Valley. The killer Nightcrawlers are hundreds of miles from there and are currently interested and absorbing as much radiation from the Davis-Besse plant as possible. I would like total silence and a private line to speak to only you and President Rameriz. I believe we will have a solution by tomorrow. It is the ideal night to deploy the formula. It is a penumbral lunar eclipse. We must deploy it between 2:34 a.m. and 4:44 a.m." President Kennedy asked if that was for the entire planet. Ciril assured her that it was. President Kennedy told her she was grateful for her help and gave Ciril her private number.

Morgan gave President Kennedy his number and recapped. "We are going to my lab in the Cuyahoga Valley National Park. We will work there and will text you updates. We are planning on deploying a solution during the penumbral lunar eclipse beginning at 2:34 a.m. with completion at 4:44 a.m.

She shook Morgan's hand and wished him luck. She turned to the Ciril. "All humanity is in your hands. Please do not let the bad outweigh the good. We hold the highest hope for both of you. Should you need anything, please text or call."

Ciril and Morgan boarded the ship, and she raised the ramp. They both noticed an extreme amount of weaponry gathered around the ship. Ciril told Morgan to sit down and use the strap to secure himself. She then slid one of the digital buttons and they were almost out of the atmosphere in less than three seconds. "That is what we call leaving them in the dust," Morgan explained. She laughed.

"Okay, shall we find your lab? I have the coordinates. Is there a parking area close by where my ship can land without being disturbed?" He told her yes, his office was next to a lumber yard. They would not have traffic to worry about. Ciril informed him that she could cloak the ship so it would not be visible to the naked eye or any radar. She recommended that they stay on the ship if he was comfortable with that. She had separate crew quarters he could use while they worked on the process. Once they landed, they would continue being cloaked; but first, she needed to contact someone who could help them. It would require travel to pick something up and then they would come back to the lab and prepare the mixture.

"We are officially settled in, Morgan. Now, let's have a discussion."

# Chapter Six

# CREATING TRUST

Jim needed to create an elixir for Kron and the baby girl. Right now both were susceptible to just about anything. Even a common cold would be bad news for Kron and her baby girl. Being locked in a cave for who knows how long and confined to this cave with no sunlight, fresh air, and fresh food would eventually affect the cave community. Jim spent most of the day in bed. It had been a busy couple of days with Kron and her delivery, plus two new babies. He was catching up on sleep. Bev was up and about and especially attentive to El to keep ahead of her needs in order to keep her from crying. She kept her in the common area with Bitty, Dorothy, and Morgan Barkley. It was a trick to keep everyone happy. Aggie was keeping Kron's babies separate for now. Marsha was in bed and not feeling well, and Bev brought her some tea a few times. She was now at the six-month mark of her pregnancy and having difficulty sleeping. Bev figured she needed some quiet time or what she called "me time." She couldn't imagine carrying twins a second time.

Bitty was a great mom to Dorothy and Morgan Barkley. They hung to her like they were baby sasquatches. It was fun to watch how she interacted with them and could sense their every need. They had built a special bond. Bev wished she had that skill. She did have a time schedule that worked well in heading El off with her need to cry. Bev hoped that Jim was actually getting some much-needed sleep. What a bunch of needy creatures we are. *Poor Jim,* she thought. *He needs a Doctor of the Year Award.* Not only was he an awesome doctor, but he was an equally awesome friend. Bev asked Bitty if she wanted anything to drink or eat. She was going to run to the kitchen. Bitty asked for a peanut butter and jelly sandwich. Bev laughed and told her she was too human and spoiled, at that. She told her she would bring her some tea to wash it down with. Bev decided she would have one, too. She wrapped the sandwiches in a paper towel and carried the cups of tea in her other hand. Bitty sat next to Bev.

Bitty hesitantly said, "MiMi," and Bev knew she had a serious question. "So, where do babies come from? I mean, I know they're in your stomach; but how do they get out of there?"

*Oh, boy,* thought Bev. *Now, what do I say to her? Okay, the truth always works best.* Bev began, "Bitty, I am so happy you trust me enough to give you a truthful answer. So the baby is in a girl's tummy like mine and Marsha's; and like Kron, one day you will give birth. There is a part of your body on the inside called a birth canal. It is like a tunnel, and the baby squeezes down and out where you pee-pee." Bitty asked if it hurt. "Bitty, I'm not going to lie. It is a horrific pain. But when you have that sweet little baby in your arms, you forget all about the pain you just endured."

"When will I have a baby?"

"Bitty, not for a long time. Plus, you must find someone who loves you and you love him. Then you have the togetherness ceremony like Virg and Kron had last year. Sometimes it takes a while to find that special someone. Never be in a hurry. You want to make sure you have the right one, like your dad and your mom had. That was probably the most special relationship I have ever seen. That should be your ideal type of relationship, Bitty."

"Okay, just wondering."

Bev pondered for a moment if anyone had told Bitty about the birds and the bees. She didn't ask, so she wasn't going to volunteer the information. In fact, that was a perfect conversation for a doctor to have. Bev told Bitty to eat her sandwich and drink her tea. Bev was feeling lucky that she got out of having to have that discussion. She thought she'd better make bottles for Dorothy, Morgan Barkley, and El as soon as she was done eating.

The cave vibrated and they heard something roar over. She hoped it did not wake any of the babies. It would be difficult to keep them quiet without a bottle. Bitty pulled Dorthy and Morgan Barkley up into her fur to snuggle. She looked at Bitty and grabbed El to tuck her in, as well. Bev whispered, "I will be right back with bottles." She went as quietly as she could to the kitchen. The vibration was just for a second, but everyone still stayed quiet and did not move around. The rangers turned off their handheld radios so they could not be traced and give away their location. Bev came back with three bottles. She took El from Bitty and fed her the bottle. She burped her, changed her diaper, and rocked her until she fell asleep. She watched Bitty feed one at a time. She laid one across her leg on its tummy while she fed the other and they burped automatically. What a great tip. Bitty cuddled them and then tucked them into her arms. They loved Bitty's soft fur.

Both park rangers came to the table. Ranger Long remarked, "It sounded like a big and low; however, it just kept going. We need to be vigilant about total silence." Bev knew they were concerned about the babies giving their location away by crying. She thought she and Bitty had been doing a fantastic job until

Ranger Long asked if they would consider giving them Benadryl to keep them quiet. Bev asked him if he was suggesting that they drug the babies. He responded yes.

She was shocked. "Wow! We have two layers of soundproofing and scan proofing up." She was unsure how any sound could penetrate through the double soundproofing and the actual heavy granite rocks. She did not understand how anyone could hear noise. But then again, she heard what went overhead a few minutes ago. She would do a better job and be more attentive.

Bitty looked upset. Bev asked her what was wrong. She responded that she was scared. "Me too, Bitty."

"No, I am frightened for Marsha today." Bev looked at her strangely.

"She is just resting, Bitty. It is not easy some days being pregnant."

"Her babies are so little." Now, Bitty had Bev's attention.

"Yes, Bitty, they are; but they will get bigger. They still have another three months in her belly to grow."

Bitty looked down and said she was frightened for her today. She would not look up at Bev but pulled the babies to her tighter. Bev asked Bitty to keep an eye on El so she would stay asleep. "I will just be gone for a few minutes. I want to check on Marsha so you will know she is fine."

She went directly to her tent and found Jim already sitting up. "Did you hear that noise go overhead?"

Jim answered, "By rolling me out of the bed."

Bev told Jim the strange thing Bitty said and how she acted. He did not say or question anything but grabbed his medical bag and went straight to see Marsha. When he walked in, she saw the medical bag. She looked up at him and watched him sit next to her. He asked, "How do you feel today? Be honest, it is important."

"I have not felt well most of the day. I spent my time in bed and Bev brought me tea a couple of times."

"And…," prodded Jim.

Marsha began to cry. "I started to spot a while ago."

"Why didn't you call me, silly? Morning, noon, or night. I am here for you. Is it light?" he asked. She nodded. "Is it pink or red?" She answered pink. "Okay, are you having any cramping?" She didn't respond. "Is it constant or here and there?"

She answered with tears in her eyes, "I am going to lose these babies."

"Now, Marsha, don't panic. This happens in a lot of pregnancies. Let's not make a mountain out of a molehill. Let's take your blood pressure." It was high, however, he said nothing. "Okay, let me check your pulse." It was high, as well. "May I listen with my stethoscope?" He laughed and said, "I knew you would agree." She relaxed some. "Yep, I hear a heart and lungs. Now let me listen to those critters. I hear two babies loud and clear, Marsha." He could see the tension and fear leave her face. "I have one last request. Knowing you, well, you flat out won't like it. I need to check to make sure you are not dilated. It will only take a second." She was clearly frightened. He told her that he would step out while she slipped off her jeans and panties.

He ran for Bev to come back with him so she could hold her hand and be her support. Jim walked in and said, "Look who I found?" Bev went right to her.

"I hate this part," said Bev. "This is when it sucks to be a woman." Marsha laughed. Bev told her about Bitty tucking the twins in the fur between her arms and body. She told her it was a sight to behold. She also told her about Bitty's burping technique.

Jim said, "I hate to interrupt you two chatterboxes, but I am ready if you are." Jim had his glove on and sat down on the cot next to her. He touched her knee first and slid the back of his hand down her leg so she wasn't so nervous. He could feel a small dilation, but the plug was still in place. "Okay. All done, Marsha."

Marsha had tears in her eyes. Jim threw away the glove and took her hand. "Marsha, you could be in the beginning of labor."

"NO, NO, NO, NO!" she screamed.

"You are on complete bed rest. I have drugs for just this occasion that will stop everything. I am going to start an IV to keep you from going into labor to buy those babies more time. We do this all the time. I will also give you something for your high blood pressure, as well as something to keep you calm. Is that okay? Does that sound like a plan?" She was crying and Bev signaled him to get the necessary supplies. He walked past the table where Bitty was sitting and thanked her for letting Bev know there was something wrong with Marsha. "We are going to help her keep those babies inside. How is El?"

"She's asleep. She is a good baby."

"Thanks, Bitty. You have been a blessing to us. I can't wait to tell Cleg what a fantastic leader and community member you are." She gave him a big smile. He went back to the medical cubby, grabbed all his supplies, and was on his way to Marsha's tent when Ranger Long asked what was going on, Jim explained that he was trying to prevent the delivery of two preemies then asked if Ranger Long would check on her a couple of times during the night and take her blood pressure and pulse rate. "If anything doesn't seem right, you come get me." He asked him to come with him to help put in the IV. That would help build trust which they would need if this turned into an emergency.

Bev stayed with Marsha after Jim and Ranger Long started the IV and administered the drugs to stop labor. Jim and Ranger Long discussed what they would do if the babies were born and how they could take care of them. She was just 27 weeks. They really need to get to 30 weeks. Jim told him they had to prepare for the worst-case scenario. They needed to build an incubator from scratch. They had oxygen; however, the cannulas were for adults. And he had five intubation kits but only one for a child, one for a baby, and none for a preemie.

Ranger Long told Jim, "We need to get this done right now." He wanted to leave the shelter and retrieve everything they would need.

"That's one of the most selfless gestures ever. Let's phone Morgan and see if there is any way of getting the supplies dropped to us here." Jim asked for Ranger Long's secure line. He was going to have to be delicate in how he told Morgan. He initiated the call. "Morgan, this is Jim. Where do we stand on getting out of here?"

"We are working on it."

"I need a few emergency things."

"What do you need?" he asked.

"Morgan, this is a precaution, I need baby incubators and ventilators from a NICU."

Morgan was silent. Jim was sure he was just processing what he said. "The babies are coming," Jim said and explained to Morgan all that had just transpired. "One of the park rangers volunteered to leave the shelter and head for Children's Hospital to bring us back supplies, but I don't want to jeopardize our safety."

Morgan just kept saying, "She is only 27 weeks."

"Morgan! Now is not the time to panic. Marsha needs your level head and so do the babies."

Blue could hear exactly what they were saying. She interrupted and said, "I have something that will help you. Let's deliver it to them."

Jim could hear her offer. "Morgan, whoever that is, please tell her we accept and to get here as fast as possible."

Morgan momentarily experienced negative thoughts about Ciril's motives, but she looked at him and said, "Trust." He looked at Ciril and asked how fast they could get over there. She answered in about a minute.

Jim was surprised by her response and asked Morgan if he was in the Valley. He replied, "Just got here to access my lab."

"Well, get here now!"

Ciril was already readying the ship for liftoff. "Will be there shortly. Have the door ready for a fast entry."

Jim hung up and immediately found Boc and Virg to have them in place to move the rock. They pulled down the tarps as the cave began to shake. Everyone in the cave was silent. Ranger Long's phone rang. "We're outside, please let us in."

Jim took the phone. "You landed above us."

"Yes, Jim, let us in. We are safe from the Nightcrawlers. There are none currently in the Valley." Jim waved for Boc and Virg to move the rock. As the rock was pushed away, there stood Morgan with his arms full of equipment. Behind him was a blue woman carrying supplies, as well.

"Jim, where is Marsha? This is Ciril. Yes, she is a Blue. She is our friend and will be pivotal in destroying the Nightcrawlers."

"This way. Boc, slide that rock back across the opening."

Morgan was surprised at how organized the community was. He put down the equipment outside the tent and ran to Marsha. They embraced as they both cried. He told Marsha everything would be fine. Marsha pushed Morgan away as she saw Ciril enter the tent. "Don't be afraid. This is Ciril. She is an alien Blue and is here to help. We brought everything we need in case you go into premature labor. You will be fine and so will our babies."

Ciril approached with a device in her hand. She asked Marsha if she could take a scan. Morgan and Jim stood to watch. It worked much like a CT scan but provided clearer and better images. It also gave vitals on both babies, as well as Marsha. Ciril stated that the babies needed more time and that she could administer something that would delay delivery for another three weeks. She asked if Marsha would permit her to inject this life-saving drug to save the babies. Marsha silently nodded, still in awe of this alien in their midst. Ciril pulled out what looked like a ballpoint pen and injected it into her neck. It felt like air. "Now, let's get the incubators set up."

She stood and looked at the door and, to her surprise, saw Virg standing there. She had seen a Bigfoot before, however, only in the wild. Morgan hugged Marsha and told her to rest. Virg carried all the equipment. Ciril thanked him and introduced herself. He nodded to her and did not seem at all bothered by her appearance or the fact she was an alien. It took about two hours to set up the equipment and hook it to a generator. She also provided solar power packs that would be placed on the cliff, camouflaged to look like a rock.

Jim asked Ciril to look at Kron and her babies. She was concerned about the baby girl absorbing necessary nutrients and gave her an injection. She stated that the babies would do better if they were now with Kron and so would she but that Aggie should continue to provide support. Kron was well on her way to a complete recovery. She could see, however, that her uterus was scarred. She told Virg and Kron that they could no longer have children because of this; however, she could help her with that after obliterating the Nightcrawlers. Virg knelt beside Kron and told her that there was always hope.

Ciril told Morgan they needed to get over to the Rainbow Trees to collect the bark and get it back to the lab to process. Morgan ran back to Marsha and kissed her and her belly. "Everything will be fine. Complete bed rest. Do you understand me? No fooling around, got it?" She nodded yes and told him to be safe and not to take chances. Jim thanked them as they walked to the mouth of the cave. Morgan told them to close and seal the door behind them. Ciril advised Jim that she was erecting a cloaking forcefield around the entire area. Not even the Nightcrawlers could penetrate that barrier. That made Morgan feel so much better.

He said one last thing to Jim. "I hope this is all over by tomorrow at this time. Take care of Marsha; and if the babies come, try your best, which I know you will." Ciril and Morgan turned and walked away. Boc and Virg were already pushing the rock back into place.

Ranger Kopchek had the tarps ready to rehang. "That fresh air in the cave was awesome for everyone," she told Jim. He agreed. "Now, we hunker down again. Kron will be up and active now that she has been cleared. We don't want to tax her too much; however, she can take over some chores. Aggie will be back at cooking for us. I see they provided food packs for everyone, as well as fresh fruit. That, my friend, is a godsend for all of us."

Jim agreed. He added, "We should have a community meeting. Let's do it outside of Marsha's tent so she is not left out." Ranger Kopchek thought that to be a brilliant idea.

Aggie came to see Marsha and could clearly see she was in despair. She solemnly stated, "Sunrise and sunset—they are free. Do you know what else is free? Happiness. You can't purchase it. It is a choice we all make. A wise human said, 'To seek happiness or even contentment in the acquisition of worldly things alone is to lose sight of the higher purpose of life.' Therefore, there is so much discouragement and it is why there is despair. Our Great Spirit loves us and would have us focus on peace and contentment and to prepare for eternal happiness." She continued, "Happiness is your choice; and right now you are choosing for the babies, too. They feel despair and unhappiness. It overwhelms them. I want you to choose happiness and be thankful for this community and the extra help that came for you. Be grateful and happy for you and the babies. Start them out with happiness and gratefulness while they are learning from you inside. You are infusing it into their very soul." Aggie knelt beside her and they hugged and cried. Marsha thanked her for her great wisdom and told her that she chose happiness and gratefulness for the love this community provided to her and her babies and that she loved her very much. Aggie jumped up and said, "I have baby duty now. I will come by later to see if you are ready for my special happiness tea." Marsha laughed and told Aggie to come by anytime.

---

Morgan and Ciril ran up the ramp. The time was 11:30 a.m. and they needed to race to the Philippines to collect a cargo bay full of bark. After that, they needed as much black pitch as they could find in one location and transport it into another cargo bay. Ciril secured the ramp and airlock. Both strapped themselves into the seats at the command console. She looked at Morgan and said, "Let's do this for not ourselves but for all life on this planet. They are depending on us. We are their hope for survival." Morgan gripped the armrests of the chair as she pushed the launch button. He felt like he left his stomach on the ground. Ciril looked at him and laughed. "You really do become accustomed to take-off." Morgan cocked his head and gave her a very doubtful look. "Okay, we are officially on route. In the compartment behind you is a flight suit that you need to put on. It has communication capabilities that can harness Terahertz frequency to communicate with anything that has a responder or receiver. This Terahertz frequency also has light-bending capabilities that will allow any object to be cloaked and appear non-visual. You must return it when we are finished…sorry. Now get going."

Morgan unbuckled the belt and walked over to the changing compartment. While he put on the suit, Ciril punched in the coordinates to the volcano where there were acres and acres of Rainbow Trees that were shedding their bark. Morgan returned, grumbling at how tight it was. Ciril told him the biomechanical structure acted as the receiver. She handed him a badge and told him to pretend it was from *Star Trek* though it would provide active communication. "Do you beam people up?" asked Morgan.

She laughed and said, "Something like that. Okay, we need to make a call; and I know this may be shocking to you."

Morgan gave her a puzzled look and told her not to keep him in the dark. "Let's hear it."

"We are tapping into the root system of the Rainbow Tree which communicates with the Baobab tree in Africa and other trees like the Corkscrew. Their roots are like our suits and that will give us the ability to talk to them. We are going to let them know the situation and that we need all the bark they can blow off their trunks. They have unique chemicals that we need to combine with the black pitch. From that, we will create a delivery spray method to deploy worldwide as well as attaching it to your satellites to spray any incoming meteors that could have other parasites attached. Earth will no longer be in jeopardy of that type of extinction-level event again. Shall we make our call, Morgan?" He nodded yes.

Morgan and Ciril listened in on a conversation between one of the Rainbow Trees and a Baobab Tree. They spoke about the destruction of the citrus trees and how the Nightcrawlers were becoming radioactive giants able to shoot poison thorns and liquefy everything in their path. They also conveyed that the killer trees moved at night and communicated only through their root system. Ciril asked Morgan if he was ready to make contact. Morgan told her to make it happen. There was a break in the conversation.

Ciril broke in. "This is Blue to Rainbow Tree. Do you hear me?" The reply was a soft yes. "As you are well aware, the Earth is under attack by microbial alien parasites that have morphed into killer Nightcrawlers. We need your help to save humanity. I am Blue. I, too, am an alien. However, I am here to protect mankind." The Rainbow Tree asked how she could help. "We need your shed bark. A chemical component of it is needed for the formula to eliminate the radioactive Nightcrawlers. Is it possible for your forest of Rainbow Trees to shed their bark now so we can collect it?" Ciril asked.

"Yes, that has already begun. I can ask them all to expedite the process," Rainbow tree answered. Ciril communicated that they would be on the rim of the volcano in 15 minutes. She wanted to know where to begin the collection. Rainbow Tree told her to begin on the northwest corner and work eastward. "I will notify the others of your mission and not to be alarmed. By the time you make it halfway in your collection efforts, the remainder of the trees will have completed shedding their bark. I am the largest of the Rainbow Trees. I am 32 feet tall. Please come to me before you leave so I may bless the success of this operation."

Morgan wondered how they would collect the bark. He was sure that all of it would fill a cargo bay. "I hope it can fill both cargo bays. Then, we can dump it and go for the black pitch." He added that humanity's welfare depended on them to get this right the first time. Ciril grimly agreed. They hovered over the northwest corner of the volcano, and all they could see was the bark dropping from trees. Stripped of their outer shell, the rainbow colors of their trunks throughout this vast forest were a dizzying sight to behold.

Ciril pushed a sensor button and a thousand drones lifted off from the hull of the ship. Morgan never even knew they were there. She told him the robots would do all the work for them. She pushed the button to open both cargo bays. She hovered 1,200 feet above the drones collecting the bark. It did not take but 25 minutes to gather it all within that corner of the forest. She pushed another button, and 500 more drones took off spraying the trees with water so they would not be burned by the sun or susceptible to forest fires. This has been a drought year, and it gave the Rainbow Tree forest a much-needed drink of water. Ciril told Morgan, "Never take without returning something in exchange for a kindness. It is a miracle that they are helping us, so we need to bless them." Morgan agreed with that mindset.

All together it took about three hours to collect the bark. It filled each bay to maximum capacity. They then stopped to thank the Mother Rainbow Tree for her and the forest's generosity. Morgan was still amazed that the spacesuit could allow him to ride the beam of light down to the ground and then back to the ship. Back on board, Ciril and Morgan strapped themselves into their chairs. They immediately headed for Morgan's lab to dump the bark and then cloak it. Then it would be off to retrieve the black pitch which appeared to be in great abundance outside of Butte, Montana.

Ciril discussed with Morgan that they may need help moving the bark from the ship into the lab. She suggested that perhaps one of the Sasquatch could come for the night while they concocted the formula. Although he agreed that they would require assistance, he felt that they didn't have the necessary manpower as it took both Virg and Boc to push the stone from the mouth of the cave, Aggie did not have the strength, and they couldn't leave the door open at night. Ciril agreed and told Morgan, "While it will take longer, we will use the drones to assist us. This ship only contains five cloaking covers for the drones, so we will have to make do."

They were approaching the Cuyahoga Valley. She explained that she would deposit the bark in front of his lab. She first needed him to access the cargo area of the ship and toss a cloaking device into each bay and then return and strap in. "This is dump and go," she explained. While Morgan completed that task, Ciril made two passes to make sure there were no trees anywhere near the Cuyahoga Valley. Still nothing. She was relieved. It was obvious they had not yet shut down the Davis-Besse plant as the Nightcrawlers continued to congregate there and grow exponentially. She knew they would not stay there forever feeding. She just needed them to stay one more day. Morgan was out of breath as he sat and buckled in. "Good job. Perhaps after this, you should engage in an exercise program with a personal trainer who will work you hard. You are a soft human." They both laughed and he agreed with her assessment. Ciril told him the dump was about 50% complete. "Just another few seconds and then we will test the cloaking and forcefield." She kept saying "almost" every 10 seconds. She finally announced that it was done and closed the cargo bay doors. She activated the cloaking devices and the forcefield. She looked down at the screen and told Morgan everything was working perfectly.

She asked if he was ready to pick up some black pitch from Montana. Morgan quipped, "Giddy up, cowboy. Let's go." She had no idea what that meant but smiled and took off straight up. Morgan looked at her knowing she did that on purpose. She looked over at him and smiled. He just shook his head. It took just 17 minutes to get to Butte, Montana. Her scanner lit up with a vast amount of black pitch in a vacant field. There must have been at least 50 acres of it. Ciril had to uncloak for about two minutes in order to employ the bending light to transport the black pitch into both cargo bays using a shield to protect them from the radium it would emit. They would need to maintain that shield to prevent the Nightcrawlers from detecting them or the military from thinking it was an incoming weapon and react by launching a missile at the spaceship. She knew this would be tricky, especially with the uncloaking. There was no doubt in her mind that they were still searching for her and would stop at nothing to stop them. Ciril thought this might be a good time to call President Kennedy and let her know what they were doing in case they encountered some difficulty with the military.

Morgan waited as the phone rang. He was surprised when she answered, "This is Charlotte." He thought to himself, *It truly is her private line.*

"Madam President, it's Morgan and Ciril. We have a solution that we believe to be viable. We are picking up the last component of what we need and thought we should inform you." She thanked Morgan and Ciril for their determination and perseverance and reminded them that the hope of mankind was with them as they strove to bring closure to this awful chapter in Earth's history. They advised her that they would require permission for one part of the deployment; however, they were still working through the problem and would advise her when they felt it to be both a logical and successful solution. They hung up.

Ciril asked Morgan if he was ready to de-cloak and begin the upload into the cargo bays. Morgan smiled and nodded. She could see great fear in his face. She knew he was thinking of those babies and not being there for them should anything go wrong. Ciril looked at him and told him, "Our God of the Universe is with us, Morgan. He will not let Earth end like this. He is watching over us and giving us the wisdom and grace to help humanity. Even with all our shortcomings, he cares greatly for us. We can and will do this. That does not mean there will be no challenges. He tests our strength and commitment on a regular basis. We put our lives in his hand to stop this catastrophic event." Ciril told him that she, too, believed in a higher power. Before Morgan realized it, Ciril told him all was done. She closed the cargo bay doors and engaged the cloaking device.

Suddenly, they felt something bump against the hull. She scanned for damage and looked at the radar. "No hull breach. It looks like we hit a drone, and not ours, as we re-engaged the cloaking device. Planes will be in the air. Hang on, this will be instant." She hit the button and it had to be 6G's. Straight up they went. "Today is your lucky day. You are an official astronaut. Look out the window, Morgan." There was Earth. He pointed to a beam of light that was coming at them. "On it!" she screamed. "Evasive maneuvers, computer." He felt a hard left. Terrified, he hung on to the arms of the chair. "MORGAN, LET GO OF THE CHAIR AND HIT THAT PURPLE BUTTON. NOW!" He did what she said and felt the ship spinning. It took a few seconds for the ship to stabilize. "We were hit with their Star Wars laser beam. Apparently, that drone attached something to the ship. I am deploying a drone to remove it and another to fix the hull and heat shields. We are out of their reach for the beam and for visuals. We are sitting on the dark side of the moon. Hope the Greys are feeling generous today. Normally, they do not take kindly to visitors on this side of the moon without their permission. I knew this was a high-risk mission; however, I never dreamed your technology could sneak up on me. We should just be a few minutes. The drone is fast. It's a small puncture in the hull. Looks like the drone removed and incinerated the tracking device. I will not be fooled again." She told Morgan he could breathe now. He looked at her like he was ready to go home. She understood. "I know, Morgan. This takes some getting used to. Most of us go through rigorous training, yours just happened to be baptism by fire. Adults are visual learners, and that's what you're experiencing. You're lucky!" Morgan could still not speak, but he realized Ciril could read his mind. She concluded, "Our solution will restore balance and defeat to the Nightcrawlers. We will not fail. And perfect timing, here come the Greys. They will especially love meeting you, Morgan. They have a thing for humans." He was clearly frightened. "No worries, I got this. You just sit there and don't say a thing, which, from what I can see, will not be an issue."

The Greys requested permission to board and were granted access. Three beings approached the command console and Ciril stood. Morgan remained seated as he stared straight ahead, too frightened to face them. He was sure his shaking was visible. The Greys spoke directly to Ciril.

"Are you aware that you did not request permission to be in our airspace?"

"Yes, but the humans deployed a tracking device on my ship and it was hit by one of their Star Wars lasers." She advised them that she was conducting an inspection and making needed repairs. They inquired about her cargo and if it contained a possible solution for the impending disaster of planet Earth. The Greys advised that it had experienced heavy casualties and was in the process of relocating to underwater bases. He advised they wanted to collaborate in this effort. They had much at stake with the mining efforts. "We currently have necessary components in the cargo bay, as well as at an Earth location. That component is cloaked and has a forcefield around it."

"What if we send a ship for it and create the formula here at our moon base? They are not going to suspect us. We already have a treaty with them and work together on DNA and human hybrids." That got Morgan's attention. All fear left. He turned his chair and stood. He spoke up and told Ciril he thought that was a good idea as their labs would be better equipped than what they had. No way was he going to say he was human. The Grey looked at him and then back at Ciril. She never turned around, but Morgan was sending her thought waves the size of a neon sign on Broadway. She continued to play it cool. She asked if, in addition, someone could repair her ship. The gyroscope was out of whack and she would have to put it into a space dock, explaining it would be easier since we would be in the dock. Grey agreed. Morgan was sending a message of great cover. I will be quiet back here. He sat back down and turned toward the console, hands on the dashboard but not touching anything. The Grey and Ciril made final arrangements, and she sat down and entered the docking coordinates. The Greys left Ciril's ship.

"That was a fine time to speak up, but good job. Proud of you. Okay, we will dock and disembark inside the moon. Their base is large and comprehensive. They have the same atmosphere as on Earth. Think of the amazing things you will see. Their lab is 500 years ahead of anything you could ever imagine. They will make this formula in no time. I would like to prepare you for this visit. You will see many types of alien beings, and some may even be shocking to you. Now the hard part, you can't show emotion. You must act like you have seen the likes of this many times. So far, they have no idea you are a human. Let's keep it that way. You can do this, Morgan. You will never in your lifetime have another opportunity to see and learn. Are you ready?" He nodded yes. "Oh, and as little speaking as possible."

"Got it, Ciril."

"I believe we should change your name; it sounds way too Earthling. I will call you Dao."

"Got it." He nodded.

"Remember, you have your communication device. It will only be heard between you and me. If we are separated for any reason, hit that communication device. I would also secure that in the secret compartment in your belt." She showed him how to slip it in the waistband. "Let's do this."

They disembarked from Ciril's ship. Morgan was in awe of the size and activity. He followed her to the elevator where she punched in the lab code the Grey had supplied. As the elevator made its way upward, Morgan pointed things out in amazement. Ciril then quickly called his attention to a large platform with what appeared to be a space shuttle containing military men. "I think that is General Crosby boarding the shuttle." She advised Morgan that this was a trap and that they needed to get off on the next level and make their way back down to the dock. "I am glad I gave them the wrong coordinates to the bark. I sent them to Antarctica. Just wait until they meet the Reptilians from Alpha Century! I would very much like to be there for that meeting. They are the most feared creatures in this solar system. They are truly vile and find pleasure in torture. Oh, yes, I wish I were a fly on the wall."

# Chapter Seven

# THE ESCAPE AND NEW ALLIES

"Morgan, we need to conceal ourselves behind this stamping equipment." The mechanical structure of the machinery hid their unique biomechanical signatures. "You and I have transponders within our electromagnetic body waves to contact the ship. It is what allows us to communicate with each other using the device contained in your waistband. It is also our way out of here because it is a teleportation device, as well. It is based on our personal electromagnetic signature. We will teleport safely back to the ship. Right now, we need to send a message to President Kennedy and President Ramirez. We will use Terahertz sound waves as they span the entire solar system. There are listening posts that are on 24x7 searching out those specific sound waves that are likely to be the frequency used. It is similar to your SETI program. It is tuned into our Terahertz frequency. We can bounce off that and make the calls. She must be made aware of General Crosby and the military that is working against her commands. The same goes for President Ramirez. After the phone call, we must crawl through the air ducts where our signatures will again be disguised by the EMP technology." Morgan complimented Ciril on her ability to take command

and act quickly. She acknowledged that she had a great amount of experience in situations like this. "We are three levels up, so we will have to access their ladders. Are you going to be okay?" she asked. He shook his head yes. "There is a duct right next to the ship. I will not turn off the force field until we are ready for that final sprint to the ship. I am sure the ramp is still down. That will be a vulnerable spot for us, but we have no choice. This will be a physically difficult climb, Morgan, but I know you can do this. Now let's make these phone calls."

It took about 10 minutes to bounce off SETI servers, but Ciril was finally able to get through to President Kennedy. She updated her of what was happening and the situation she and Morgan were in on Grey's moon base, as well as the treasonous activities of General Crosby and those working with him. The conversation took 20 minutes due to the details and questions. In an effort to bypass going back to Morgan's lab, which she was sure had been compromised, she advised the president on how to contact the Rainbow Tree and to inform her that they would need more bark in the same quantity. She understood perfectly and told Ciril she would be like a snowplow and pave the way.

The next call was to President Ramirez. Her plan was to move the lab and she would be asking President Ramirez if he could accommodate them. It took almost 15 minutes of bouncing off SETI receivers to reach President Ramirez. She explained everything to him just as she had with President Kennedy. "We are asking if you can assist us in developing the formula in a secure lab." He responded that his country would be honored to help humanity and that he would provide coordinates to the secure lab once he made the proper arrangements to protect their safety. He would have the current lab personnel transferred to a different facility while Ciril and Morgan prepared the formula. He assured Ciril that they would not be told the reason for this action so that there would be no leaks, and no traitors could impact the development of the formula.

She received the coordinates and told President Ramirez that she was grateful for his assistance and that they would send a message when they landed. They would first deposit a load of black pitch at the lab and then retrieve the other component needed to concoct the formula. She told him these items would be cloaked and undetectable, just like her ship. He assured her that they would be prepared for their arrival.

Morgan asked Ciril if she felt that both presidents were genuine and trustworthy. Her response was an immediate yes. She asked Morgan if he was ready. He took in a deep breath, let it out slowly, and nodded.

"Let's do this safely. Remember, be careful of how and where you're stepping. We need you to make this formula." Ciril stood looking carefully and then turned and pulled the grate off the air vent. She leaned over and climbed in, then helped Morgan in, and they both pulled the grate back into place. "Now, let's head to the ship." Morgan was able to keep up on the first level and climb the metal ladder to the next level. She told him to stop and catch his breath before proceeding further. As they rested in the air duct, they saw troops searching for them below. Morgan was shocked to see U.S. troops accompanying the Greys. All personnel searching had some type of small weapon. Ciril tapped Morgan to get his attention and indicated that they needed to get to the next level. Morgan was slower on this leg of the escape. They both felt a vibration just as they approached the ladder. Ciril put her finger to her lips to warn him not to speak. The vibration grew stronger. She pointed to the grate. Ciril pushed it and rolled out, but Morgan could barely make it out of the shaft. Ciril almost yanked him all the way out and she threw him a bit off balance. She noticed a small compartment in a nearby piece of machinery and dragged Morgan into it. It was very tight quarters. She felt it start to move. Morgan snapped his head to look at her. She put her finger over his mouth and then pointed to his head. He knew that meant for him to talk to her through the thought process.

"Where is this thing going?"

She whispered into his ear, "To the same level as the ship but to the medical hospital. It is down the hall from the bay where the ship is docked."

Morgan said, "I bet this is where they bring the humans they abduct to experiment on." She nodded yes. "Will we be able to get out?" She nodded her head. They felt the machine roll over a bump. They both assumed it was the medical lab. They could hear talking and then humans screaming to stop and let them go. They were pleading, and the screams were making Morgan's blood boil. He felt the urge to jump out and free them. Ciril took his arm and shook her head no.

They sat cramped in the small cubby within the machine. After a two-hour wait, it grew quiet. Ciril took her scanner and looked for life forms. She was unable to locate any. She put her finger up to have Morgan wait until she rescanned the area. It still showed nothing. She gently opened the compartment, and it was dark and quiet. She told Morgan to stay put. She pulled herself partway out and looked around the lab. It was empty. She stepped fully out and turned to offer Morgan her hand to assist him; however, she heard something and quickly shut the door with Morgan still inside. She cloaked and squatted down beside the machine. She stayed quiet and slowed her breathing while she waited to see what the noise was. It didn't take long to see a Grey walk in to pick up an instrument he must have left on one of the tables. Ciril watched him take the instrument, look it over, and then leave with it. She waited a few minutes to make sure he was not coming back and decided before she opened the door, she would also have Morgan cloak himself. She considered transporting to the ship from that location, but she feared they may track that wave frequency, intercept them, and pull them right into their Brig. She opened the door and directed Morgan to press the button to cloak. She grabbed his other hand so she could help him out. They somehow had to get down the hall and into the ship without being detected. All she could do was hope that they had not captured her or Morgan's electromagnetic signatures.

So far, they appeared to be undetected. It was still dark and quiet. She decided that they should transport directly to the command center of the ship. She sent the signal and, in a snap, they found themselves there. Ciril told Morgan to buckle in. She lifted off and did a turn as she was exiting. They cleared the moon base. She thought to herself, *That was too smooth. This is not right.*

She warned Morgan, "We are in for something; that was way too easy." He looked over to her. His face was pale, and his look was that of a very frightened human. She had seen that look when the Greys strapped a human on the table and began their experiments with no sedation. She attempted to reassure Morgan that they could get through anything if they stuck together. He nodded his head in agreement. Morgan leaned back in his chair and thought of the twins Morgan and Dorothy. He loved them so much. He thought about Marsha and the twins she was now carrying. She was in a precarious situation, attempting to stave off the early birth of the babies.

He heard a scream from Ciril and quickly sat forward, searching for the cause of her concern. "It's two ships of yours. We're safe!"

"I wish that were so; however, those are the ships captured by your military. The nefarious co-workers of mine." They began firing weapons at them. She engaged the forcefield and returned fire, concentrating on the weak spots she detected from an obvious crash. She picked one off immediately. Morgan watched it disintegrate in front of them as they flew through the left-over particles and debris. She instructed Morgan to put on the glasses that were sitting on his console. It would allow him to see cloaked ships. "If you detect one, call out where and an estimate of how far away it is from the ship."

Ciril maneuvered around two ships from Rasalhague. They were two hulking crafts. She managed to slip in between them by flying the ship on its side. This would hide their signature. She told Morgan, "This will take us out of our way; but, we can most likely hitch a ride on one of their jump stream ships. It will take us right to Earth. It will cost something precious to them, which we happen to have, black pitch. They use the barium for cleaning their atmosphere. For now, we sit back and enjoy the ride to Rasalhague." She told Morgan that was sheer luck so far.

Morgan was still recovering and grimly observed, "I hate to point out the obvious, but couldn't the other ship just be setting us up again?"

"Nothing is impossible, but the Rasal beings are totally devoted to transmitting a clear message of peace and unity to the entire universe. They have the ability to read waves generated from people's hearts. Our hearts are already speaking to them. They are hearing our hope for humanity and speaking to them about their help. We need them now to help with the formula to save mankind. So we will have a nice chat with the jump stream ship and ask for its help.

"Not to rain on your parade, but who is to say that your co-worker has not commandeered that jump stream ship?" She explained that the Rasals can hear a black heart, and she was sure they had already attempted something deceitful. She explained that they should start sending signals to the Rasal beings about Earth's perilous situation and our attempt to save mankind from the evil Nightcrawlers. "We should explain what happened on the moon base and how the traitors are trying to block our attempt for peace and unity by killing us, thus stopping our goal to save sentient lifeforms on planet Earth."

Ciril was busy making calculations for weights and then inputting it into the navigation system. Her concentration was disrupted by a voice that said, "This is Ground Control for Rasalhague. Please identify yourself."

Morgan looked at Ciril, "Ground Control, this is Blue requesting your assistance for restoring unity and peace on planet Earth. They need your help to prevent a catastrophic event from destroying all sentient life on that planet. Please allow us to land and collaborate with the scientific experts within your community. Time is not on our side. Please, sir, help us."

"Ground Control to Blue, you have permission to land. Follow the landing beacon. Please set down your craft next to the Ministry of Immigration building."

"Thank you, sir. Out."

Ciril asked Morgan his thoughts, He responded, "I believe them to be of good faith. They are not disingenuous. I think they are truthful, Ciril. I have been sending positive messages for hope and restoration for our planet. My heart has been screaming it. My wife and babies need us, and we need their help."

Ciril looked at him and could feel his sincerity. She assured him they would make it back in time. "The species on this planet are givers, not takers." As they landed, they were met by an immigration liaison. Morgan looked at Ciril as they were guided into the building. She nodded her head in assurance. He kept playing over and over in his mind everyone hiding in the cave and the Nightcrawlers that were now radioactive killing machines that would be after everyone and everything living.

The liaison had them sit at a round table and informed them that someone would be in to assist them. Morgan was still overwhelmed by the events of the day. A woman with the whitest hair he had ever seen walked in and sat down. He looked into her eyes. The pupils were shaped like daisies and the iris was the clearest blue he had ever seen. They waited for the woman to speak first. She looked into Ciril's eyes and then touched her heart. She then turned to Morgan who had tears welling in his eyes. She tilted her head and touched his heart. Tears then welled in her eyes. She touched his head and closed her eyes. That lasted nearly three minutes. When she finally opened them, she introduced herself as Talia. She had been assigned to assess the situation and lend any help needed to resolve the problem involving planet Earth. Ciril introduced herself and explained that she had been sent to Earth from her planet to help prevent an extinction-level event. Talia then turned to Morgan, who had tears flowing. She gently addressed him and told Morgan he had the purest heart she had ever touched. His soul once lived on their planet and was rejoicing at being home again. "I also see your wife and children, but not just them. I see the entire community in that cave. I can see the horrific monsters that are gripping your planet. We will aid you in a formula that will eliminate the awful Nightcrawlers that are ravaging the planet." She looked at Morgan then revealed, "It is not just the Nightcrawlers. There is a nefarious military group attempting a world takeover. This poison must also be addressed." Both nodded as she spoke. Talia told them they had encountered the microbial alien parasites before they discovered that radiation gave them the ability to obliterate any living thing on the planet. She informed them they already had a sufficient formula to eliminate them. She laid out a plan using satellites and decontamination ships that would also have the ability to spray.

Ciril contacted President Ramirez to provide direct phone access to coordinate efforts. Morgan wondered why she did not give President Kennedy's phone. He said nothing, however, Talia turned to Morgan and advised him that she had received intelligence that President Kennedy's phone had been compromised. She told him not to worry. They had a plan to expose the traitor General Crosby and his companions.

Ciril brought up her co-workers that were complicit in the treasonous act. Talia expressed that her heart was saddened that neither peer lived to see the sun across another horizon. Confused, Ciril explained that she had only taken out one of the ships. Talia nodded and said, "How that must burden your heart to kill any living thing." She then revealed that the Greys accidentally destroyed the other craft. They assumed it was you and Morgan.

Talia told them they would be taken to freshen up while arrangements were made to begin work on the formula. It would take a few hours to notify and prep the lab. Making a planet-wide batch of C14 would take some time. Morgan's mind went right to Marsha. Talia tried to reassure him they would work as fast as possible.

Someone came to take them to a resting area. She invited them to enter and showed them how to operate the lights, shower, food, and door. Morgan looked at Ciril as the liaison left. "Well, here we are," said Morgan. He invited her to go first because, after all, that was the right thing for a gentleman to do. While she was in the shower, Morgan explored the room. He found the button to extend out the water and basin for the kitchen sink. He found the refrigerator that opened by waving his hand in front of the sensor. He had no idea what the items within there were, so he shut the door. He looked in the cupboards, however, they must not have ever had a human there. He was in search of a peanut butter and jelly sandwich and potato chips and a nice big Diet Coke on ice. Ciril walked out and told him it was his turn. He was still looking in the cupboard and told her what he was craving. She told him she would take care of that while he was showering.

He turned around and stood there. He was speechless. He looked down and cleared his throat and asked if she was going to dress. She told him their species had to air dry because their thin layer of skin tends to rip open if dried with a towel. The biomechanical suit protects it. To put the suit on, the skin must be completely dry and devoid of any moisture. As he walked past her, he said to himself, *Who knew.*

Morgan turned on the shower, undressed, and stood under the hot water for a lengthy time. He washed his hair with something gooey. He hoped it grew hair on his head. He looked suspiciously at the bar of soap and shrugged. "Oh, well, let's do this. As he was rinsing off, Ciril came in, still not dressed, and stood there looking at him. He turned and saw her and she told him his meal had arrived.

She then walked slowly over to Morgan, looking deeply into his eyes. Morgan was mesmerized and couldn't move or think. She approached him and entered the shower with him. She stood in front of him and then pressed into him. Morgan fought hard, thinking of Marsha and the babies. He closed his eyes thinking only of that. Ciril stood there for about four minutes, pressed into him, staring in his eyes. She never put her arms around him, nor did she kiss him. Morgan tried not to think about what was happening. He opened his eyes and then he felt it. He did not know what that was. She stepped back and walked away dripping wet. He couldn't make sense of what that tradition was, but he was glad it was over.

He jumped out and dried himself off. He quickly dressed, looking forward to this alien attempt at a peanut butter and strawberry jelly sandwich. He couldn't wait to drink a Diet Coke. Well, at least he hoped that was what it would be since he was on an alien ship. He sat down at the table as Ciril started preparing something from the refrigerator. She still was not dressed. He looked back down at his food as he attempted to swallow the next bite. He thought it was not nearly as good as what he had at home. He wasn't so sure if he would order it again. Ciril was still mixing a few things just as he finished. He took his plate to the sink. She turned to him. Morgan looked into her eyes and told her to please get dressed. She acknowledged his request and walked into the other room. Morgan thought, *These aliens have no modesty, that's for sure.*

Ciril came back out with her biomechanical suit on. She went over to the counter and picked up her plate and sat at the table with Morgan. Morgan looked at her and asked what she was eating. She told him it was a platameyer, which was like Earth's pheasant. She asked Morgan if he would like to taste it. He said sure. She cut off a piece and handed it to him. Morgan popped it in his mouth and the meat melted. *This is heavenly*, he thought. Morgan said it was the best thing he had ever eaten. He told her he was exhausted and wanted to lie down and asked how to work the bed. She walked in with him and pushed the button on the wall and the bed extended out into the room. He was feeling dizzy. She helped him lie down and undressed him as he slept. She undressed, as well, and pressed against him. He, however, was unconscious and had no idea that she was helping herself to pleasure and, more importantly, that this was her fertile time. She knew Morgan would have the perfect DNA to match hers. She thought he felt so good next to her and fit her body perfectly.

The door buzzer rang. She jumped up and stated that they would be right out. Ciril suited up and then woke Morgan. She told him it was time to go. Morgan sat up and realized he was unclothed. Morgan jumped up out of bed and dressed quickly. He was ready in three minutes. Ciril was impressed. They both followed the liaison to the lab. The hall was pure white with wonderful paintings in bright colors. He couldn't wait to see their equipment. The airlock opened and the lab was massive. The outside wall was all glass which increased the brightness of the lab. Morgan thought to himself that the lab had to be 25 feet in height and the size of three football fields. Morgan had never seen a lab of that magnitude. He could see drones and satellites against the wall and there were three large steel drums that contained what appeared to be a green liquid. They were just inside the airlock when the liaison handed them each a strange-looking mask. Morgan watched Ciril place it close to her mouth and nose. In an instant, it sucked against her face sealing the mask to her face. He followed her lead and made a complete seal against his face. The liaison signaled for them to come through the second airlock. Ciril and Morgan entered the lab. The liaison walked them over to the front of the lab where their lead scientist Turok greeted them.

Turok toured them through the lab. He gave special attention to the satellites and drones, showing them the spray mechanisms, cloaking technology, and for some of the drones, an avoidance system. Because of Earth's meridian lines, a few needed to have a weapons system; and at certain points, their cloaking was rendered useless. Then he showed them the handheld spray gun mechanisms that had laser weaponry, as well. Ciril asked how many ground troops he was going to deploy. Turok indicated that he thought the first wave would be about 5,000 and the second wave would drop to around 3,500. He said that, in addition, they were waiting for a shipment of 2,000 spray cannons for the ground troops to deploy.

Morgan voiced his concern about the amount of weaponry that the troops would be employing and feared that the casualties would be substantial. He urged Ciril and Turok to mitigate the number of injured or fatalities. Turok reassured Morgan that they had special suits coming from another planet, named Scheat, that had encountered this microbial alien parasite before and had successfully worked through this war.

He explained, "They have specially designed suits that can withstand radiation and the acid that drips from these monsters and are equipped with monitors to measure their levels. Once they reach a critical point, those troops are recalled and a new regiment is sent forward. The troops pulled back are sanitized and their suits reset. Then the cycle starts again. No one is exposed to the radiation or acid for more than 30 minutes, and even less if the suit displays a warning of being beyond the acceptable levels of either the radiation or acid. We have many protocols in place as well as processes for the protection of all." He went on to explain that the entire operation would take three to four days. "Of course, that includes the expunging of all radiation and acid. If a human comes in contact with either, that is a death sentence. We will also clean up Fukushima, Three Mile Island, and Chernobyl. We will not permit an extinction-level event on this planet. We will conduct a planning meeting in five hours with departure the next hour. Until that time, we will continue to prep the drones, satellites, handhelds, and cannons. Until the meeting, you will go back to your ready room and wait for your liaison to bring you back for your assignments."

The liaison escorted them back to the ready room. Ciril knew this was a fortunate opportunity to gather more DNA and fertilize more of her eggs. Morgan was not only saving his own civilization but hers, too. Ciril asked him if he was hungry and ordered some refreshments. She was surprised the liaison was back so quickly with the order. She placed it on the table. Morgan ate his peanut butter and jelly sandwich and began sipping his tea. They did not talk much. He told Ciri that he needed to shower again and to sleep and asked to be awakened an hour before the briefing. Ciril could sense Morgan's stress. The shower stayed on for 10 minutes. She heard it stop and Morgan yelled, "Where are the towels?"

"Lie down on the bed. It auto-dries you." He commented that all of this new technology was great but he still liked towels. She laughed and told him after a while you can't live without it. She then laughed harder as well as louder. She was testing to see if he was asleep.

There was no response so she disrobed as she walked to the bed where Morgan lay asleep. She climbed on him, pressing against him, and whispered to him, "If you only knew you were saving a civilization, my civilization." She decided that she would enjoy the human way of transferring DNA. It was faster and much more pleasurable. She had 3.5 hours to fertilize as many eggs as possible. As the time passed, she was envisioning all the children that would come from these sessions. Some would have the skill set of her people—empathic, telepathic, teleportation, hypnotic, and, for females, the ability to produce thousands of eggs with each fertile session. Females did not come along that often. There was high hope that this would result in a very large population of females that could produce more offspring. She was enjoying this session. She could see why humans transferred this way. It was addictive and she did not want it to end. It had been over three hours. She needed to stop. She thought, *Any longer and he might feel something. He could become suspicious.* She climbed off and retrieved the cleaning light. It was like a shower only you did not get wet. She ran it over Morgan and herself. She saw him stir. She put the light away, hurried to the kitchen, and got dressed. She started the coffee and tea.

Morgan opened his eyes. He could smell the coffee. He dressed and went out to the kitchen. "Well, you are becoming domesticated. I guess I am training you to be a good wife for someone."

She laughed and handed him his coffee. "Drink up, Soldier Boy." Morgan laughed and told her it was better than being called Nerd Boy. Morgan expressed that the suits needed to be redesigned or he needed his underwear back. He was complaining the crotch area was rubbing certain man parts.

She laughed and said, "Now you are a couture clothing designer?" They laughed again. She was happy that was what he thought caused the chafing. At that moment, she knew that many eggs had been fertilized and was hoping for more over the next few hours. This was a critical time for the fertilization to take hold. She knew that somehow she had to get them reassigned to the cargo ship that would take them out of harm's way.

The liaison would soon return to take them back to the lab. She advised Morgan it was getting close to the time for the detailed planning review for the mission. "Let's clean up the kitchen for them." They stood and sanitized their cups with the cleaning light. Ciril then went in and ran the light over the bed. She then made the bed and pushed the button that pulled the bed back into the wall. A large screen information center dropped into place. She asked Morgan to come into the room to watch the people assembling for the meeting. They could also see that most of the equipment had been secured onto long trolleys that floated in their air. Morgan asked why didn't use wheels. She laughed and told him that it was so twentieth century. He laughed and told her he was just an old-fashioned guy. They heard the door buzz and the airlock release. The liaison asked if they were ready, and they both responded with an enthusiastic yes. They walked the long hall again. Morgan loved looking at the paintings and stopped again at the lady in blue with the red flower. Morgan told the liaison that he would love to have this painting and she should wrap it up and give it to him as a gift. The liaison smiled and told him she was happy that he appreciated the work of their artists. They continued to walk to the lab.

They entered the airlock; and as it swished open, they could see most people had already been seated. She escorted them to the front row and seated them. Morgan noticed there were many different kinds of species. Some looked as if they should be in an ocean. Morgan stared in amazement at the species seated in the lab as well as the drones, satellites, and hundreds of tables with metal cases stacked 25 high along the back wall of the lab. He saw 200 or so large steel tanks encased in a moving glass-like substance. He could not even imagine what that was. Then he realized that there was a man up front speaking. Morgan began listening, wondering what he had missed. The gentleman looked to be in military dress and conveyed an air of self-assurance in his voice. He looked confident as he went through the battle plan. Morgan was surprised to hear that alien bases on Earth would be assisting. The bases at Mr. Baker, Utah Four Corners, Davy Crockett National Forest, Cuyahoga Valley National Park, Italian Alps outposts, Interlaken, Switzerland, Malta, the arctic region of Norway, Lake Titicaca, Tiwanaku, and Antarctica. All had their assignments as did the underwater outposts in the Mariana Trench, Catalina Island in California, Tonga, Iceland, Japan, China, India, the South African coast, and the Coast of Australia. Morgan could not believe all the alien bases and outposts on the planet. There must have been something going on in the ocean with the microbial alien parasites.

The alien ambassador for Earth stood alongside the military leader, and the holographic images of the Killer Citrus Tree Nightcrawlers appeared. It was horrifying, and there was a gasp from the room. Then the next holographic image appeared. This was from the ocean. Giant coral reef monsters had formed mostly around Fukushima, Malta, and Australia. However, there appeared to be one that was covered in black oil in the Gulf Of Mexico close to Texas. The military person advised that all necessary equipment and supplies for these bases and outposts left for planet Earth an hour ago. The remainder was for our attack by land, sea, and air.

The ambassador spoke again, pulling another holographic image that showed a giant bird. It resembled a chicken hawk, but its toes looked like shiny steel points. It looked to be the size of an aircraft carrier. He advised that they only had intel on one of these creatures that was causing havoc on Japan. The concern would be for the drones as well as ground troops. The military person informed everyone in attendance that they had confronted this enemy on three other planets, and they had the experience to defeat this parasite. There would be casualties; however, all personnel were devoted to the peace and unity of the galactic federation. He reminded them that this was a young planet just starting out exploring the stars, so no equipment should be left behind. That would be against the Prime Directive.

"Currently, we are awaiting the radiation and acid suits from the planet Scheat. They are experts in the development and production of this specialized protection suit. It will be here in two hours. We leave for the mission in three hours after the troops and personnel have been outfitted." The ambassador told them that this was a top-secret mission and only President Kennedy of the United States and President Rameriz of Honduras had been briefed. Surprisingly neither took questions. The liaison was there to take them back to the ready room. Ciril was still unsure how she would have them reassigned to the cargo ship that would carry ground troops and all their equipment. The other two cargo ships would carry the drones and satellites, as well as the extra formula.

Ciril's fertility drive went right to how she could obtain another session of DNA transfer. At present, she was only sitting at 159 eggs fertilized. She needed many more. She knew that Morgan would suspect that something was going on if she drugged him again, and it was too soon after the previous dose to risk it. She decided she would use her hypnotic powers to do the transfer, all with Morgan not knowing anything about what she was doing. They went through the airlock of the ready room. She laughed and told him they cleaned for nothing. Then she acted like she had something in her eye. Morgan pulled her close to the light to look in her eye, as she had hoped he would. She gazed into his eyes with a trance-inducing stare, and she could immediately see that he was in a state of near-paralysis. She quickly moved him to the bedroom and pushed the button for the bed. The monitor went up and the bed extended out from the wall. She laid him down. She did not speak to Morgan as she undressed him. She climbed back on and continued his DNA transfer the human way. This was so much more effective than her species' way to transfer. She continued to look deep into his eyes to maintain this level of mental unconsciousness. Every so often, she would close her eyes to release more eggs to be fertilized. She was having difficulty without the drug to keep Morgan's human transfer instrument up and functioning. She sent him pictures telepathically to stimulate that transfer. This method appeared to work. She couldn't imagine not having this method available during her next fertile period in three years. Smiling, she looked at Morgan and thought, *I will see you again in three years should this produce the offspring I believe it will.* It had been over an hour. She climbed off and grabbed the light to clean her and Morgan once again. This time she grabbed the skin healing wand and ran that over Morgan, as well. She thought he should perhaps have an energy infusion so she pulled the air injector from the bathroom and injected it into his nose. She knew there was no smell and he would never know. She redressed them both and had him stand. She pushed the button for the bed to retract and the monitor screen to drop. She then turned it on and snapped Morgan out of his hypnotic state as she spoke about the troops and the new protection suit. Morgan watched the screen and said nothing. She knew his mind was blank from the moment they walked in the door, and this new memory of watching the screen was implanted into his mind. They stood there and watched the troops being fit for their individual form-fitting suits. It somehow engulfed the soldier and fit like a glove. He was impressed. When he saw the wings unfold from the suit, he was in total disbelief. He asked Ciril if they could fly with those wings, She shook her head yes. Morgan was in awe.

The buzzer went off for the door. They walked into the kitchen and the liaison entered. "I am to take you for your fitting of the protective suit in the lab and last-minute deployment instructions and assignments." They followed her, and Morgan made one last stop at the blue lady painting. *Wish this was mine.* He then continued to walk with the liaison and Ciril. They approached the lab airlock. As they entered, a soldier took them to a side room where two suits were waiting to be fitted to them. The soldier instructed Ciril to stand in front of the suit facing forward with her back to the suit. He then asked her to take one step backward, and the suit was attracted to her like a magnet. It enveloped her and then conformed to her body. There was a glow of sorts in the abdomen area. The soldier said nothing. He let her get the feel of the suit as he turned his focus to Morgan and gave the same instructions. Morgan was surprised at the ease of the envelopment and fitting to his form. True to Morgan's sense of humor, he asked if it made him look skinny. Ciril laughed. The soldier did not. The soldier told them both to remain there for further instruction.

A female liaison walked into the room. She smiled and told them the protective suit fit well. She continued with their assignments to the cargo vessel which carried the drones and satellites. There was also refill capability with formula onboard. Ciril thought this was a miracle. She did not have to maneuver a reassignment. The liaison stressed the importance of wearing the protective suit as well as the helmet while in the cargo bay. However, while in the ready rooms that would not be required as they all had individual force fields and were designed as escape pods. Morgan thanked her for the detailed instructions and would follow them implicitly. Ciril also agreed. The liaison turned to Ciril and took both hands into hers. She told her the reason she had been assigned there was because her species took pregnancy as a critical event for the survival of their species; and since she was carrying multiple fertilized eggs, the plans changed to accommodate her condition. Morgan looked shocked. The liaison moved to Morgan and took both his hands. "You, my new human friend, are not familiar with this technology or fighting. You are also assigned to this cargo ship. While you are highly intelligent, you are not yet up to speed with the technology. I hope this is acceptable to you." Morgan smiled, shaking his head in agreement. It was clear that Morgan was relieved their duties were to be far less dangerous than the previous assignment.

An audible voice directed all troops to proceed to their assigned ships for departure. Both Ciril and Morgan stood in line with soldiers as they waited to board the shuttle to take them to their assigned cargo ship.

# Chapter Eight

# MISSION ERADICATE

As they boarded the ship they found there were no seats, only straps hanging from the roof to hang on to. It reminded Morgan of a city bus. Ciril could see his concern and advised him not to worry as it was only a 10-minute journey. Morgan shook his head that he understood. The shuttle ride was really fast. He felt the bump as the craft put down in the cargo bay. The back of the shuttle opened and everyone disembarked. The soldiers formed two lines. Morgan and Cirl stood between them. *This is an impressive display. I wonder how many ground troops the cargo ship can hold? Enough for a massive invasion is how many*, thought Morgan as he watched in awe.

Ciril looked at him and told him this species would never invade any planet. Same with the special forces taking part in this mission. "Everyone is committed to peace and unity of the Galaxy Federation. Earth is off-limits except for the science contingencies of the outposts and bases. Even then, they have limits as to what they can accomplish without human contact. Now I know the Reptilians and Greys push the envelope on this "no contact" declaration. They are, however, penalized for each interaction with humans. There are tracers and monitors in place that look for alien biosignatures. Should they find one, it is tracked and they are picked up immediately and charged with the crime of human contact and trying to influence technology advancement against the Prime Directive. Morgan shook his head, acknowledging he understood.

Three military officers came to meet the ground troops, as well as Cirl and Morgan. Two of them took groups that were already lined up and waiting for instructions. The other officer approached Ciril and Morgan and asked them to follow him. He took them forward to the ship's Ready Rooms. He explained that these also doubled as escape pods. He wanted them to stay inside this room until otherwise directed. Ciril asked if they could remove their protective suits.

He snapped back, "Of course." Morgan thought his tone was harsh and uncalled for. Ciril touched his arm. He sensed then not to address this officer's rude manner. She thanked the officer and assured him that they would be compliant with his instructions. He nodded and left. Ciril walked to the door and turned the locking mechanism.

"They will not enter uninvited, Morgan." Morgan felt relieved and Ciril anticipated an opportunity for a lot of DNA transfer. She told Morgan that they should take turns keeping watch and that he should lie down for a couple of hours before the intensity heated up. She explained that the war on the microbial alien parasites would need their full attention. "Now is the time for you to rest. We will need our strength for later. Plan on being up for maybe 24 hours." Morgan was surprised. He asked her if she was sure that she wanted him to go first. She assured him that she did. He moved closer to her and asked her why she did not trust him enough to tell him she was pregnant. She shook her head and explained that pregnancy was not the same for her as it was for human women. She only carried the eggs, the incubation period was done by machine.

Morgan laughed and said, "Well, no stretch marks that way." She laughed. She turned to him and gave him a push toward the bed. Morgan laughed as he gave in and laid down. She then told him that he needed to take a pill for space sickness. Morgan insisted he was not sick. She advised him that when they started physically working with the cargo bay doors open, he would find himself not feeling well from being exposed to the force field. He complied and popped it in his mouth. She sarcastically said, "Swallow it, nerd boy!" and walked out of the room. She knew it would take a little while for the pill to take effect.

Ciril spent the next 15 minutes looking out the window as shuttlecraft moved troops to the planet. The mission had begun. The deployment of satellites would be ongoing for the next 15 hours. She thought she would peek in and see if Morgan was asleep. She opened the door gently and looked in. She approached the bed and called softly to him. He did not respond. She lifted his eyelid to see if he was under. She could tell by Morgan's eyes that he was unconscious and would be out for at least four hours. She slipped off her suit and climbed on. Her goal was to achieve another 200 eggs fertilized. She had hours to do this. She pressed into him to start, but it didn't take her long to move onto the human way to transfer DNA. She knew this was her last opportunity. She would have to deposit all fertilized eggs in five days. She thought she would have a total of 400 eggs to be incubated, an amount never produced by one female. Ciril decided this time she was going to let herself go and enjoy this human way. The next few hours she intended to block out everything except unadulterated pleasure during the DNA transfer. After two hours she could tell she was at the maximum amount she could safely hold. She extricated herself and went into the bathroom to access the sonic cleaner, then returned to Morgan and used it on him. She retrieved the skin wand for fast repair and ran it over him then returned it to the bathroom. She slipped back into her suit and redressed Morgan. She was grateful she had this opportunity. If humans only realized how many times aliens took their DNA to help populate their civilizations. Her species will be much improved from Morgan's DNA. She waited for him to awaken then she would rest for a few hours. She wondered how Morgan would react when she gave him one of the offspring. It only took one week to incubate. She would bring him a male child. She knew she could never tell him he was the father to 400 children. She decided not to worry about it until then. It was the sovereign duty of her species to present one of the male offspring to the father. She knew there was no escaping this obligation when it came time.

Morgan awoke and went into the bathroom to shower. He quickly dressed and returned to the kitchen area in 10 minutes flat. Ciril was waiting with a hot beverage and handed it to Morgan as he sat down. She told him the satellite would finish deploying in about 11 hours and that ground troops continued being deployed and the drones had all been released. She told him to wake her in three hours. Morgan smiled and told her he would. He asked Ciril what he should do while she was resting. She reached over to the wall and touched it. A view screen extended from the wall.

"This is like your touch-screen computers. You can search for anything you want; and since we are within your television waves, you can watch any program or news. She turned and walked into the sleeping area. Morgan noticed the glowing abdomen. He thought it was brighter and bigger. He wondered how her pregnancy worked and what the gestational time was. One thing he did know, she was not concerned so he was not going to worry about it.

Ciril awoke and thought, *That was a fast three hours.* She decided to shower, as well. She undressed and stood under the hot water for 15 minutes then walked into the kitchen. Morgan asked her if she ever wore clothes

"I am drying off," she explained.

Morgan asked if he could touch her glowing belly. She walked over to him. He gently touched her stomach and could feel it moving, almost like a vibration. He asked her how long the pregnancy lasted. She explained that the machine develops the fetus into a child in approximately one week and that the eggs spend the first little bit of time with her. The fertilized eggs, once stable enough to transfer, then go into a receptacle. He asked her how they extract the eggs. She told him, like human birth, the female pushes the eggs that are fertilized out through a birth canal. Morgan then asked where she was in the process. Ciril looked at him and told him not to worry. She had plenty of time before that would occur. She told him when the belly became clear and the eggs could be seen, it would be a matter of one day. He then asked if they ever came early. She told him she never knew that to happen and that females only have fertile time every three years.

Both Ciril and Morgan heard an alarm blasting throughout the ship. Ciril told him to put on his protective suit and that they should stay in this protective pod. She did not want to risk exposure with babies on board. He agreed. They both donned their suits and proceeded to the window where they could see what was going on. They were surprised to see a space shuttle attempting to enter the cargo ship bay. The next thing they saw was the space shuttle firing a laser-type weapon at the ship.

Ciril exclaimed, "Fools! This ship will blow them into eternity." Morgan suggested that they reach out to the shuttle and find out their intentions. Ciril looked at Morgan and told him she pretty much could guess their intention. "They will have troops board that shuttle with weapons blazing." She walked over to the table and pulled down the view screen and called up President Kennedy's personal line. Morgan walked over to the table. They stood, waiting for her to respond. She did not answer. Ciril said to Morgan, "She has been compromised." She tried connecting to President Rameriz. He answered. "Mr. President, this is Blue and Morgan. I hope the troops are making headway." He told them it was amazing and that the entire area was free of the Nightcrawlers. He informed them that he had seen drones in the air, as well as ground troops. Then, he advised them that he had seen U.S. jets firing on the drones to no avail.

"Thank you so much for the intel. I will pass it along to the appropriate chain of command." She disconnected the viewer from that channel and spoke to the command center to inform them of the information received from President Rameiz. She advised that she had been unable to reach President Kennedy. The space shuttle was not friendly fire. She recommended boarding the shuttle and taking everyone prisoner until it could be sorted out.

He advised her that the plan was in motion. "We expect to have all aboard the shuttle in the bay within minutes. The prisoners will be taken to a secure ready room and scanned for weaponry. After that is cleared, we would like you to join us for a chat with the prisoners."

"Let us know if you have any questions regarding the prisoners prior to us joining your interrogation."

# Chapter Nine

# THE BIRTH

anger Kopchek and Ranger Long kept the community quiet as they could hear the drones buzzing overhead. They also heard heavy scraping sounds above them and knew it was dark and that the Nightcrawlers were moving. Everyone pitched in to keep the babies quiet. Bitty and Aggie had a special connection with them, knowing when to have their bottles ready and diapers changed. Marsha was still on strict bed rest. She had not spotted since Morgan left. The drones overhead was stressing and the sound of the heavy dragging was scary. All in the cave knew that it was the Nightcrawlers traveling through the park. The rangers were not only concerned for the humans but all the wildlife within the Cuyahoga Valley.

Bev came in to sit with Marsha. She knew that she must be worried sick about Morgan on top of being confined to bed, and she wanted to help Marsha stay calm so that she could buy the babies more time in her womb. She brought the book *Little Women* with her. It was her favorite book and she enjoyed reading it to Marsha and Bitty. Bitty spent most of her time with Marsha caring for baby Morgan and Dorothy- Alice. Dorothy-

Alice cried when anyone but Bitty or Marsha held her. Bitty held both babies nearly all the time. She was trying to teach them to hold on to her fur. Marsha told Bitty that human babies did not have the strength to hold on like a Sasquatch baby. Bitty was determined to continue trying. Marsha and Bev reminded her constantly to never let go of the babies as they would fall and hurt themselves. She understood that, however, she just wanted to feel them latching onto her. She told Bev and Marsha it would make her feel complete. Bev started reading to them at a whisper level. Jim came in shortly after and signaled Bev that she should go back and lie down. He instructed Bitty to take the babies to the cubby farthest back and under the most rock to care for them with Aggie. Jim stacked diapers in her hand along with two bottles.

He then leaned forward and asked Marsha in a whisper how she was feeling. He went down the list from dizzy to headache, to cramping to spotting. She shook her head no to all. Jim felt something was off. He took her blood pressure and found it to be high. Marsha knew just by watching Jim that something was wrong. He took her pulse and it was fast. Jim was now concerned. He looked at Marsha and moved to sit beside her on the cot. He asked her again how she was feeling and told her to tell him the truth. She told Jim she was scared and that she had felt twinges earlier. He put his hand on her belly and said, "I asked you to tell me if you felt anything new. I must check you, Marsha. This could be serious."

She began to cry. "No, no, my babies. Morgan will be so upset for losing our babies."

Jim took her in his arms and hugged her. He whispered in her ear, "We are not losing these babies, got that?" She continued to cry. He told her the babies needed her to pull it together. "No more crying. I need you to be strong for them." She pulled away, wiping tears from her face. Jim held her hand for a minute while she continued to calm down. He asked her if she was okay. She shook her head yes. He asked her to lie down for a fast exam while he donned a glove and added some goo, as Marsha called it. He asked if she was ready as he sat down next to her on the cot. She took in a deep breath and let it out and then took in another. Jim told her to take her time and let him know when she was ready. She took in a few more deep breaths and blew them out slowly. She told him she was okay and to go ahead and see where they were. Jim smiled and told her she was brave. He checked and it did not take him long. He told her to remain lying down. He removed the glove and looked her in the eyes, explaining that she was dilated three centimeters and the cervix had effaced, meaning she would be giving birth soon. He needed to move her to the very back in the medical cubby. First, however, he needed to get the incubators and the room ready. He reminded her to not scream out. It would give away the hiding place and put the entire community in jeopardy.

He got Ranger Long to assist him, then had Bev go back to sit with Marsha. Jim and Ranger Long spent over an hour getting everything in order for both babies and Marsha. He could not allow her to experience full labor because she would not be able to remain totally silent in the final stages. He would let her go as long as possible without giving a general anesthetic. Jim was the most worried about starting an IV in preemies that small. He told Ranger Long how important it was to keep a confident attitude, especially in front of Marsha. Jim hoped that Ranger Long had exceptional skills; they both would need them to deliver such premature babies and keep them alive. Jim told Ranger Long it was time to get Marsha; however, he wanted to stop at each encampment to let everyone know what was happening. It was important that they stay away from the medical area so as not to contaminate it.

Jim entered Marsha's tent while Ranger Long remained at the doorway. "Okay, Marsha, everything is set up. We are going to walk with you back to the medical area."

Ranger Long stuck his head in and asked, "Why don't we carry her back? We can each take one end of the cot and Kron can support it in the middle until we get to just outside the sterile area. Then it would be up to us to carry her the rest of the way." Marsha laughed. Bev told them she would go get Kron to help and was back with her in less than three minutes. Kron walked in and immediately put her hand on Marsha's belly. She looked at Marsha and told her the babies were ready and that she should not fear. They are ready and they are true warriors. Marsha began to cry and thanked Kron. Jim told Kron that she needed to let go of the cot before they got to the room because she was not sterile and would contaminate the room. She told them she understood. They picked up the cot and transported Marsha to the medical cubby. Bitty called out to Marsha that the babies were fine and not to worry. Jim turned his head and warned Bitty not to yell.

Kron let go of the cot. She put her hand on Marsha's head and whispered to her, "Peace, know peace, my friend." Marsha felt a wave of calm come over her. Jim told her to roll onto the table and not to roll off. She laughed. Jim thought to himself that it was great to hear a laugh. Kron had a wonderful effect on Marsha's attitude. He thought she should be there for Marsha and instructed her to bathe, then he would provide a sheet covering to keep her sterilized. He called for Kron and instructed her what to do. Kron told him she would do it right away. He hoped that this was the right call.

Marsha asked what was next. Jim told her he would allow her to go into labor until the pain could no longer be controlled. At that point, he would give her anesthetic and she would go to sleep. Then he would go in and get the babies. He said a scream would give away their hiding place, and he was sure that she would never want to endanger the entire community. She agreed. He asked if she was comfortable on the table and she said yes. Ranger Long took her blood pressure and pulse while Jim listened to the babies. He told her the babies sounded great. Ranger Long informed Jim that her blood pressure was elevated, as was her pulse.

Kron approached the medical cubby after bathing. Ranger Long sprayed her with disinfectant and then wrapped her in a sheet and tied it on her. They put surgical cloth boots over her feet, as well as a surgical cap. Marsha looked over and started laughing. She asked who had a phone to take a picture of this sight. Kron came in and asked if she was pretty. Jim laughed and said, "Of course, you are the belle of the ball." They were all laughing until Marsha experienced her first real pang of labor. She winced and groaned.

Jim looked at Ranger Long who said, "They kind of sneak up on you, don't they?" She nodded and told Jim she would not be vocal again now that she knew what to expect.

Jim laughed and said, "Yeah, sure. That's what they all say." Kron began to stroke her hair. She looked at Jim and told him she would not cry out again. Jim then told Ranger Long to time the contractions. It was so quiet in the cave.

Marsha asked Jim if she could have tea. He looked at her and said, "What do you think my answer will be because I am sure you know it is NO! Now, we start an IV and give you fluids." He was wondering if he should give her something for her blood pressure. "Marsha, I am going to give you something to bring down your blood pressure."

Kron asked him not to give her that because she could help bring that down for Marsha. Jim told her that would be better all the way around. Kron put her hand on Marsha's forehead and told her to close her eyes. She then touched her heart and lifted her hands away and told her to open her eyes. She smiled at Kron. She felt such love, warmth, and security. Ranger Long stepped over to take her blood pressure. He told Jim it was normal, as was her pulse. He looked at Kron in amazement. Marsha thanked her and told her she would hold a special love in her heart for her always. Kron could feel her hand tensing as she held it loosely, allowing for her to squeeze as tightly as possible. Kron looked at Jim and knew another contraction was coming which made them six minutes apart. He thought that labor was progressing along faster than he had anticipated. He took Marsha's other hand and told her she was doing great. She smiled at him. Kron put her hand back on Marsha's heart and kept it there for a minute. Jim thought that to be odd. He looked at Kron and she nodded to him and then looked back at Marsha. He grabbed his stethoscope and put it to her chest, listening. He then walked over to the cabinet and pulled out a vial of medicine. Marsha asked what was wrong with her. Jim told her it was probably nothing; however, he may have heard a skip in the beat of her heart. He wanted to give her a little medicine but was sure Kron already took care of it for him. He was also going to hook her and the babies up to a monitor to make sure all three were safe.

"Okay, Jim, but I do feel fine."

"Wonderful, Marsha, music to my ears".

Kron felt her hand squeezing, and this time it was much harder. Kron looked over at Jim who turned and looked at the monitor. "Alright, Marsha, you are four minutes apart now. Good job. How bad are the contractions?" She told him they were not bad. Kron gave Jim a look that signaled to him that Marsha might have reached the maximum level of pain she could tolerate. He would see what the next contraction would be for her and how far apart. It had only been two minutes and she began another contraction. This one she struggled with and fought hard to not cry out. At the end of the contraction, she could not hold it. Kron sensed it and placed her head down on her mouth to absorb the scream. Jim looked her in the eyes and told her it was time. They could not allow her to go any further. He was going to give her medication to make her sleep. When she woke up, she would see her babies. He moved to above her head. She whispered to Jim to tell Morgan she loved him very much in the event something happened. Jim assured her he would but that nothing was going to happen. He pushed the propofol and watched her drift off to sleep. He then pushed some additional drugs, intubated her, and put her on the ventilator. He asked Kron to leave the cubby and then told Ranger Long to get the incubators ready. He needed the babies out now. Jim grabbed two blankets and laid them on Marsha's legs while Ranger Long prepped the incubators. Jim pulled the surgical tray to his side and cleansed her belly with betadine. He took hold of the scalpel and made the incision. He then used his spreader and reached in to pull out the first baby and break the amniotic sac. It was going perfectly so far. The first baby out was Zoey Grace. He laid her on the blanket and told Ranger Long to rub her and get her breathing and then to suction her. Jim thought she was a viable weight of maybe 2.5 pounds. He heard her cry. He looked over and Ranger Long was putting oxygen on her. Jim asked about her O2 level and heart rate. She was at 92% and 123. Jim told him to keep with her and to clean off the top of her head so he could start the IV there.

He finally had a hold of baby Liam, pulled him out, and laid him on the blanket. He was blue and not breathing. Jim went right to work on the baby knowing Marsha would be okay for a few minutes. He rubbed him and flicked his heel. Finally, he cried out. Jim lifted him into the incubator and told Ranger Long to help baby Liam and let him know his levels as soon as possible. "85%, Doctor."

He had to get Marsha taken care of. He finished with her while Ranger Long got the intubation tube ready for baby Liam. Jim asked Ranger Long to put on new gloves and stitch Marsha up. He responded, "Right away, Doctor." Jim looked at baby Liam who was still blue. He gave him oxygen and then worked on an IV for him. He got it on the first try. *What a stroke of luck*, he thought. He immediately attempted to intubate him and was also able to obtain his airway on the first try. He taped everything down. Jim decided to increase the heat in the incubator. With the oxygen and airway, he started pinking up. He moved to Zoey Grace. Her saturation level was better at 98% so he was not going to intubate her; however, he wanted to get IV access. He wanted to get them both started on steroids. He listened to her breath. She sounded good. He went back to baby Liam and listened to him. He thought that he should have a round of antibiotics. He pushed the steroid and waited on the antibiotic.

He went to see how Ranger Long was doing and put on a clean pair of gloves to help him out. As they finished, Marsha's heart alarm went off. Jim looked up and said, "No, we will not be having this." He gave her more medication for the arrhythmia.

Ranger Long looked at Jim and said, "Doc, we would convert her in the squad with an arrhythmia like hers." He watched the monitor and never looked away from it as he told Ranger Long to charge the paddles. He pulled down her gown and told him to clear. He watched her jump and her heart went back to a normal rhythm. Jim was relieved. He gave her more meds.

"I would like to keep her under anesthesia so her body can rest. Let's leave her under for a couple of hours. Would you sit and monitor her while I am observing the twins? Let's get Kron to come back in and hold her hand. She has a gift so let's have her use it." Jim knew he would find Kron outside the door. She had already grabbed a clean sheet and was wrapped in it and tightening it in place. Kron entered the room and pulled a chair alongside the bed. She held her hand and rubbed her head. Jim looked over at Marsha, then at the monitors. Everything looked good. He was glad he had Ranger Long to help him. Ranger Long sat with a pad and paper writing everything down. He thought this was a good time for Ranger Long to take a break. Jim spoke in a low voice and told him to go get some coffee and something to eat. He would get something when he came back. He stood and gave Jim a brief report. As Ranger Long exited the cubby, Jim could hear whispering outside the room. He was sure Ranger Long was giving everyone an update. He turned back to the twins. Jim heard a soft voice call out to him. He turned and there stood Bev just outside the door wearing a mask, surgical gown, hat, and booties. She walked in and went directly over to Marsha. She looked at Kron and asked how she was doing. Kron told Bev she was resting very well. She could feel a stirring within her. Jim heard that and looked at the monitor and gave her more medication to keep her asleep. He told Kron when she felt anything to let him know.

Bev walked over to the babies and said, "They are so tiny, Jim." She asked him how they were doing. He told her Zoey was doing well so far. Liam, however, needed breathing support but was hanging on. He hoped he was a fighter. She looked at Jim and tears flowed freely. "What about the equipment the Blue brought?"

"I was concerned about using it; however, I believe when Ranger Long returns I will be ready with one of the incubators for Liam. Blue stated it was to be used for total life support and speeds up development and the repair of vital organs, but I know so little about it, only the brief summary she gave me. However, I believe it is Liam's only hope at the moment."

Bev looked at Marsha and began sobbing, Kron stood and touched Bev's head. She took her hand and told her that Marsha would be fine. "The baby girl will be fine and the baby boy is struggling. Jim should try whatever he can to save him." Bev began crying. Jim took her in his arms. He let her cry as he held her. He pulled her back from him and told her to go lie down and let him get to work on baby Liam. She took another look in at both babies and then walked over and squeezed Marsha's hand. She turned one last time and looked at Jim and Kron and told them she would have everyone praying for little Liam.

She looked right at Jim and told him she loved him and to please let her know when he brings Marsha around. She wanted to be there with her. "She will need both Kron and I to be her support." Bev turned and walked out removing her gown, mask, and shoe covers. Jim removed his as well and put on fresh. He looked at Marsha's monitors and then put his stethoscope on and bent over to listen to her lungs and heart. Everything sounded good. Her blood pressure was perfect. He looked to see if her conversion with the paddles left burns. Her skin was red for sure. He applied a soothing aloe to the burned area. He marked it on her makeshift chart, along with the medication he administered He documented everything that had happened thus far. Ranger Long had also documented the medication amounts and times. He had also documented the time of each birth. Jim filled in the rest of the information on what he had done for each baby, including the medication given.

Ranger Long appeared at the door as he was gowning and masking. He asked if anything had changed while he was gone. Jim updated him on Marsha's condition. He asked Jim if he knew when he would start to rouse her. Jim looked down at Marsha and told him he was not comfortable yet with that idea. He wanted her calm for as long as possible. Jim knew the minute she saw the babies there may be screaming which, of course, would be a natural reaction to seeing her premature infants. He told Ranger Long that he wanted to put baby Liam in the Blue's incubator. Ranger Long did not look surprised. He told Jim he thought he would do that from the get-go for both babies. Jim set up the incubator device as Blue had instructed. They put it right beside the incubator that Liam was in. The device was on and already warm. He could hear a buzzing-type sound. Jim carefully picked up Liam and laid him in the incubator device. A screen immediately popped up and gave a visual read-out of the vital signs. It also showed his internal organs as well as generating cells to help his underdeveloped lungs and eyes. It showed everything, including the lab values.

Jim looked at Ranger Long and he looked at Jim. He said to Jim, "Let's fire up the other one." They worked hard and fast setting up the other incubator for baby Zoey. It took about half an hour to prepare it for her. Kron called out as softly as a Sasquatch could, Marsha was stirring and near awake. Both turned and quickly tended to Marsha. Jim was grateful he had the syringe already drawn with the meds to give her. As he was administering it, she opened her eyes and tried to speak. Kron covered her eyes and told Jim that Marsha was fighting this. He looked at Kron and asked her to be more tuned into Marsha so he could do a better job of keeping her sedated. Kron removed her hand from Marsha's eyes. She looked relaxed and was once again asleep.

Kron began stroking her hair and placed her hand on her belly. Jim looked at Kron and immediately asked her if something was wrong. She shook her head as she started humming gibberish. She looked at Jim who was clearly worried and pulled back the blanket and sheet to look at the incision. It looked fine to him. He looked back to Kron who had her eyes closed and continued humming. Ranger Long looked at Jim as he handed him his stethoscope. Jim put them on and listened to her abdomen. It sounded quiet. He did not like this. He kept listening and nothing. Jim walked around the table to Kron. He took her arm and turned her head toward him. He said in a very controlled voice I need to know what is wrong with her. She looked into his eyes and said, "Same as me. You fixed everything like me." Jim's heart sank and he thanked her. He told Ranger Long that they needed to open Marsha back up because she had a bleed. "First, let's get baby Zoey in the other incubator." Jim carefully picked her up and placed her inside, the screen flipped on with the readouts. She looked great. The lung cell generator came on for her, as well. "Okay, she's stable. Let's change our gowns and gloves and then prep the surgical tray.

Kron sat there with her while they quickly completed each task in preparation for another emergency surgery. Kron stood with her hand on Marsha's abdomen. This time Jim stepped back and she said forcefully, "Hurry, there is another baby." Jim looked shocked and asked her if she was sure. Her answer was a very loud, "NOW!" She repeated it again, "NOW." Jim picked up the scalpel and cut through the stitches quickly. He retracted her belly back. How on earth could he have missed this? He said OMG and quickly pulled out another little girl. He wrapped her in a blanket and laid her in with Zoey. It gave an immediate display. She was in worse shape than Liam. Jim was visibly shaken and crying for this little baby girl. The display showed it was generating lung, heart, and brain cells at an expeditious rate. The incubator was breathing for her somehow without a ventilator. She had been in her own little sac, and most of the fluid was all over Jim and the baby. He turned back to Marsha, searching for the bleed. He found it and tied it off. He then delivered the afterbirth and made sure there was none left. The bleed should not affect her ability to have more children; however, with five who would want more? Jim stitched her closed again. He looked at Kron and thanked her. Without her quick response, that baby, and probably Marsha, would have died. Jim was wondering if he could take care of them and not do any more harm. He was devastated by missing something so simple.

He saw Kron stand again and his heart sank. He looked down at Marsha and then at the monitor. Kron walked around the table to Jim. She told him this was a mistake and happened more than he would think with multiple babies. "One sometimes is in hiding to give her brother and sister time because she is strong enough to survive. Please know she loves you and thanks you for saving her brother and sister. She wants you to know it was her choice after discussions with her brother and sister. Their future path was more important than the one she needs to walk right at this very moment. While it is an uphill battle, she knows the way and is walking it now. She told him he must believe in her path, as well as her brother, sister, and mom's future paths. Sometimes when faced with a difficult decision, the road looks dark, but you know it is the right path. She feels just that way. Believe in her choice. That it is the right choice." Jim looked into Kron's eyes and gave her a hug. She touched his head. He closed his eyes and stood there for a moment. He felt a calm come over him, a feeling that everything would be fine. He opened his eyes and pulled his mask down so Kron could see his smile. She smiled and nodded at him.

Ranger Long told Jim that Marsha was moving and that he'd better sedate her again. Jim turned to reach for the syringe, but Kron put her hand on his arm shaking her head no. She told him Marsha was strong and deserved to be part of the struggle for life, good or bad. Jim walked around to the top of Marsha's head and unhooked the breathing tube and extubated her. He put an oxygen mask on her and gave her pain medication. He knew she would be in terrible pain from two surgeries. Jim called her name, but she didn't respond. Kron let out a loud whoop and she opened her eyes. Jim looked at Kron and reminded her that they needed to be quiet. He looked back down at Marsha as she struggled to say, "Babies." He got close to her and told her all THREE were alive and being supported. She stared at him, not moving for a second, then repeated, "Three?"

"Two girls and a boy. Better think of another name for the wee one." She tried to sit up and screamed in pain. Kron moved Jim aside and picked her up in her arms and took her to the incubator. Jim remarked, "Well, that is one way to do it."

Marsha reached out and touched both incubators and marveled at the screen and technology. She turned to Jim and asked, "Blue?" He nodded yes. She turned back to the babies and began moaning and grabbing her belly. Kron brought her back to the table and gently laid her back down. She was clearly bleeding as there were bloodstains on Kron's gown. Ranger Long slid a chucks under her. Jim realized the exertion of trying to see her babies caused it. The intense pain took over and she fainted. They hooked her back up to the monitors and saw that her blood pressure was low.

"Let's give her some blood we have stored. Pull out A positive." He started the blood and directed Ranger Long to watch her vitals closely.

He turned back to Kron who was now standing over the babies. He told her that she could be his assistant anytime. She replied that many have talents such as hers and confided that even Merlin of King Arthur's day was a Sasquatch species. Jim and Ranger Long were surprised. "We have many advanced skills, like cloaking and interdimensional travel."

Jim said out loud, "Good to know. Do you happen to know how the rescue of humanity and, well, every living creature is going?"

She looked at him and told him they were battling for each success. He asked how long it would take and she thought several days. He looked into Kron's eyes and asked, "Morgan?"

She responded, "Well and safe." Jim nodded in relief. He asked if there were any monsters in the Cuyahoga Valley. She responded that they had been eradicated; however, there were evildoers in the Park from the military.

"Are they looking for us?" She did not know that answer; however, she felt the urgency to remain silent, including Marsha. Jim looked at her. "Should I medicate her heavily?"

She responded, "Yes." She explained to Jim that she knew at the moment Marsha awakened that she needed to see her babies to give her the strength to go on, as well as to give the babies something to fight for and to save the third baby. She pulled off her sheet as she walked out the door, telling Jim and Ranger Long that she must remind everyone that no noise will be permitted in order to keep the community safe.

Jim drew up a strong dose of medication to keep her asleep just enough so he did not have to intubate her again. He turned his attention back to the babies and the vital screens. It showed Liam to have gained over 30% more in lung cells and capacity. He looked so much better. It showed some dehydration so Jim adjusted the drip of the IV. He went to see the new baby and Zoey. Zoey was at full lung capacity like a full-term baby. He decided to continue the oxygen support. The new baby was still struggling. Her lung capacity was only at 28% and her heart rate was good; however, the regeneration was still in the upper 20's. Her brain function was tremendous. It was that of a full-term infant. Her eyes were showing zero. He pressed on the screen and another popped up. He pushed the button to make a new one. He had no idea what he just did but it was better than zero. She was barely hanging on to life. Even with this advanced technology, she could still slip away. Jim knew that was a definite possibility.

Kron came back into the room tying her gown in place and putting on a mask. She used sanitizer all up the fur on her arms. Jim and Ranger Long watched her walk over to the incubator with New Baby and Zoey. "Okay, big sister, time for you to help little sister," she said. She unwrapped the new baby and Zoey. She placed them so that they were almost lying on top of each other and put Zoey's arm around the new baby. Her vitals immediately elevated. Jim was amazed, as was Ranger Long. Kron turned, shutting the lid to the incubator. She told them the new baby would be fine now and that she would be able to see. Jim asked Kron if the baby was blind and she told him yes; however, the machine fixed them. Jim was grateful for that. Kron added that she would have the ability to see things humans cannot. "Her spectrum for light is bendable, and she can see into other dimensions, as we do."

Jim told her that was good to know. He thought, *Maybe, I'll just keep that information for Morgan.* He wondered what else he could enhance on the new baby. He went back to the monitor and pressed "Functions" and then "Improve." It appeared to boost the development of both babies. Their strength increased dramatically, as did both of their brain functions. There were a few functions he was unsure of but pressed "Improve" anyway. The babies were out of danger and all weighed in the five-pound range which put them small but still considered a normal size birth. Ranger Long remarked that he wished he had this on the squad and that he also had Kron as a paramedic and healer. The incubators were insulated and, therefore, could muffle any sound to almost any level. Ranger Long joked that he needed one of those for his kids so that he could muffle or eliminate their sound for 10 minutes. Jim asked how many he had, and he responded with four boys. Jim shook his head and told him he must be overwhelmed at times. Ranger Long laughed and nodded his head in agreement.

Baby Liam's incubator gave a short ding. Jim went over to check it out while Ranger Long stayed with Marsha. "It is telling me to extubate him. Okay, let me do that for you, little fella." Jim removed the breathing tube but put on a nasal cannula for light support. "Okay, let's see how you progress so I can remove the IV. That, my little friend, is your next goal." Jim looked at all the feeds on the babies and told Kron he would need three bottles and three diapers. Kron said nothing as she got up to retrieve them. Jim looked at Ranger Long and remarked that he loved this community and would miss it when things went back to normal. Ranger Long agreed.

Kron soon returned with bottles and diapers. Jim diapered each one and told Kron and Ranger Long to pick a baby to feed. Kron took the new baby although Jim was a little hesitant about letting her feed the sickest one. However, if it had not been for her, there would be no baby to feed. Jim took Zoey and Ranger Long took Liam. Zoey kept turning toward Kron and the new baby. Jim brought her over to the new baby, and she settled right in. Kron told him to place her right beside the new baby and she would feed both. He laid her gently in the crook of Kron's arm, and with ease, she fed both babies. She turned both onto their tummies to lay on her thighs. She bounced them a few times and both burped. Ranger Long told Jim he never saw that technique. He started to say he would try it until he saw both spit up a little and spatter the fur on Kron's leg. It did not bother Kron one bit. She picked up both babies and held them tightly together. It was amazing to watch Kron cradle the babies and respond instinctively to their every need. Jim walked over to Kron and told her the babies needed to go back into the incubator to finish their regeneration process. Kron placed both at the same time holding each other inside the incubator. You could see it pained her to put the babies down. Jim pulled up the view mode to see how well they processed the milk. Zoey was fine; however, the new baby needed regeneration of the digestive system. He pushed that display to begin.

They heard a loud boom above them. It had to have been in the air because it did not vibrate and shake the cave. They heard it again. Ranger Kopchek ran back to check on things, She stood at the door with a mask over her mouth. "It has to be the evildoers trying to prevent the good guys from taking them prisoner in an effort to reveal their treasonous acts against the

United States, well, actually against all sentient life on this planet."

"I hope they string the traitors up and let them hang," said Ranger Long.

Ranger Kopchek warned, "Silence is golden at this point since they are in the vicinity of the cave. It is imperative that we maintain total silence. What about the babies?" Jim told her the incubators would mask their cries and they were keeping Marsha sedated for now. She turned and walked away.

Ranger Long whispered, "On the outside, she is gruff like a lion. However, on the inside, she is like a pussycat."

The cannon fire continued for another three hours. It was intense. Jim could hear a buzzing sound, which he assumed were the drones that had weapons on board. He hoped Morgan was safe.

Kron put her hand on Marsha's belly again. Jim caught it out of the corner of his eye as he was tending to baby Liam. He turned to look at Kron and thought, *Is there nothing that can ever be easy? Can't anything go smoothly?*

He put down the diaper and turned his complete focus on what Kron was doing. He stood by Kron and asked her what was going on with Marsha. Marsha awoke and looked at Jim and Kron. She said, "Babies." Jim took her hand and told her they were beautiful and doing well and had even taken a bottle. He asked her how she was doing. She told him she was so tired and her stomach hurt very badly. Jim asked her if it was her stomach or the C-Section incision. She replied that it was her stomach. "What is wrong with me?" she asked.

Kron stood and Jim looked up at her. She grabbed a basin as Marsha started to throw up. She then began moaning. "Marsha, I want to roll you onto a mat." He told Ranger Long to grab the mat that Blue left and slide it under Marsha. She rolled and moaned loudly. Jim told her that the Monsters were right above them and that she had to try her hardest to not make a sound. He told her he understood if she could not stay quiet and would give her something. She didn't answer him. Kron pointed to one place on her belly. They rolled Marsha back down on top of the mat. A screen came up and showed her entire inside in 3-D color. He could clearly see an obstruction. He pressed on the screen and it flashed, "Resolve." It didn't indicate that, like for the babies, it would take care of it. He had to resolve it.

"Okay, Marsha, we have an answer. You have an obstruction. I am sure it is from all the work we did in your abdomen. I need to take care of this or it could be life-threatening. I am going to insert an NG tube. You will not like this at all, but it is necessary. It will go down through your nose and into your stomach. I will give you a glass of water to drink as I push it forward down the back of your throat and into your stomach. It should resolve this situation. It happens a lot. Let me get everything together and we will do this." He was back in no time and laid out on a tray. "Alright, here is what it looks like." Marsha kept shaking her head no. He told her it was not a choice. She still was not talking, just uttering soft moans. "Marsha, Kron will hold you up and I want you to drink water. Do NOT stop. Continue to swallow. Alright, tip your head back just a bit. Now, swallow, swallow, don't stop." She began to shake her head no. Kron put her head against Marsha's head and Jim kept saying swallow. She tried to push his hand away and Kron grabbed it and held it. "Okay, I believe I am in. Lay her back down on the mat and let's see if it is in the correct position. Actually, it looks like it is in a perfect spot. Ranger Long, turn on the suction please". Marsha heard a machine go on. She was gagging. Kron began rubbing her head. Jim could see how miserable she was and decided to not even ask. He continued and asked Ranger Long for an intubation kit. Jim turned and pulled meds out of the cupboard. He drew them up and turned to her. She looked miserable and just plain awful as she continued to gag and try to breathe. He injected the meds through her IV and she drifted to sleep. He stood above her head and intubated her again. He taped it down and Ranger Long turned on the ventilator. She looked so much better now. He kept Marsha on the mat so he had continual readouts. She was still obstructed; however, it took a bit of time to resolve. He knew if this did not work, he would have to go back in and surgically remove it. He did not think Marsha was strong enough to undergo yet another surgery. He asked Ranger Long to run and get a hot vanilla latte with an extra pump of vanilla and something to eat. He looked at Jim and laughed and asked if they had opened a Starbucks in the cave. He removed his surgical gown, hat, and shoe coverings and said he would be back shortly.

Kron pointed to Marsha's gown and said, "Wet for babies."

Jim looked and knew exactly what she meant. "I need to collect this for the babies." He opened the breast pump and began pumping. He showed Kron how to do it and then fill bottles with what she pumps.

Kron looked at Jim and pointed to her breasts and said, "I have plenty."

Jim shook his head and told her, "No, the babies needed the antibodies in Marsha's milk." She continued to pump and was able to fill 12 bottles. Jim looked at the body scan and the obstruction was resolved. *Wow, that only took 15 minutes.* He decided he would keep her under for the next couple of days or until they were rescued. The display indicated that she would be fertile again in 3.1 weeks. He would need to tell Morgan that he must abstain from intercourse for the next six weeks to give her time to heal. Jim knew he had to come up with a rotation plan for him and Ranger Long. Both would sleep in the room with

Marsha and the babies; however, one would have sleep time for a four-hour period. He knew he was exhausted and Ranger Long had to be, as well.

Ranger Long returned with his coffee, some beef jerky, and bowls of spaghetti for them both. They were so hungry and ate quickly. Jim asked Ranger Long to retrieve two cots with pillows and blankets. He did as requested and put them against the wall. Jim told him that they would sleep four hours at a time, one person on and one person off. If an issue arose, the other person would be there to help get the situation under control. Jim suggested that Ranger Long take the first sleep period. He thanked him, laid down, and zipped up the sleeping bag. He turned on his side, facing the wall. Jim was sure he was asleep before his head hit the pillow.

He couldn't believe how fast Liam had progressed. He was a normal newborn and then some. Whatever the machine fixed made it better than human. He moved onto Zoey and the new baby. He thought, *This baby needs a name.* He looked back at Kron and asked what they should name the baby. "Her name should mean brave. Caci. Yes?"

He said, "Marsha will love it. Caci it is." He turned to look at the infant. Jim could not believe how much she had improved. Her lung function was 79% and her eyes now registered as completely whole. Her strength was that of a full-grown child. He was unsure how that could be, but he was glad for it. He did not understand the uterus care. He wanted that whole, too, so he pressed "Accept." It was now working on that. And once again, the incubator also did it for Zoey.

Kron spoke and pointed to Marsha, "Wet." Jim thought that was odd. She had just pumped 12 bottles. He looked at the screen and pulled up breast milk production. It had set it for "Continual." He decided to turn it off and let her dry. They would give the baby formula. He looked at Kron and thanked her. He asked her to help him change Marsha's gown and, while doing so, applied aloe to the burned area once again. Jim thought it a good idea to bind Marsha to help her dry up and stop milk production. Jim and Kron wrapped gauze tightly around her chest and Jim slid in pads to prevent the milk from running through binding. They laid her flat on her back. He was going to have to begin turning Marsha to prevent bedsores. He looked at the projection of vitals, which was steady and right in line with where they should be. She was still obstruction-free. Her screen still requested approval for uterus repair. He punched "Accept" again. A message popped up that milk production was stopped. Jim thought, *Great, they would not have to deal with that.*

He looked at Kron and told her she should get some rest and to have Aggie care for the babies. She said nothing but removed her mask, gown, hat, and shoe covers. She looked exhausted. He knew he would not have gotten this far without her. While Ranger Long slept, Jim sterilized the surgical tools and wiped everything down. He wished Bev would come for a visit. He sat down and charted everything he had done and every button he pushed on the displays. He was caught up in charting. He glanced at Marsha, and she looked peaceful. He was so sorry this whole ordeal did not turn out the way they planned. He wondered how things were going outside the cave. He had not heard anything in hours, for which he was thankful. He stood to check Caci. She looked as if she had grown longer and had filled out. He could not believe she had gained so much and was now weighing in at 5 lbs. 2 oz. Amazing since she started at 1 lb. 1 oz. He wished that humans had this technology. He knew he would have to return it to Blue so as not to violate her Prime Directive. All three babies were sleeping, and Marsha was resting comfortably.

It was just about time for Ranger Long to wake for his four-hour shift. Jim was looking forward to sleeping. He heard Ranger

Long's watch ding and vibrate as he stood stretching. Jim told him to get something to eat and drink then bring back Bev with him. "Please ask Bittty to take care El." He was gone for 25 minutes and returned with Bev in tow. She gowned up, as did Ranger Long. She ran to Jim and hugged him. He told her it was time for him to sleep, and he wanted her to lay beside him and fall asleep in his arms. She smiled and laid on the cot next to Jim's. He put his arm around her and fell asleep.

Both woke suddenly to a soft alarm. Jim jumped up and found that Marsha was experiencing a cardiac event. Jim started barking orders for different drugs to Ranger Long. Marsha was once again having an arrhythmia issue. Jim looked at Ranger Long and said, "We must convert her again." Ranger Long charged the paddles. Jim took them in his hands, told everyone to clear, and then zapped her. She jumped; however, it was still not in sinus rhythm. Jim told him to charge it once more and then zapped her again. This time she converted. All he could think of was that he could not help her past this. He did not have an external pacemaker to keep her in rhythm. He started her on a blood thinner so she would not have a stroke. Jim and Ranger Long stood for a moment, looking at each other. He asked how long he had been asleep and Ranger Long told him it had been six hours. He knew he was exhausted and wanted him to rest.

"I appreciate that gesture; however, I'm concerned about Marsha so please keep it to four hours." Jim heard crying behind him. Bev stood there looking at Marsha. He turned back and covered her, then walked to Bev's side. "She will be fine. I don't want you to worry. Come and see the babies. They are doing great."

She looked in and could not believe how well they looked. "Marsha will be so happy." He told her that Kron named the surprise baby Caci, which translated to Brave.

"Perfect! May I sit with Marsha and hold her hand until Kron comes back?" He nodded his head yes. She sat down next to her, took her hand, and started singing an old hymn that Marsha loved called "It Is Well With My Soul." It was beautiful.

*When peace like a river, attendeth my way,*

*When sorrows like sea billows roll;*

*Whatever my lot, Thou hast taught me to know*

*It is well, it is well, with my soul.*

*It is well, it is well,*

*With my soul, with my soul*

*It is well, it is well, with my soul.*

*Though Satan should buffet, though trials should come,*

*Let this blest assurance control,*

*That Christ has regarded my helpless estate,*

*And hath shed His own blood for my soul.*

*My sin, oh, the bliss of this glorious thought!*

*My sin, not in part but the whole,*

*Is nailed to the cross, and I bear it no more,*

*Praise the Lord, praise the Lord, O my soul!*

. . .

*For me, be it Christ, be it Christ hence to live:*

*If Jordan above me shall roll,*

*No pang shall be mine, for in death as in life,*

*Thou wilt whisper Thy peace to my soul.*


*But Lord, 'tis for Thee, for Thy coming we wait,*

*The sky, not the grave, is our goal;*

*Oh, trump of the angel! Oh, voice of the Lord!*

*Blessed hope, blessed rest of my soul.*


*And Lord, haste the day when the faith shall be sight,*

*The clouds be rolled back as a scroll;*

*The trump shall resound, and the Lord shall descend,*

*A song in the night, oh my soul!*


Kron stood at the doorway listening as Bev sang to Marsha. Soon, the entire community stood there singing softly along with Bev. The Sasquatch all hummed to the tune that the humans sang. They closed their eyes, sending beautiful thought waves into the universe. Most were crying. Jim turned and wiped away a flood of tears.

# Chapter Ten

# HOPE OF A SPECIES

Ciril picked up her head and tuned in on those sound waves. She knew where they came from. *It was a sad song,* she thought. Her hope was that the babies made it, as did Marsha, and that song was not for anyone's death. Morgan was looking out the window as ships came and went. He heard that it was going slower than expected because the U.S. military was shooting down ships and also firing on ground troops. The European Union stood up to the U.S. military-industrial complex. The mission was moving along a lot faster in Europe because the country's military joined forces with the Galaxy troops. At the same time, they were fighting against the treasonous forces within the U.S. military. South America had just about obliterated the Nightcrawlers. Most of the traitor forces were focused in Europe, as they were not interested in the poor countries of South America.

Morgan would give anything to be with the group. He was worried sick about Marsha and the babies, and he felt it in his very being that there was something wrong. Ciril knew his thoughts, but she had no idea how to fix it. Ciril stood up to go to Morgan. When she did, her stomach felt like it was dropping out of her. It took her to her knees. Morgan turned to see her falling to the ground and clutching her stomach. It was glowing brightly. He ran to her. She asked for Morgan to help her to the bed.

Morgan said, "Your stomach is glowing so brightly, and it is much larger than it was previously."

She closed her eyes and thought she must have overfilled with fertilized eggs. "I need the incubator on board in the ship's sickbay. These eggs are about to be delivered, and they have to be delivered into a special receptacle and placed in a special incubator."

"Isn't this early for you?"

She screamed, "Yes!" He asked her if it was a pain level like human childbirth. She gritted her teeth and said, "Yes," and urged, "put your suit on, Morgan."

He met the liaison in the hall and asked where the sickbay was and if they had a doctor on board. He answered, "No doctor, but there are holographic instructions on how to handle things." Morgan directed the liaison to take him there but then stopped and asked for help in transporting Blue. They grabbed her and almost dragged her into the sickbay. There were a few soldiers lying on cots healing themselves with the holographic guides.

He laid her on a bed and the screen lit up with information showing both her heart rate and blood pressure were up. It indicated that it was stabilizing the patient. Morgan was relieved. Then it advised, Egg delivery is imminent. Please have a receptacle and incubation pod ready." The liaison knew what to do and brought the receptacle to Morgan.

"Shouldn't I scrub to be sterile?" The computer determined there was no time.

"Have the patient disrobe and start to push once the receptacle is in place." While she was taking off her suit, Morgan asked for the how-to guide on situating the receptacle and placing it in the incubator. She laid back on the table, screaming. He asked the computer for pain control. It gave a location and the liaison hurried to get it. Morgan did not know how to administer the drug, and a soldier came over to assist. He told Morgan he was a medic. He took the med gun and administered the pain control. Morgan asked about the receptacle. He told Ciril to bring her knees up to her chest, and he put the receptacle in place. Morgan told her to push. The soldier and liaison could see it would take another two receptacles. Morgan removed the filled one and replaced it with a fresh one. He then repeated the process. Her stomach was no longer glowing, and she was non-responsive. Morgan asked the computer if this was normal.

It responded, "The patient has imminent life failure." Morgan asked how to resolve life failure. A guide dropped with step-by-step instructions. The soldier pushed Morgan aside and started CPR and began yelling orders of what to load in the medication pen. The liaison handled that task. He asked Morgan to grab the red cart displaying a black circle with a red dot.

"Bring it now!" he screamed. Morgan pulled the entire cart over and handed him what he asked for. He placed it in the center of her chest. It was doing the compressions. He grabbed a mask and it adhered to her face. The computer registered her oxygen level at 98%. Music to Morgan's ears. He opened the drawer to the cart. It had a section for the central line. He handed it to the soldier but was told that only a doctor could do that procedure.

"Move over," he commanded as he pushed the soldier aside. "While I am from the Stone Age as far as you're concerned, I am a licensed physician." He felt her neck then cleaned it. He put on gloves before he opened the sterile kit. He picked up the needle and punctured her neck. He saw the flash of blood and knew he was in the vein. He advanced the catheter and then stitched it in place and put a dressing over it. The soldier had already gone and picked up two liters of fluids and tubing. Morgan hung and connected it. The computer told him to administer blood pressure medication. The liaison handed him the pen the soldier had loaded.

The computer indicated that the patient was stable. "Please attend to the eggs according to protocol." He requested the instruction guide for the incubator. Most of it was visual. He walked over to the incubator, and the soldier was already setting the panel. Morgan looked at the receptacle's content. The soldier stated that he had never seen that many fertilized eggs from one fertile period.

Morgan thought to himself, *They looked like human embryos.* He asked how many eggs were typical. He told Morgan that 200 was average but there appeared to be approximately 450. He revealed that females usually had only three fertile periods in their entire life. They occurred every three years within a 10-year span, and that was the only time children could be produced. The soldier explained that they remain in the amniotic fluid for one week and are then transferred to individual development containers. Morgan asked if they had 450 containers.

"Wow, you are from Earth. We replicate them in about an hour. They are then hooked to a circulating liquid and the children are born in one week." Morgan was shocked. He asked why they had no doctor on board. The soldier told Morgan he was accidentally killed when the liquid-filling dispenser backfired and the pump flew back and hit him in the head, decapitating him. Morgan raised his eyebrows and shook his head. The soldier asked if he could stay in the sickbay to assist if badly wounded soldiers were brought in. Morgan looked at the soldier and told him he was now promoted to assistant. The soldier replied, "Only if my commander approves."

Morgan looked at Ciril who appeared to be stable. "we are going to go for a visit with your commander."

Morgan walked across the cargo ship bay to a very large entity. He had no idea what his species was. He introduced himself and informed him that he was a doctor and requested the soldier be reassigned to assist him in taking care of troops. The commander agreed. "Good luck, Doctor."

"Thank you, sir." They returned quickly to the sickbay and walked through the airlock door. Two soldiers were lying on cots, the displays projecting their vital signs. He told the soldier to tend to those patients. He then checked on Ciril. It projected all life functions normal—uterus function normal, hydration 50% complete, maintaining a state of stasis. He touched the exit command and walked over to the incubators. The screen popped up. It indicated that all was normal and the eggs had advanced in embryonic development and had the gestational age of a multicellular embryo of one week. Morgan took a good look at the eggs in the receptacle and could see them changing as he watched. He found it most interesting. He walked back over to Ciril. Everything still looked good.

He then went over to the soldier tending to the patients currently occupying the medical bay tables. One was in serious condition with a hole in his gut. The vitals display was blinking and providing an alert, "Unstable–imminent life failure. Please repair the transverse colon and infuse blood." He looked at the soldier tending to him and asked where they performed surgery or if there was some sort of robot to handle that.

The soldier turned to him and told him his name was Tig and the surgical area was right here. "A sterilization wave sweeps the area. Then we move a device over to the bedside that will illuminate the area that is in need of repair, in 3-D." Morgan asked him to get it. He wheeled it over to the bedside.

"Cut his clothing off, Tig."

"No need." He pushed on the screen and it dissolved the clothing. He activated the sterilization field. Tig then moved the surgical machine into place. Morgan looked at him and waved his hands. Tig put his hands under the sterilization field and then nodded his head for Morgan to do the same. The injured soldier asked if they intended to do this without anesthesia. Morgan looked at Tig then told the soldier to lay back and close his eyes. The soldier asked why. He pulled the anesthesia screen up on the display and pressed the Dispense button. He looked over to the soldier and said, "Nighty-night" in the most sarcastic tone he could muster. The panel flashed, "Anesthesia complete, continuing to maintain the patient." Morgan stepped to the table and looked into the device that was over the open wound in his abdomen. He turned to Tig and asked where the surgical instruments were. He instructed him to hold his hand out with his palm up and ask for the instrument needed. Tig stepped to the other side of the table. He asked for wound sterilization and sterilization on the inside of the open area.

Morgan said to Tig, "Let's begin."

It turned out that the Medical Bay was extremely busy once word got out there was a doctor on board. Morgan learned so much, and Tig was a good teacher. He had just finished a case when he heard the display on Ciril's bed announce, "Patient awakened." Morgan and Tig both ran to the bed. They stood there as she opened her eyes. Morgan told her to stay still as she was recovering and attached to the bed with a central line providing much-needed hydration.

She smiled and then asked about her eggs. Morgan told her they were multicellular embryos. "All of them! Within the next day, they will need to be in the full development cycle." She closed her eyes and tears ran down her face. The projection indicated her hydration level was now at 79%. He told Ciril she would remain there overnight to complete the hydration process and to watch for anything else out of the ordinary. He asked her to remain on the medical table until he felt she was ready. She lay with her eyes closed and tears flowing. She knew she had to tell him and explain the importance of this mission to save their civilization with a new DNA infusion. She opened her eyes and could see there were three receptacles full of her fertilized eggs. Her abdomen felt warm, and she looked down to see a faint glow. She thought to herself, *Oh no, another fertile cycle. They must have engaged in uterus healing and it made me fertile again.* Her drive would soon take over again and she would not be able to control herself. Morgan checked on his other patients and discharged two of them.

He walked back over to Ciril. Her eyes were open and staring upward as she lay there. He hit a medical scan, hoping hydration was at 82%. At that point, he could pull the line and send her back to the ready room to rest. It flashed, "Active fertile period at present. Engage in fertilization." He looked at her and told her he thought the fertile period was once every three years for a 10-year period.

She looked at him with tears in her eyes and said, "That is correct. This somehow healed the uterus and activated a fertile period." She explained that it was an absolute blessing as her civilization was on the brink of extinction because of the lack of viable DNA.

Morgan turned to the receptacle. "The incubator display indicates there are 409 total eggs fertilized. That is amazing." He said that he would pull the central line; and while there was a lull in soldiers needing his assistance, he would go back to the ready room with her to make her comfortable. He pulled the line and dressed the wound. Morgan told her she may have a scar.

She laughed and said, "No, we will wave the skin repair over it."

"Ah, another new bit of technology."

He helped her off the table and they put on their protective suits and walked back to the ready room. She could already tell she was in the stage of seek and find. She closed her eyes as they walked. Morgan noticed and asked if she was okay. She responded, "Yes. I'm glad you are with me and grateful you took care of me." Morgan smiled and took her hand as they walked. She was secreting hormones to have him ready to submit. They entered the airlock and into the ready room. Both took off their protective suits. She could not hold back. It felt like the first time she went through a fertile cycle. Her drive was massive. She did not understand what was going on. She told Morgan to sit and she would make him a latte and her some dandelion tea.

"Now, you should be resting."

She said, "Sit!" He laughed and sat down. Both beverages were ready in a couple of minutes. She set hers down on the table and handed Morgan his. She sat down and began to drink her tea. She told him it tasted so good. He finished his and she asked if he wanted another. He declined but said he wanted a shower.

She smiled and said, "You may want to lie down for a bit. I promise to leave my clothes on if I come and lie down, too." He laughed as he made his way to the bathroom. She heard the shower turn on. He stayed in for almost 20 minutes. She was about to check on him when she heard him lie on the bed. She was trying to fight this urge but could not control it. She sat down beside Morgan on the bed and ran her fingers through his hair calling his name. There was no response. She then put her hand firmly on his head to read his thoughts. There were none. He was in a totally unconscious state. Ciril stood, disrobed, and pressed herself on top of him. Once again, she opted for the human way of DNA transfer. Her head back and eyes closed, she continued the transfer for two hours. She rolled off the bed and grabbed the skin healing generator and waved it over them. She didn't have to dress him as he had not bothered to dress prior to lying down. She suited up and realized she must hide the glow in her abdomen. She asked the computer projector in the bathroom to disguise it which sprayed a fabric that blacked out the light. Going forward, she could not be alone with Morgan. She knew that Tig had a DNA match with her. She would seek him out. It would be up to her to obtain a receptacle for incubation when her biological impulse told her it was time to deliver the fertile eggs. She knew how to bring it on after one day. She decided that she would do that and claim they were not delivered prior because they were not ready. She would not allow uterus regeneration. She would let that happen spontaneously.

She sat back down at the kitchen table catching up on news and how the troops were doing on the monitor. Morgan had been asleep about four hours now. She thought she should wake him. Tig was probably wondering where he was. She walked into the bedroom and, before she woke him, she made sure her glowing abdomen was hidden through her clothing and camouflage. She called out his name. He woke and sat up on the side of the bed. "Hey, sleepyhead. You have been asleep for four hours." He looked shocked and then realized he had no clothing on. As Morgan got up, Ciril left the room so he could get dressed in private. He came out from the bedroom adjusting his top.

"Wow, I didn't realize how exhausted I was." He stopped in his tracks and looked at Ciril as her eyes closed and she collapsed on the floor of the kitchen. He pushed the medical emergency button on the wall intercom. Tig and another soldier came running in, forgetting to don their protective suits. Tig had brought with him a portable diagnostic reader. She had begun to convulse. He ran the scanner over her; and when they got to her abdomen, it revealed fertilized eggs. He advised Morgan that she must not have expelled all of the eggs. The other soldier had a long black roll in his hand. He pressed the red button and it unfurled into a litter. Morgan grabbed the portable diagnostic machine, and they all ran to the medical bay. They laid her on the table. The projection screen showed that her blood pressure and heart rate were low. The projection also displayed, "End of Life Imminent."

Morgan was going on gut instinct that there must be a leak somewhere, or perhaps she had suffered a stroke. He scanned her head and abdomen. Tig was having blood work run, as well. The medical projector advised of a cerebral vascular incident. "Clot elimination beginning now. Hydration critical." It specified three drugs to be administered immediately. Tig loaded the med gun and administered the injections. Morgan was angry at himself for removing the central line. He began working on the other side of her neck and was able to access the vein on his first try. The projector flashed, "Access Successful," and directed that two additional drugs be administered with urgency. The display read, "Life Signs Stable." It then advised that the patient be put in stasis for the safety of the fertilized eggs until her brain had time to heal. The estimated duration was 7.5 hours. Surgical extraction of the eggs was recommended at that time. Removal of the uterus was strongly suggested.

Tig told Morgan that her species was on the brink of extinction, and a loss of a female uterus would be devastating.

Morgan looked back at the incubator where he could see substantial progress in the growth of the embryos. "There are 409 eggs, plus what we will extract later. That should be enough for one person to contribute to her civilization's survival."

Tig turned to look at Morgan squarely in the eyes. "This new batch of eggs had to have been fertilized in the last five hours. Morgan, she was with you. Ciril transferred your DNA to fertilize her eggs. Rather than let the eggs die, she risked her life for the good of her people." Morgan was shocked. "Your DNA must be a perfect match to hers. That is a very rare find. If you object, we can destroy the embryos."

Morgan stared pensively at the incubator. "No, I can't be the cause of an entire species becoming extinct; but I am surprised. Shocked! Tig, how does she obtain the DNA?"

"She only has to press against you."

"Wow," exclaimed Morgan, suddenly remembering what transpired between them earlier in the day.

"DNA transfer can occur that way; however, it is a slow process. The other way when combining with humans is the Human Transfer method."

Morgan turned to him and said, "I can assure you I never had sex with her."

"We can scan you and see. You know, you don't have to be awake for that to happen." Tig grabbed the scanner which confirmed that a mass extraction of semen had occurred. Morgan turned and looked at Blue, confusion and horror swirling through his brain. *She wouldn't have.*

Tig implored him not to judge her. "Her entire species needs this. Would you have given it voluntarily?" Morgan told him he was married and would consider that act to be cheating on his wife.

"It wouldn't be if she just did a basic extraction, without the sex act." Morgan agreed.

The projector flashed and directed him to add a different kind of fluid that contained minerals and vitamin D. Morgan and Tig prepared and hung what was requested. Morgan noticed Ciril's abdomen was glowing and in the last few minutes had extended. They needed to physically see and watch the abdomen so Tig pulled up the screen and pressed the button to remove her clothing. Morgan covered her with a sheet. He asked the computer if while in stasis Blue could possibly know when it was time to deliver the eggs. It responded back, "Unknown." They agreed that they would have to watch her closely. Tig recommended that Morgan monitor her while he cared for the two men and one woman who just entered seeking treatment.

Morgan pulled up the instruction guide to search how to surgically extract eggs in the Blue species while in stasis. It walked him through the procedure step by step; however, he really needed to see physically what was being referenced. He pulled the sheet down on Ciril and went through each step. The first step was much like a human birth—check vaginally for effacement and plug loss. Tig returned as he was walking through the process visually and suggested that Morgan check her now. He donned a glove while Tig put her in the proper position. Morgan noticed that her female anatomy was similar to a human. He asked the medical projection unit for a speculum. He held his palm up and it materialized. He inserted it and asked the computer medical bed unit to illuminate the vaginal area. A brilliant light illuminated the specific area. He could see the plug was clearly gone and was leaking fluid. He also noticed her vaginal area was torn. He sat up for a moment and thought to himself, *OMG she did obtain my DNA this way.*

Tig asked for her status, and the medical computer responded, "Patient stability and stasis continues. Eggs must be surgically removed within the next 10 minutes to maintain viability of fertilization." Morgan blocked out the personal information that he just discovered and directed Tig to assemble everything they needed as well as a collection receptacle. Morgan pulled the surgical machine over her and sterilized her and their hands. He and Tig followed the instructional guide to the letter. Tig grabbed the collection receptacle once all the eggs had been expelled. He told Morgan it looked to be around 80. He placed them in a separate incubator so they would not mix with the previous batch. Morgan ordered the medical projection device to close the surgical incision. He looked to Tig and told him her uterus could not be saved.

Tig looked thoughtfully into the incubators at the hundreds of new lives that were quickly developing and told Morgan that his DNA donation would undoubtedly save the species. He grabbed hold of Morgan's shoulder and told him it did not matter how she did it, what mattered was the humanity it took to give their civilization a fighting chance. Morgan asked how many females would come of 500 eggs. Tig told him, if they were lucky, no more than 12. Morgan did not respond. Tig added, "I will send some DNA with Blue to donate to another female when she comes into her fertile period. They have so few females; and so few men like us, Morgan, can donate to this species." Morgan asked Tig the name of his species. He replied that he was from the planet Gienah in the star system Cygnus and was half-human. That was why he could donate his DNA. Morgan then asked if he should donate more. Tig said the Blues would find it to be an immeasurable kindness. For the entire day, Tig and Morgan donated their DNA several times. Both made sure to mark whose DNA it was.

The computer advised them that Ciril could be brought out of stasis; however, she would need several drugs administered prior to that. Tig administered the medication, and Morgan asked him to stand by with a seizure drug as well as a blood thinner. Once safely roused from her unconscious state, she slept peacefully for an additional half-hour. Morgan and Tig were charting when she stirred. Both went to her bedside. She looked at Morgan and asked what happened. He explained to her she had a small bleed and a clot in her brain. "In humans, we call that a stroke. Your blood pressure was too high. In addition, you were carrying more fertilized eggs. We surgically removed them and placed them in incubators. During all of this, and in order to preserve your life, we had to remove the uterus. I'm sorry, but it could not be saved."

Ciril began to cry. Morgan put his hand on her arm, as did Tig, as he told her they donated enough DNA for other females to use during their fertile periods. They pointed to the receptacle marked DNA. Ciril looked him in the eyes and said, "You know, I am so ashamed."

Morgan reassured her that he understood it was something she did to save her species. "I can't fault you for that. I would have freely given it to you the way your species does, just not in the way we humans procreate. That ritual is reserved for my wife only. It is done, and we will not speak of this again. The focus is on saving your civilization."

Ciril continued to rest in the sickbay. She told Morgan she was experiencing much pain. He told the medical computer unit to scan her for anomalies. It responded that the patient was stable. He told Tig to draw up a dose of pain medication for her species. She asked if she could view and access the news.

Tig told her, "Of course. However, this medication will make you sleep."

She sounded indignant when she responded, "Why did you give me that type of medicine?" Tig told her to be quiet and enjoy it. Ciril responded with, "Typical military man response."

Morgan intervened, "We will have no spats with our patients, Tig."

He walked over to Ciril and asked her to lie back and let the medicine do its work. She smiled and laid back down. He told her to stay in a vertical position. "Please, please do it for me, okay?" She nodded and grabbed his arm as he walked away, pulling him back to her. She told him she loved him as she looked deeply into his eyes and thoughts. Morgan told her a lot of patients feel that way after a doctor saves their life. He told her he was deeply flattered, however, he loved his wife Marsha with all his heart.

She smiled. "Marsha is a lucky woman." She knew that was the deep and loving truth about Marsha.

---

Jim was sitting beside Marsha as she awoke. "You are doing fine now. I want you to remain still. We have a tube inserted to help you breathe." She reached her hand up, and he pulled it down and told her not to pull it out as she could damage her voice box if it was not extracted properly. He explained to her that she had a heart arrhythmia issue, but for now, it was stable. He told her all three babies were fine and that he didn't foresee any long-term issues and that Kron, who was now sitting beside her holding her arm and stroking her head, had named the third baby Caci. "It means Brave One. I thought it was perfect for her. We have not heard from Morgan yet. We expect that communication soon. Okay, this is taking a toll on you. I want you to rest again. I am going to have you sleep so that your body will have time to heal. I just wanted to wake you to give you a report that the babies are absolutely fine and are even eating. Don't worry about anything now."

Jim began pushing the meds as Kron continued to stroke her hair and hold her arm. Jim told her to close her eyes as he gave the last push of the drugs. She tried to pull her arm away from Kron, but the drugs that were administered to her were too powerful and she succumbed to induced sleep again.

Jim looked at Ranger Long who shook his head and said, "Now that is one heck of a fighter." Jim shook his head yes. Both looked at each other and then looked at the monitors that Marsha was hooked to. All seemed stable. Kron had been out of the room for most of the day and this was the first time she was sitting with Marsha in over five hours. Kron stood and Ranger Long quickly called out, "Early alert system!"

Jim asked what was wrong. She lifted Marsha's leg and pointed to her calf. Her leg was swollen. "Great catch, Kron." He asked Ranger Long to draw up some additional blood thinner to administer to Marsha. "This has been a long and arduous journey for her. The last delivery was easy breezy. She used to tell everyone labor and delivery were nothing. Totally easy to do. I believe just about everything that could go wrong has. I will be glad when this is behind us and she is cuddling those babies in her arms. That will be a joyous day for sure."

Jim looked at Kron and asked her how Marsha was doing. "Fighting a fierce battle. She will win!" Kron began humming the song "It Is Well With My Soul." She did that for hours. Jim did not want to tell her to stop. He did ask her if Marsha could hear her. She never stopped the humming, instead just nodded yes to him.

It was Jim's sleeping time. He was looking forward to four hours of rest; however, he was nervous to leave Marsha without his full attention. He knew, however, he would be no good to any of them if he could not think clearly. He was almost finished with his rest period when it sounded like a bomb went off next to them. The cave shook and debris flew everywhere. Kron instinctively jumped on top of Marsha. Ranger Long covered the incubator with the two girls in it. Jim jumped up and ran to Liam's incubator to shield him from the rubble. When the shaking stopped, Kron ran immediately out of the room and Jim knew she was headed to her babies.

Jim told Ranger Long to check the community for injuries and to make sure they were not exposed in any way. Jim grabbed a tarp and put it up over the door and placed another on the floor to keep the dust to a minimum. There was a double tarp on the ceiling and one on each side. He wondered how many millions of humans were dead and how much animal life was destroyed. He had to stop and wonder why Princess Celia was not intervening with peace treaty attempts. That was her major role to perform for humanity. Maybe she felt humanity could handle this even with a mass death toll and that humans had to learn the art of a treaty.

Then they were rocked with another explosion; however, this one sounded like it was close to Everett Covered Bridge. He thought about Freda the Great Blue Heron and her newborn. He wished Bev would come to him. He needed her support and love right now. Ranger Long returned and was glad to see Jim at the door.

"I have a patient that will not allow me to treat her."

Jim turned around from the incubators and said angrily, "Who?" He pulled Bitty in. Jim ran to her and dropped to her level shouting, "Bitty the Brave!" He could clearly see that her arm was broken. "Looks like a broken arm, my precious one."

"I had to save my baby El."

Jim pulled her to him and began to cry. She hugged him and let him cry. After a minute, he asked if El was okay. She told him she was fine and was with Bev. "Thank you, Bitty, for saving El."

"My mom was with me so I knew we would be fine."

Jim pulled her in again and gave her a kiss on the cheek. "Now, Bitty The Brave, I need to align those bones so they knit together correctly. Ranger Long is going to help me. Since you are a big girl now, I am giving you two choices. The first is you grit and bear the procedure because it will hurt. You can't cry out as we must continue to be quiet. The second, and this is the one I vote for, is that I give you just a little bit of medicine to make you sleep and help with pain." Bitty asked if she had to have the tube in her throat.

"Yes, but just for a little bit, until we are all done. Deal? After all, you are Bitty the Brave." Jim asked Ranger Long to get a blanket and a pallet for Bitty to lie on. He asked her if she was in a lot of pain. She looked down and scuffed her foot. "No worries, my precious daughter, you got this." Jim laid out everything that they would need to set the break along with the IV and pain control medication so that she would not cry out when she awoke. Ranger Long brought in the pallet. Jim was happy to see Bev right behind him carrying a blanket and El in her arms. Jim kissed them both. Jim told her to wash the dust off her and the baby. "In fact, everyone should because the explosion probably shook a lot of the spores loose." She agreed.

He said to her. "I really need you! This has been brutal."

"I know, love," she replied. "We are all so grateful for your generosity in helping us through this crisis."

"Go and make sure everyone washes and that all the tents are cleaned inside and out, especially the kitchen. Everything in there needs to be disinfected." Bev told him she understood. She kissed him again and left.

"Okay, Bitty the Brave, we are ready for you. Lay on the pallet and I will be right next to you while Ranger Long hands me everything I ask for." He remembered where the vein was from before and accessed it quickly. Bitty regaled Jim the entire time with all the things baby El had been doing and what she had been teaching the baby. She told Jim that El knew how to growl.

Ranger Long said, "Just what every baby should know." Jim and he laughed. Jim hung the fluids and then asked Ranger Long for the medication. He had two syringes in his hand.

"Do you remember these, Bitty?" She shook her head yes. "Okay, are you ready for Ranger Long and myself to fix your arm? When you wake up, you will have a hard cast on your arm to protect it. I can see Ranger Long selected purple for the color." She smiled and thanked him, stating that purple was her favorite color.

He responded, "You're welcome. You will get to wear that for six weeks. Lucky you!" Bitty looked overjoyed that she would have it on her arm for six weeks. Jim took over the conversation and asked again if she was ready. She looked down and shook her head no.

"We can wait for you, Bitty. You let us know when," said Jim. Bitty said nothing for five minutes. Jim rubbed her arm and told her to relax while he checked on Marsha's monitors and the babies. He had seen this before from Bitty and knew she was wrestling with her brave Sasquatch side and the human feeling side she had learned from Bev. They gave more meds to Marsha, and the babies looked fine. Jim sat down on the pallet beside Bitty again. He didn't say anything as he rubbed her arm.

She looked up and him and in a shaky voice said, "Ready!" Jim said nothing to her as she laid back on the pallet. He pushed the syringe full of meds and she was asleep in no time.

"Okay, let's fix this arm." As they both worked on it, Ranger Long remarked that he wished they had an x-ray machine. Jim said, "I wish I had a million dollars. I think there is a good chance neither of us will get our wish today." They did the best they could and hoped it was straight and aligned. The cast looked good, but Jim wished he could have shaved her arm before they cast it. "Okay, let's clean up everything and let her sleep. Knowing Bitty, it will not be very long before she is awake."

Kron was outside the door and gave a soft whoop. Jim told her she could come in. She sat beside Marsha and looked over at Bitty and the cast on her arm. She looked at Ranger Long and growled. Alarmed by her reaction, he stopped and stood still. Jim turned to Kron and said, "Hey, we fixed Bitty's arm." She growled again. He knew then that it had to be the cast. He explained to Kron that it was there to hold the bone in place. She still looked concerned. He suggested to Ranger Long that help to clean the kitchen. Still afraid to move, Jim walked him to the door and told him not to come back for an hour.

Jim turned around and asked Kron how Marsha was doing. She looked down at Marsha and stroked her head and hair. She told him very well. That was music to Jim's ears. He asked her to sit with Bitty until she woke up, which he thought should be any time, and to hold her for comfort. Kron moved to the pallet, pulling Bitty into her arms. Kron no sooner did this when Bitty awakened. Jim had a syringe of medication ready for her, if needed; but it took only but a few seconds before Bitty started roaring from the pain. Jim thought, *Oh, no. They will hear this!* He quickly injected it and she was out again. Everyone came running to the door. Jim met them and explained that Bitty was in pain from a broken arm that was just set in place. Aggie asked Kron to change places with her. She handed her the babies and Kron walked back to her teepee with them. Aggie sat down on the pallet cradling Bitty like she did when she was barely holding on to life sick with sepsis. Jim thanked Aggie for all she had done in taking on the lion's share of work within the community. She shyly smiled at him.

He turned and filled several more syringes. He wasn't sure how long the meds would work on Bitty. He had to wait and find the right mix. Jim sat in the chair next to Marsha. Aggie looked at Jim and told him he looked exhausted. He smiled and nodded in agreement. She told him that Marsha would be fine and was doing very well and that the babies were in excellent condition.

She advised him that two were ready to come out of the incubator as they had gained a great deal of strength. Aggie advised Jim that she and Kron had plenty of milk and had been feeding all the babies. Jim sat up, shocked, and asked if she meant the human babies, too. She shook her head yes and told him they had almost the same kind of milk; however, theirs was higher in vitamin D and antibodies to fight off disease. She asked if she could take the boy child and the larger girl child. Jim hesitated and told her she could do so once Bitty was settled into a routine. They would start with baby Zoey.

Aggie told him Bitty was stirring and needed more medication before she cried out with another roar. He walked around and pushed the entire syringe into the tubing. Aggie began stroking her arms and head. She told Jim this would help her to sleep. He asked Aggie to let him know ahead of time when she was going to wake and he would give her more medicine. She nodded yes. He noticed her blowing gently on her face as she stroked her head and fur. He wanted so badly to sleep for a few hours. He would ask Ranger Long when he came back in to take over. He got up and pulled four syringes for Bitty and two for Marsha. He just needed two hours. Just about half an hour passed when Ranger Long returned and announced that the kitchen was clean. He looked at Jim and could see that he needed some sleep. Jim gave him the syringes for Bitty and for Marsha and had them clearly marked.

Just then, Aggie announced, "Now." Jim went over and pushed the entire syringe. He filled another syringe and marked it with Bitty's name, then told Ranger Long to wake him in two hours. "Then it will be your turn to take a two-hour siesta." They both laughed.

Bev fed baby El, who seemed to know she was not Bitty or Aggie. She thought, *Oh great, she forgot me.* She cradled and sang to her and then changed her. Virg came to her tent door and asked if she wanted to rest and have him take over baby duty. She thanked him and requested that he come back in an hour. At the moment, she just wanted to sing quietly and cuddle with her. He agreed that he would come back in an hour and advised her that he had strict orders from Jim to not allow her to overdo it as she was supposed to be on bed rest. She smiled and promised him she would just sit with the baby, not stand or walk with her. He gave her a quick nod and turned to return to his teepee.

Next in line to take baby El was Ranger Kopchek. Bev laughed and asked her if this was a conspiracy.

Ranger Kopchek grinned. "No, but, we promised Jim that we would help you. Everyone loves that piece of sugar with all their hearts. She has become the community's baby."

Bev told Ranger Kopchek she had promised Virg that he could take El. "After he does a couple hours, maybe he will let you have a turn."

She laughed as she left the tent. "Okay, spend time with your precious one."

Bev looked down at El and wondered if she should take bets on who was going to be next. She didn't have to wait long as Kron arrived with both of her babies. Kron didn't even ask if she could come in; she just walked in and sat down on the floor. Her babies were crawling all over her. Bev asked if she had names for them yet. She nodded and told her that was why she was there. She asked Bev if she could name her girl baby after Bev's family name, Grissom. Bev started to cry and told her she would be honored. Kron told her the boy child would be named Mottice.

"Wow, wait until Jim hears that. He will be so thrilled. Thank you for such an honor. We are humbled. We love you and the babies." Kron replied that she loved El like she was her own. She then observed what a special time this was for both tribes with the next generation forging bonds together as one tribal community. Bev agreed. Kron told her she would let her rest and that she would take El and have her sleep with her and the babies. They needed to nurse. Bev never dreamed that meant El. She gave the baby a kiss and told her that mommy loved her and she would see her in the morning. As she laid down in the bed, she thought to herself, *Just wait until Jim hears this.*

She was reading her book again for the third time. She saw a shadow pass by her tent and was surprised when she saw Jim walk in with his black medical bag. She rushed over and jumped up on him holding onto his neck with her legs wrapped around his waist. Jim kissed her and said, "Really, Bev! You will not be doing that again! Hear my words, little missy. Well, it appears I have not examined you in over a week, plus it's a good excuse to see you." They both laughed. "So, my wife, how have you been feeling lately?"

"Tired but good."

"Let's listen to you." He listened to her heart and lungs, then listened to her belly and the baby. "All sounds good. Staying in bed is paying off for you. Okay, blood pressure time." He put the cuff on and was surprised and re-took it. She could tell just by looking at him that he was not a happy doctor. He looked at her and said, "Terrible blood pressure. Very concerning." He asked her if she had been taking her medicine and she admitted that she didn't always remember. "Okay, will have someone come by twice a day now and watch you take your pills. I just happen to know the perfect drill sergeant for that duty." He looked at her ankles and saw that there was swelling. "Okay, now seriously, no getting out of the bed except to use the bathroom that will now be bedside. Someone will come with water for a sponge bath daily." He could see Bev was frightened. "It is okay, honey. We just need to be more careful, that's all."

"How are Marsha and the babies?"

"The babies are fine and Marsha is much better. And our furry daughter is sleeping after resetting that arm bone. Bitty saved El's life."

She literally laid on top of her and pushed me out of the way or I would have been hurt or worse. Oh, and while I'm thinking about it, Kron was in with her two babies and has taken El for the night to sleep with her two. Surprisingly, they now have names." Jim asked what they were as he was putting his medical equipment back in his bag. "Grissom for the baby girl and, get this, Mottice for the baby boy."

Jim spun around, laughing. "Wow, that is amazing." She agreed. He pointed to the bed and told her to get in and stay there. He sat down next to her and gave her a passionate kiss. "You're fine, Bev. You just can't forget your meds. I will be back tomorrow with a vitamin shot."

"A shot!" she cried.

"Baby!" he teased. Both laughed.

He stopped at Ranger Kopchek's tent and asked her to check on Bev twice a day to make sure she took her medication. "Also, would you find a bucket which she will not like and will adamantly object to using for her bathroom?" Ranger Kopchek laughed and told him that she had a portable one with a seat in Ranger Long's truck. She would go and get it right now.

Jim also instructed her to give Bev water, not coffee, to drink with one of her blood pressure pills. "No more coffee for her. She can have dandelion tea because it has no caffeine and it is also a diuretic. And no salt for her, either." Jim stopped by

Kron's teepee while she was playing with the babies. He thanked her for taking care of El and then asked her to check on Bev and to let him know if she found anything worrisome. He stopped for a bathroom break and then to the kitchen for a cup of coffee and a fast cup of mac and cheese. He walked back into the medical area attempting to carry the coffee, mac and cheese, and his medical bag. He put everything on the side counter away from any machine. He asked Ranger Long how it was going. He reported he had already used both syringes for Bitty and administered Marsha's meds. He asked how Bev was doing. Jim told him he was worried as her blood pressure was sky high and her ankles were swollen. He told him he would check on her twice a day going forward. He went to the medicine bin and filled four more syringes. As he turned, he looked down at Marsha.

"Is that her wheezing? Sounds like she needs suction." Jim grabbed the suctioning device and sucked the mucus from her throat. He instructed Ranger Long to keep an eye and ear out for any more wheezing and would show him next time how to remove it. Ranger Long asked Jim when he was going to pull the NG tube.

"Well, let's take a listen to her belly and see if we hear anything." Jim pulled out his stethoscope and put it in his ears. He listened and told him things were moving great. "Let's pull it when she wakes up. As long as I am giving her pain meds, she is susceptible to an obstruction."

He no sooner said that when two big roars came from Bitty. He gave her another injection. Aggie said she never even felt her stir. Jim walked back over to the medicine bin and pulled out the big guns. He did not know why the other was not working. That is what he used last time on her. He gave her a dose of the new drugs and hoped that would hold her for a few hours. Ranger Long asked him if perhaps the bone was not set in place. Jim looked at Aggie and asked her what she thought. She told him the bone was crooked and the cast was too tight. "Okay, let's fix it. Good catch, Ranger Long." Aggie told them she would continue to hold Bitty.

She slept through the reset and recast. This time, they shaved off the fur so they knew how tight they would need to make the cast. It took about two hours to cut the old one off, shave her, and then reset the bone. Jim asked Aggie if she felt Bitty stirring, and she told them she was just beginning to come around. Jim was not risking another roar and administered heavy-duty medication. Ranger Long laid down for his four-hour sleep period. Jim decided that when Ranger Long got up, he would allow Bitty to wake so they could see where she was pain-wise.

As Jim charted everything, he heard the wheezing again. He pulled the suction over and sucked out the thick mucus. Aggie had been sitting quietly for the last three hours, allowing Jim to get his work done. She told Jim she didn't need that anymore. "Let her wake up. She will be tired but fine. These babies will give her great strength." While Jim respected her opinion, he was not ready to pull everything just yet. He told Aggie he would pull it when Ranger Long woke from his rest period.

He then asked Aggie if she thought Marsha's heart was fine. She replied, "Only with the help of your medicine. It will never be fixed except through medicine." He knew deep down that she needed a pacemaker. And Aggie added, "No more babies. She will die if she tries." That confirmed what he thought, as well.

"So, you still think it is safe to wake her? She needs a pacemaker which I do not have."

"Restriction is what we do with our tribe members that have issues such as this. We also use organic medicines like you to help regulate the rhythm."

To Jim, this was a risk he was not willing to take. On the other hand, he did not like the thick mucus. He said out loud, "I sure hope this is over tomorrow or the next day. It has been two weeks of struggles."

Before he slept for a few hours, he wanted to see Bev. He thought he would sit with her for a while. Jim finished giving a report on his patients, administered another dose of medication to Bitty and Marsha, and changed the babies. All was good. He grabbed his bag and headed for his tent. It was quiet in the camp as he walked through. He arrived at the tent to find Bev sitting at the table. He came in and said, "Bev, what are you doing?"

"Having breakfast. Here she comes now."

Ranger Kopchek arrived with water, dandelion tea, and Cream of Wheat, then grabbed the pills from the nightstand, put one in her hand, and handed her the glass of water. "Bottoms up." Bev took a sip and Ranger Kopchek barked, "All of it!" She drank the rest of it.

"Is that a good, Master Sergeant?"

"It's a start! I expect to find an empty bowl when I return for the tray."

"Okay, thanks," responded Bev.

Ranger Kopchek left and Jim sat down on the bed and pointed to it. She got in and sat up in bed. He arranged her pillows. "Let's take your blood pressure this morning." He put the cuff on and listened as she said nothing. When he was done he looked at her and said, "Just as high as yesterday. You will stay in bed. I could have Virg or Boc come and sit with you all day."

She looked at him and said, "No way. Have you lost your mind? Another man in my tent, what will people think?" They both laughed.

Jim then stepped over to the table and brought the tray to her. "I will be back later, and we will take your blood pressure again. Only this time I had better see improvement." She saluted him like the military does. He shook his head and laughed and went back to the medical cubby.

He spoke with Ranger Long who told him that everything was fine and that he should take his rest period. He assured Jim that he would wake him if any situation arose. He laid on his cot and fell asleep. Time flew by. He woke suddenly and asked how long he had been asleep. Ranger Long told him it had been four hours. He got up and looked at Marsha and then went over to Bitty and Aggie. He then told Ranger Long that he was going to check on Bev. As he turned to leave, he heard Marsha wheezing. He suctioned her and asked Ranger Long how many times he had to do that while he was sleeping. He told Jim twice. He shook his head and walked out the door. It was totally quiet.

As he neared his tent, he thought he detected talking outside the cave. He quickly entered the tent and Bev looked panicked as she stood with Ranger Kopchek. Jim whispered to quickly tell everyone not to make any movement or sounds at all. She ran from tent to tent and teepee to teepee and then to the medical area. Jim thought of Bitty, as he started to say her name out loud. He ran for the medical cubby just as she was stirring and grabbed the syringe and pushed it hard. She was back out in seconds. He whispered to Aggie and Ranger Long that they heard voices close to the cave but on the other side of the waterfall. He was certain they still did not know where they were hiding as this cave was not marked on any map. Jim filled another syringe and handed it to Ranger Long. He started for his tent and Bev. When he got there, she was in tears. He could just imagine her blood pressure. He sat her down and held her tight. They could not hear anyone; however, they sat listening intently for any sounds. Jim turned and kissed Bev and then turned to look at the cave entrance. Still, they heard nothing.

Jim started rubbing Bev's back to help her relax. She leaned against him, and he played with her hair. He knew he had to take a chance and sedate Bev to get her blood pressure down. He told her to lie down and that he would be right back. He needed to check on Bitty so she would not give them away with another roar. He was back in a few minutes which, to Bev, seemed an eternity. She was sobbing into a pillow so no sound would be heard. Jim did not speak; he sat next to her and hugged her, holding her tightly. He pulled her away and kissed her. Then he pulled the syringe out of his pocket. He put his finger on her lips to signal no talking. He opened an alcohol swab and cleaned her arm, then aimed for the vein so it would work fast. He finished and wiped it again with the alcohol swab. He scooted back next to her and held her tightly again. After about 10 minutes he could feel her relaxing, he laid her back against the pillows for her to sleep.

Ranger Kopchek came to the door. She said nothing as she entered with an outdoor magazine and sat at the table. Bev was sleeping. Jim stood and mouthed the words "thank you" to her. He ran back to the medical area and looked immediately at Bitty to make sure that fast push did not overload her. He asked Aggie in the softest whisper how she was. She nodded up and down. He felt relieved. He then asked her to lay Bitty down and nurse the two girls. He went to the incubator and pulled them out. Both were free of their IV and could be moved readily. Jim placed them in Aggie's arms and they immediately latched onto her. After about 20 minutes she asked for Liam. He lifted him out and handed him to Aggie. To his amazement, the girls were hanging onto Aggie like one of her own. Aggie reached up with one hand and pulled them both down and nuzzled them together in the crook of her arm. Caci latched back onto Aggie and decided she was not through eating. Aggie nursed and cuddled them. She did soft whoops to them as they slept in her arms.

Aggie started shaking her head toward Bitty. Jim went to her and gave her more meds. He knew he had to do this until they were absolutely certain no one was outside trying to root them out of their hiding place. Jim felt safer with the babies in the soundproof incubators. He took baby Liam, who was fast asleep, and put him back in his incubator. He then picked up Zoey, who was also asleep, and put her in the other incubator. He came back for Caci, but she had latched onto again to Aggie. She cradled her deep into her fur as she nursed. She was responding and bonding with Aggie. He decided to let her sleep in Aggie's arms. Although she was still latched onto Aggie, she really was no longer feeding. Aggie moved to Bitty and took her in her other arm. Jim and Ranger Long were both impressed at how Aggie could tend to both with almost no effort. Caci was moving her little finger through the fur on Aggie's arm. It was so cute. Jim wondered if they could make a papoose sling carrier for Caci to keep her at Aggie's breast. It appeared she did not want to be pulled away. Aggie did not mind keeping her where she could stay latched on to nurse freely when she wanted. Ranger Long made a sling out of a sheet that wrapped around and under her arm and tied at her shoulder. They pulled Caci away, and she started to whimper at being removed from Aggie's breast. Once placed in the sling and right at the nipple, she latched on again and closed her eyes, content as she could be. Jim quietly asked if that was something she encountered with the babies in her tribe. She whispered, "Yes, all the time." He smiled as he watched Aggie. Jim knew Aggie loved nursing the baby and caring for her.

Ranger Kopchek appeared at the medical area door, and she didn't look well. Everyone turned to look at her, and Jim jumped up from charting. She turned her head aside, coughing and sneezing. He whispered for her to wait outside and grabbed a chair and pulled it out for her. They were still in the vicinity where it was the thickest rock and virtually soundproof. He then retrieved his bag to examine her. She displayed a fever of 101.2 degrees, her blood pressure was elevated, and her heart rate was fast. Jim's mind went to the spores. He listened to her heart and lungs. Her lungs were congested. He thought it might be bronchitis but was concerned that she had a fever. He instructed her to quarantine in her tent and gave her acetaminophen and an antibiotic shot, along with antibiotic pills and cough syrup with codeine. He told her he would come by her tent later that evening. She thanked him and went back to her tent, zipping it shut.

Jim came back into the cubby and told Ranger Long that his partner had bronchitis and was running a fever. "Make sure to take her some green tea later and then sterilize yourself before you come back in." Jim knelt down beside Bitty. He had to let her wake so he could see if she was recuperating. He noticed her stirring when he came back in from examining Ranger Kopchek.

She opened her eyes and saw Jim. He smiled and said, "Hey, Bitty the Brave." She said nothing. He knew that was a terrible sign. She coughed. Jim asked her about the pain and she remained silent. He told her she had to talk and use her words so Uncle Jim would know. Again, she said nothing. Then she coughed again. Ranger Long wiped down the stethoscope and handed it to Jim. He listened and she, too, was congested. He asked Bitty if she was in pain. No response. He stood and she closed her eyes. *No, this can't be happening.* He asked Aggie if Bitty had a fever. Aggie said that she did. He put his head back and closed his eyes. Ranger Long stood ready. Jim said, "Okay, either Bitty has what Ranger Kopchek has or she is septic. I do not like either diagnosis." He knelt down to Bitty and once again asked how she was feeling. She did not answer, and her eyes remained closed. Aggie gave her a stern whoop and a low growl. Bitty opened her eyes and told him that her arm hurt and she felt sick and cold. Jim shook his head with concern then walked out of the room. Aggie followed. She put her hand on Jim and told him Bitty was strong.

"Her arm hurts very badly. We see infection after many of our tribe breaks bones. Not uncommon. She is using everything within herself to not cry out. Please make her sleep and give her medicine for infection." Jim turned and smiled at her. He thanked her for her help. Aggie looked into his eyes and told him they would have to open the door for fresh air within the next few days or the spores would cause them all to be sick, including the babies. Jim knew that was true.

He walked back in and told Ranger Long to give him an intubation kit and to mix another antibiotic bag and meds to put Bitty under. He was glad he had that line in place, but he was concerned that his unfamiliarity with the Sasquatch anatomy would cause problems with intubating her. He explained to Ranger Long that the way their heads sit, he didn't know how hard it would be to insert. He decided to try a pediatric kit first. He started the antibiotic, then pushed the meds. When she was under, he tried for several minutes to intubate her with no success. He asked Ranger Long to try. They switched spots, and he was successful with his first attempt. They hooked it to the ventilator, and they both watched and monitored Bitty. She seemed to tolerate the level she was on. Aggie sat stroking her hair and humming Bev's hymn.

Once Bitty was stable, Jim went to check on Bev. He asked how she was doing. And told her about Ranger Kopcheck and that she was confined to her tent. He took her blood pressure and found that it was pretty close to normal. Jim was smiling so she knew it was good. He told her he would get her some tea and water to take her pill. He came back with dry cereal, dandelion tea, and water. He opened the pill bottle and handed her the pill. She put it in her mouth and dutifully drank all the water.

Jim smiled and gave her a kiss. She whispered, "Are you training me like our dog?"

"Which one?" he asked. She laughed. "Now, little miss snuggle bunny, back under the covers. From now on, I want you to start wearing a mask at all times to help filter out the spores."

She told him she was going to miss him and had one request. "Give Bitty a kiss for me. Pinky promise you will do that." Jim laughed and said that would be the first thing he did. She smiled and told him she loved him.

He turned back to her and said, "Stay in bed!"

"This is so boring," whined Bev. Jim mouthed the word BED.

Jim stopped by to see Ranger Kopchek. He sat next to her at the table in her tent. He took her temperature and it was 102.4 degrees. He said nothing and asked her if she was short of breath. She nodded her head yes as she coughed into the crook of her arm. Jim put on his stethoscope and told her to take a deep breath, then another, then a normal breath. Then he listened to her heart. He pulled the stethoscope from his ears and asked her if she had taken her medication. She told him that she had. He directed her to stay in bed and not worry about her security duties. She looked horrified that he would suggest that. "Really, I don't want you to pass around what you have. Your temperature is high. I will have Virg bring you some hot tea. Please sip on that. He will also bring you some cool water and an inhaler to use. Do you know how to use one?" he asked. She nodded yes. He handed Ranger Kopchek a mask and told her to wear it to keep spore contamination at a minimum. She shook her head yes. Jim told her he would check on her later. He looked back at her as he turned to leave. "In bed and no rounds today." She nodded.

As he was walking out, she vomited. He rushed back and pulled her hair aside as he reached over and grabbed a tissue for her.

"I'll have Virg drop off some nausea meds that dissolve. Only take two per day. How long have you been experiencing this?" She said for the last couple of hours. "If this continues, we will need to place an IV for hydration. Virg will be in shortly with your inhaler."

Jim was very concerned. He had bags he could use for fluids and plenty of IV catheters, but that did not help him in determining what was going on. He went back to the medical cubby and took off his gown and gloves before entering. He had already removed his mask. He stood at the doorway and turned as Virg approached. "I need several things, Virg. Are you up to doing a few errands?" Virg agreed but revealed that he had come because Boc was sick. Jim washed and sterilized his hands, then put on a clean gown, gloves, and mask. He asked Ranger Long for a pack of Zofran and an inhaler for Ranger Kopchek and said he would return after checking on Boc.

Aggie sat up with a look of concern. Jim told her he would be back shortly and would let her know what was going on. He took Ranger Kopchek her meds. He did not enter the tent, just laid them on the table near the doorway. He went to Boc and Aggie's teepee and asked him if he could come in. Boc waved him in. He was lying listlessly on a pallet. Jim asked what was bothering him. He sat up and began coughing. He told Jim it was difficult to breathe and that he was cold and hurt all over. Jim told him he would be back soon and returned to the medical cubby for a full syringe of antibiotics and a bottle of cough medicine with codeine. Jim arrived back at Boc's teepee and gave him the medicine and a small plastic cup. He told him to fill the plastic cup and drink one every couple of hours. He then asked if he could give him an antibiotic shot. He nodded. Jim did not bother with cleaning; he just poked and injected. He told Boc to rest and he would return later to check on him. He told him to keep away from the babies.

Jim returned to the medical area. He stripped and asked Ranger Long to get him a change of clothing and some soap and to do the same for himself. He thought it was a wise idea for both of them to shower and wash their hair. Ranger Long was back in no time. Jim took the items and left to clean up. When he returned, his dark hair was still wet and he pushed back with his fingers. He told Ranger Long to get going and be thorough and fast.

While he was gone, Jim checked Bitty and pushed more meds. He then turned his attention to Aggie. "How are you feeling?" Jim asked. She responded that she was fine. He asked if she had a cough, fever, headache, or sniffles. She responded that she did not. Baby Caci was moving around; however, she still had a tight latch on Aggie's nipple. Jim cleaned the stethoscope and listened to her. She sounded perfect. She was nursing as though she had never eaten before. Jim laughingly remarked that she was a hearty eater but reminded her that human babies should not be allowed to nurse constantly. He also thought that the babies should have their lungs scanned and asked her opinion. She told Jim they all needed to have their lungs cleaned and reluctantly admitted that Caci should join her siblings in the incubator. He asked Ranger Long to bathe the babies while he programmed the incubators to clean their lungs and sinuses. He told Aggie that Caci needed to be kept in for eight hours. Jim could see that she was upset. She absolutely did not want to give her back and reluctantly gave the baby to Ranger Long. He cleaned her as she cried and then he put her into the incubator. Jim pulled up the medical screen and pushed the selection for detox of lungs and sinus cavity. In addition, he set hers for sedation and decided to do that for the other babies, as well. He pulled up the diagnostic panel for each. The display showed lung infections from unknown spores. It recommended the elimination of spores to begin in 10 minutes. He pressed yes. It would take 10 minutes to cycle through the process to eliminate all spores.

Ranger Long saw the display and asked, "Do you suppose there is a way to pull these incubators together and clean the rooms and all of us?"

Jim wished he could speak to Morgan. "Yes, I do believe we should be able to wire them together using the holographic projector to scan and sterilize the entire cave. Then, one by one, we could each lie on the three incubator mats together and have it perform a scanning and sterilization procedure. He suggested that Ranger Kopchek go first. If that worked, they would tackle Boc, then the rest of the community.

Jim fixed two slings that crisscrossed so the babies could all take turns nursing with Aggie. They would stay in the clean unit. Jim slid a chuck in each sling that could easily be removed and a clean one inserted. Each baby weighed approximately 7.5 lbs. It was remarkable the gains they made while in the incubator. Aggie began to cry and actually picked up the incubator and put it to her heart so the baby could hear her heartbeat. Jim and Ranger Long were touched at the level of love Aggie felt for that baby. They moved a chair over to her and let her hold the incubator with Caci asleep inside.

He put the slings on Aggie with chucks inside. She immediately pulled them out. "I will take care of the potty. No need for that." Ranger Long whispered to Jim that he wondered what they did with the scat.

"Guess we are going to see first hand how that happens," replied Jim. He told Ranger Long he wanted to check on Bev for a few minutes. He grabbed his bag but stopped at Bitty. He heard her wheezing. Jim did not have to say anything. Ranger Long told him that he would suction her.

Jim walked through the tent door and pushed the screen out of the way. Bev smiled and sat up. He went to her and held her. As he did, she started coughing. Jim's heart sank. He pulled her from him and said, "All right, missy, when did the cough start?"

She responded, "An hour or so ago."

He pulled out the thermometer. Thankfully, there was no fever. He thought for a moment and then grabbed a few tarps for protection from the spores. Jim explained to her that the tent windows and door must remain covered. "These tarps will keep the mold out. As soon as I rig up the incubators to help Marsha and Bitty, you are next in line. It will scan your lungs and the baby's lungs and fix the spores damage. Bev, we have to get out of this cave and soon. I hope Blue and Morgan are finding a way to win this war."

"How are the babies?" she asked.

"Becoming little fatties. Aggie is nursing them but has a special bond with Caci. She latches onto Aggie and doesn't let go. Guess that is what babies of her tribe do."

"That is a lot of milk to produce for Marsha's three and her two."

"I hear you. Her milk is high in so many things and those babies are thriving on it."

He took Bev's blood pressure and it was normal, as was her heart rate, and the swelling had gone down in her ankles. He told her he would be right back and quickly returned with green tea and water. He opened the bottle of medication and handed her one pill. She popped it in her mouth and drank the entire glass of water. He smiled and thanked her. She held the teacup in her hands tightly, enjoying the warmth and the aroma. He showed her the bottle of Manuka honey and the lemon bottle. He squeezed the lemon in first. Then took a giant spoon full of honey and stirred it into the tea. "Just a little sweetness for my sweetie." He told Bev that he had to get back to his patients. She smiled and told him she would see him later. He walked out and zipped the tent closed.

He walked back to the medical cubby and stripped off his gown and mask and then sanitized and donned clean protective clothing. He walked over to the incubators and pressed the display on the projection diagnostic screen on each incubator. They were now clear. He lifted each baby out and placed them in the slings. He put Zoey and Liam together and Caci by herself. She immediately began nursing voraciously. Aggie winced for a second, and then again. Jim pulled her off Aggie and ran his fingers over her gums. Sure enough, five teeth. He checked the other two and they each had three. However, they did not nurse as hard as Caci. Jim asked Aggie if she was okay. She nodded. He then asked if her tribe young nursed that hard. She shook her head no, then added verbally, "Much harder. I am just out of practice." Jim put Caci back into the sling and she needed no help in finding the nipple. She again was aggressive. Aggie gave her a growl and light tap and she slowed down. Jim was amazed at this entire episode of feeding.

Ranger Long said, "If we don't wake Marsha soon, her kids will be in college." Jim looked at him and began laughing.

"Okay, let's take a look at the how-to guide on connecting the incubator beds together to form a large one for an adult patient."

Ranger Long said, "Bing! Here it is."

Both read and re-read the instructions. Jim thought it to be very straightforward.

Aggie spoke loudly, "Now, now, now!" They both turned to find Bitty struggling to sit up, but Aggie attempted to hold her down using her leg while pinioning her arms as she flailed.

"We should have been watching her," Jim said as he sat on her and injected the medicine into her tube. "I hope it did not dislodge. Let's take a look."Jim told Ranger Long to examine it while he continued to restrain her just in case she woke again. The ranger took the light and looked down. It was still in place and her oxygen level was perfect. "This medicine is becoming less and less effective. I am going to have to increase the mix. I had this trouble with her last time and found that if Morgan or I slept beside her, she did much better. We do not have the luxury to do that this time."

They checked Marsha gave her more meds and suctioned her once again, then turned their attention to incubator mats. It took about two hours but they finally had it complete. "Let's try this out with Bitty first, then Marsha. It will be easier to extubate Bitty and keep her settled." They rolled Bitty onto her side and slid the mat under her, then hooked up the wire to the incubator. Jim sat on the pallet beside her.

He pulled up the projection screen. Its diagnostic capabilities revealed a few things they didn't know. Bitty had an eye injury and was nearly blind in her left eye. The computer advised it was regenerating the eye cornea. The next projection notified them that the radius was broken in her right arm. "Generating healing bone cells now." As those cells were being generated, it alerted, "Eye cornea cell generation complete and at 150% of the original eye cornea." Then it scanned her lungs. "Spore infestation in both lungs. Sterilization and elimination of spores. Regeneration of lung tissue commencing, approximate time 20 minutes to completion." It continued to scan. It stopped over the abdomen and reported, "Fertile cycle in 2.2 weeks." Jim glanced at Ranger Long and then at Aggie. She shook her head, acknowledging the importance of that information. No one said anything. The next report indicated that it was regenerating cartilage in the left knee. "Four minutes to regeneration and completion." It then alerted, "Uterus correction complete." They looked shocked. It then announced, "Knee cartilage repair complete." Five minutes later it reported,

"Lung sterilization and elimination of spores complete. Commence rest period of five hours. Patient to be intubated. Please administer the following drugs." Ranger Long wrote down what was required and retrieved the med gun to load it. Jim administered them to Bitty along with additional medication to induce sleep.

When they were finished, Jim discussed with Aggie the need for her to have a reproductive health talk with Bitty as soon as possible. Aggie acknowledged that she was probably already emitting a hormone that would alert the males that she was ready. "They will be pulling at her and attempting to impregnate her. We must keep that from happening," she said. "Bitty is far too young to have that happen to her right now."

Jim told Ranger Long he was ready to help Marsha. Ranger Long rolled her onto her left side so Jim could slide the mat under her, but Jim pulled it up to have her head scanned, as well. The medical projection screen started its diagnosis. "Cerebral clot pressing on the eye nerve and is a high probability for depletion of life." Jim pulled it up to the screen to ask for repair. The computer announced, "Clot elimination in process. Eye nerve repair in process." Seconds later it notified, "Potential imminent life-ending event. Brain aneurysm detected. Repair underway. Please turn up the ventilator and oxygen at this time." Jim immediately complied. He was soaked in sweat. "Left heart ventricle contains a hole. In the process of repair. The approximate time for completion is 9 minutes." That explained the arrhythmia. "Vagus nerve damage. Currently regenerating nerve. Time to completion is 15 minutes." It scanned down and stopped at the uterus. "Uterus beyond repair. Please remove expeditiously to prevent an internal bleed." Jim lowered his head. "Please leave the patient intubated until removal of the uterus is complete. Heart valve hole repair complete." Jim saw it rescanning. Voicebox repair from mucus and intubation is requiring both cell and arterial repair. The time to completion is

7 minutes. Please prepare for surgery. How-to guide is shown above."

The surgical tray was at Jim's side. He was sick with worry but knew he had to do this. The computer advised, "Aneurysm repair complete, clot illumination complete, vagus nerve repair complete. Please prepare for uterus removal." He looked at Ranger Long who told Jim there was no choice. She and Morgan had five children, three of those being his biological children. Jim hoped Marsha and Morgan would forgive him for this. He made the incision and proceeded to remove everything—her uterus, tubes, and eggs. Instead of disposing of the eggs, he asked Ranger Long for a storage container and then deposited them into the receptacle. It self-sealed and the projection screen instructed to place it in an incubator and provided the proper settings. Ranger Long did that while Jim closed and attempted to make the stitches small and close just like a plastic surgeon would do. They had completed the surgery. The computer instructed them to keep her intubated for an additional four hours, at which time a face mask oxygen dispenser would be sufficient. Jim admitted to Ranger Long that he did not realize she was not only knocking on death's door but had one leg actually inside.

"All right, it's Bev's turn and then Ranger Kopchek's." Jim looked around and pushed Marsha's table over to the wall. He pulled out a cot and had Ranger Long disinfect it. He then pulled the mat out from under Marsha and laid it on the cot. As he left to get Bev, Jim told him to move the cot into the middle where Marsha's table had been and to give Bitty another dose of medication.

Jim had Bev by the hand and guided her to the medical cubby. When they got to the door, she froze with fear and could not move or talk. Jim pulled back the curtain and asked Aggie if she could carry her in and lay her on the cot while holding the babies in the sling. She nodded and crossed to Bev. She easily picked her up and gently laid her down on top of the medial diagnostic pad. Aggie informed Jim that Bev was very warm. They pulled up the diagnostic projection device and it began its scan of her head and then worked its way down, stopping at the lungs. "Spore infestation. Beginning lung sterilization and elimination. Completion in 7 minutes. Vagus nerve inflamed. Repair with new nerves. Completion in 12 minutes. Uterus inflamed, embryonic sac in distress with potential delivery. Not yet at a viable gestational age. Please administer the following drugs. Generating a protective new embryonic sac. Embryo distressed. Please administer the following drugs directly into the 14-week gestation embryo. Once the abdomen is punctured, the needle will guide itself to the proper insertion site. Please mix all drugs into one delivery needle."

Ranger Long saw Jim's tears flowing and assured him that this would work. Jim resolutely mixed all the drugs as Aggie began softly humming "All is well with my soul." Ranger Long quietly said a prayer as Aggie continued to hum.

*God our future is in your hands today. In all matters, we have stored up the truths of your work in our hearts. We are prepared for whatever we are called to do. We realize that you can impact this event we are about to go through. Please help Jim and me through any uncertainty. We know that not all things in life are easy, but one thing we do know is that we won't be alone. Guide us please, Lord, in all we do today in the name of Jesus Christ our Lord and Savior. We pray this. Amen.*

Jim asked the computer if he could administer pain meds safely. The computer responded with the exact amount to give her. Jim followed the instructions given. She was asleep within one minute. Jim cleaned the site and inserted the needle. He felt the needle move from his hand and watched the medication being administered. He took the needle in his hand and removed it, then cleaned the site again as Ranger Long dressed the puncture wound. He stroked Bev's hair. He looked at the vitals of both her and the baby. They looked great. The computer scanned again and reported, "Burns on cornea. Repairing and completion in 3 minutes." Jim knew that Bev sustained this damage in the recent past when a misguided lab experiment created the Hornet Queen Hybrid, an evil creature who failed in her attempt to take over the Cuyahoga Valley National Park. This half-human, half-hornet planned to cause total devastation of the forest and a complete environmental disaster and attacked anyone who stood in her way, including Bev. Thankfully, her malicious plan was thwarted in time.

Jim asked the computer how long before they knew if the embryo would continue to develop. The computer responded, "It continues to grow and is currently on schedule to deliver at full term." Jim closed his eyes and thanked God for His mercy.

# Chapter Eleven

# BRUTALITY OF WAR

Morgan asked Tig about his species. He explained that he was a human hybrid that was mated with the Rasalhague species. Both were very similar to each other. Their species was all about balance, peace, and hope. He told Morgan he used to gaze at the bright stars above him at night and found hope in what he saw. "That hope has always been stronger than any fear I could imagine. I always run toward the stars every chance I have. The military gave me the opportunity to help others with the same mindset. Now, we help planets such as yours that find themselves, through no fault of their own, experiencing an extinction-level event. They do not yet have the technology to overcome the situation. The Galactic Federation has certain guidelines that, if met, allow us to intervene. So, here we are.

"The war against the microbial alien parasites that have irradiated themselves is proving to be more difficult than we anticipated. Your traitor, General Campbell, and his followers are protecting the alien parasites; however, the alien parasite Nightcrawlers are killing them, too. The treasonous military men are running to us for the acid and nuclear burns. It is rather interesting how this is turning out. We have provided many shelters for the people of Earth that are proving effective in protecting them. So far, that has been a very positive workaround for buying time to exterminate the Nightcrawlers. We have eliminated those on the African continent, Australia, New Zealand, Antarctica, the Philippines, South America, Central America, Mexico, most of the Caribbean, and all of Russia. We continue to have major infestations in the United States, American Samoa, Guam, Tonga, Canada, Japan, China, and the European Union. We are making considerable progress in Alaska, the Yellowstone area, and into Wisconsin, Iowa, and Upper Michigan. Most of the military traitors have been turning themselves over so as not to be killed by the Nightcrawlers. We are about 95% clear of these parasites. Yellowstone had considerable loss of animal life that we could not prevent because of your military. An additional cargo ship has been dispatched to begin cloning the bison, elk, and prairie dogs. They are nearly extinct. Only one wolf and one mountain lion remains. So, they are at the top of the list to clone. We also believe there is only one living Snalleygaster and one living Dogman. We are awaiting permission from the Government agency to clone both. The Dogman is really an alien from the Kraz. We are awaiting permission from that planet to proceed with cloning. We are unsure about the Skinwalkers' safety. They are also aliens operating on this planet illegally. So obtaining real numbers of fatalities is difficult."

Morgan was unsure what to make of all this information. He mustered the courage to ask about the Cuyahoga Valley National Park. Tig told him it was clear; however, there was considerable infestation in the Toledo and Detroit areas because of the Davis-Besse Nuclear Plant. Tig told him there was a 30-foot Nightcrawler in the Cuyahoga Valley National Park that they hit with an EMP and laser that killed the tree. The cleanup took two days. In addition, they went back a day ago to sweep the entire park for spores to eliminate. It is 100% free of any Nightcrawlers and has a protective shield over it, as does any area that has been cleaned and all Nightcrawlers exterminated. Morgan asked if he could be taken by shuttle to the cave in the park and if it would remain protected by the force field that would hold against the Nightcrawlers and U.S. treasonous troops. Tig assured him it would and that he would pilot the shuttle.

"They now have a trained physician who can run things for a short time. Let's go, get into your protective suit. Let's take supplies with us to help them until the mission is complete. It could take another week, maybe two."

Supplies were loaded as well as an extra forcefield so they could leave the cave door open with no fear of attack. They also took additional medical supplies in the event the babies had been born. They brought a medical support and projection mobile bed. As Morgan and Tig were in flight, Morgan told him about the Sasquatch and that some had taken refuge in the cave with the humans. Tig told Morgan they were also aliens that had been brought to the planet by the Anunnaki to mine gold and had been on the planet 100,000 years or more. Morgan remarked that he was not surprised. Many humans thought that way. They circled in the ship over the park for 15 minutes looking for any telltale stragglers. It looked clear. Morgan inquired if the military could track the ship. He told Morgan they had multiple cloaking devices engaged. He had Tig land in the gorge that surrounded the falls and which provided automatic protection from visible detection and tracking as it was surrounded by high cliffs.

Morgan knew they had to have heard the approach and landing inside the cave. He picked up his phone and called Jim. He answered. It was good to hear his voice. He advised Jim that he was outside with supplies and news. Jim was elated and ran to get Virg and Boc. As news spread, many of the community ran to the cave entrance to greet him. They watched as Boc and Virg pushed the door and saw the shuttlecraft and Morgan standing there. They ran to Morgan who gave hugs all around.

Jim approached Morgan who quickly asked, "Where, where is she?" Jim told him she was in the back of the cave in the medical area. He also informed him that he was the father of one boy and two girls. Morgan stood there, dumbfounded, and finally asked, "Three?" He stepped forward and asked Jim if they were alive. He smiled and said yes. Morgan ran past them and back to the medical cubby where Ranger Long was suctioning Marsha's trach. He began to cry and knelt beside her, then looked up at Ranger Long and back down at Marsha.

Jim walked in and said, "She is so much better now, but we nearly lost her several times."

Morgan wiped his eyes and told him they had lots of supplies and medical equipment. "Have Virg and Boc bring everything in. Let me see my babies."

He told him that Aggie had all three and was tending to them. Jim took him to Aggie's teepee. As they entered, Aggie pulled Liam out of the sling and handed him to Morgan. She said, "Your precious Liam."

Morgan gazed at him with such love. He looked at Jim and said, "He is so big. He must weigh eight pounds." Jim agreed. Aggie pulled Zoey out of the sling and handed her to Morgan. Jim took Liam. He smiled and called her his little Princess Zoey. Jim handed Liam back to Aggie and she returned him to the sling. Morgan looked at Aggie and asked her if she had another in the other sling. She pulled Caci out and she immediately began to cry.

"She has some lungs. A little wildcat." Jim told him that her name was Caci which means Brave. He cleared his throat and told Morgan she had bonded with Aggie and nurses non-stop.

"Her ability to stay latched is remarkable. It's like a locking mechanism. There is no letting go for her. Oh, you are a fighter. Yes, you are, and you have a loving, loyal personality. I like that in a woman. You will fit in with both tribes. You are our warrior princess." He gave her back to Aggie and she almost attacked her nipple, aggressively sucking. Morgan smiled and asked if that was painful. Aggie answered that all the young in her tribe nursed the same way as baby Caci. Morgan turned to Jim and asked how Dorothy-Alice and baby Morgan were doing. He told them both had a sort of bronchitis. Morgan told him they brought all kinds of medical supplies.

He turned and stepped in closer to Jim and had a tear in his eye. He asked just one word, "Marsha?"

"She is stable for the most part." Morgan listened as Jim relayed the series of events. He advised Jim that he brought a portable medical bed and wanted Marsha on it as soon as possible. He left the teepee and returned to the mouth of the cave where Tig, Virg, and Boc were unloading supplies from the shuttle. Morgan and Jim pitched in to help. They had just completed the unloading when Morgan looked at Jim with a frightened look.

"Bev?" Jim explained that they used the incubator bed mats that Blue left and were able to stabilize her. He related that most of the residents were sick with a bronchial-type of inflammation from continuous exposure to mold spores in the cave. That, along with the lack of fresh air, was causing a lung infection and that he needed advanced technology to cure them. He told Morgan that the open air was a godsend for their health. He also let Morgan know about Bitty's brush with death due to the spores and a severely broken arm.

Jim, Morgan, Tig, and Ranger Long stocked the supplies, triaged patients, and looked after the serious to critical patients they kept in the medical cubby. Marsha was still what they considered critical and decided to keep her intubated and sedated. They extubated Bitty but decided to keep her semi-sedated and in the unit. Bev absolutely had to stay on a medical bed. There was no other choice for her and the baby.

Ranger Kopchek came running with her service weapon drawn. Tig stepped in front of everyone and drew his weapon. She screamed that a blue-white light with a high screeching and scraping sound was getting louder—a Nightcrawler! Tig ran for the mouth of the cave and ordered them to seal it shut again. Now! He would take the ship and attempt to eliminate this predator. The shuttlecraft took off as Boc and Virg rolled the rock across the mouth of the cave and sealed it shut. The force field was still engaged. Tig communicated to Morgan through his biomechanical suit that they had been found out and that it was our military that were dropping trees to destroy the community. He radioed for troops and ships to be deployed to eliminate this alien and the traitors. Tig told them not to worry because they had a force field inside and out.

He instructed them to seal the cave with the spray they brought so as not to allow any nuclear particles from infiltrating the space. "Have Virg do it because he can reach every corner of the cave." He directed them to have all babies moved to the medical cubby and to turn on the extra force field within that space. Aggie and Kron should remain with them to nurse the babies. Virg sprayed every inch of the cave in less than an hour. They covered all water holes with the tarps. They moved the truck into the back of the cave and installed the tarps across the cave to put an additional barrier between them and the mouth of the cave. They put cots in the back of the utility truck and hung a tarp securely over the opening. Everyone not in the medical cubby felt better with extra protection.

Tig updated Morgan that he took out the military transport unit that was dropping the Nightcrawlers. He had not seen such evil in a very long time. He was now joined by other crafts that were vaporizing the trees and ground troops that were surrounding the cave. He advised, "In addition, a large medical cargo craft is coming through the atmosphere to pick up everyone in the cave. The troops will help move everything aboard and will take them less than 15 minutes. Everyone can jump on a medical bed and be rid of the spores in their lungs and whatever else they have. Get everyone ready. Ground troops are already stationed outside the cave. Shuttle crafts that are armed with deadly laser cannons are hovering above for protection. Get everyone ready. I can see the ship coming through right now. They should land in a minute or so. I will escort you back in space and will dock in the bay. Will be right in to help you guys again."

The ship was massive. The community residents hurried from their hiding places and into the ship for safety. It took 12 minutes to load everyone as well as some of the medical equipment, including the receptacle. The ship thrusters propelled the giant craft up into the sky as the U.S. military fired upon it. The shuttle crafts swooped in and destroyed the traitorous military craft and tanks.

Morgan, Jim, and Ranger Long settled the critically ill patients into medical projection beds and got the receptacle into the incubators. Bev was having difficulty maintaining a stable lung function, and Marsha appeared to be having the same issue. Everyone was placed on a medical projection bed and their lungs were cleaned and the mold spores eliminated. It was found that Aggie was pregnant. She was so happy.

Kron was diagnosed with a severe urinary tract infection, and the bed healed her. It also recommended hydration because her level showed that she was only at 54%. In addition, she had a broken rib. Jim could not understand why Kron did not come to him with her symptoms. He did not know how she broke a rib. He volunteered to start the IV on her and run a bolus of fluids.

Several of the community members on the ship were diagnosed with major issues. They had radiation burns, acid burns, and broken bones. One child had a T3 break and was in critical condition from that injury plus acid burns. There were three doctors in addition to Morgan and Jim, three physician assistants, and medics, Tig, Ranger Long, and Kron. Kron would stand next to the physician pointing out things the medical bed was missing. *With medical training, Kron would be unstoppable*, Morgan thought.

Morgan sat in between Marsha and Bev while Jim slept for a couple of hours. Marsha was still listed by the medical projection bed as critical. Bev was listed as stable. Aggie entered the Medical Care Bay. She still had the babies in the slings. Morgan jumped up thinking something was wrong with one of the babies. She told Morgan that she had begun to cough and had a fever. He had Ranger Long put all three babies together in an incubator to scan all three. Caci was screaming at the top of her lungs. He asked Aggie to lie down on one of the beds for a scan. Morgan pulled up the screen while another physician looked after the babies. Morgan told Aggie she was really sick. She had pneumonia. She would have to stay at least overnight to receive medicine and proper care. She would need oxygen therapy and hydration because she was only at 72%. With feeding five babies, she needed to be hydrated. Morgan cued in everything into the projection monitor. He got everything he needed to start an IV.

The physician advised Morgan that two of the babies had mold spores and had begun therapy to eradicate them and that the baby named Caci had begun teething. Morgan asked him to repeat what he just said, explaining that the baby was premature and was only two weeks old. The physician looked puzzled and went back and pulled up the incubator screen. As Morgan continued to work on Aggie, he could hear Caci screaming. Aggie started to get up, and Morgan pushed her back down. She shoved him away, and he flew against the wall. She pushed the other physician away and picked up Caci, nestling her in the sling where she latched onto her nipple with such ferocity the physician thought she would rip it off. He helped Morgan up and asked if he was hurt. He shook his head no. Aggie got back on the table and laid down with Caci in the sling. He decided to leave things as they were for now. The physician came back over and told him the incubators were programmed for the Blue species and had changed all three babies into a hybrid human and Blue, particularly Caci, who was almost entirely converted to the Blue species. He had never seen this before. Morgan asked what that meant for the babies. He told Morgan he did not know and would need more advanced research. He also pointed out the babies had been nursing with a different species, as well, and that Caci was displaying behaviors of Aggie's species. He did advise to not break the bond between Aggie and Caci at this point. He told Morgan that, going forward, all incubators would be programmed for the human species. He nodded in agreement.

Morgan continued to care for Aggie. He was able to start the IV and had the medical projection device induce sleep which would also have Caci sleep. Mogan pulled the sling down and looked at his warrior princess sleeping while still latched to Aggie. He decided to pull her away from Aggie's nipple to give it a rest. He pulled the sling back up over the baby after he unlatched her. He also upped the medication to make them sleep. The physician walked over to Morgan and told him now would be the time to put her in the incubator that was set for a Blue and help her sleep. The physician pulled her from the sling as she slept and carried her to the empty incubator and placed her on the mat. The projection screen popped up. He could see the physician pushing six or seven screens. He asked Morgan if he wanted to look in on the babies while he made a few adjustments for Aggie to accommodate her species. Morgan walked over to Liam. He thought he looked just like him when he was a baby. He was smiling as he slept. He then looked in on Zoey and she looked so peaceful and sweet. She was laying on her back. The more he looked at her, the more he thought she looked like Marsha. He went over to Caci and she was also on her back. The screen was still up. It showed the same reproductive composition and positioning as Ciril. He looked at her and, while she looked like Morgan, he could also see tints of blue in her hair. He wondered if the physician left the screen up on purpose so he could take that information in and process it by himself. He was sure that is exactly what he did. He appreciated his gesture for allowing this privacy. He asked, "Computer, is Caci human?" The display showed that her blood type was human. Her breathing function was that of a superior human swimming athlete. Her skin makeup was that of a human. The read-out ended there. He asked the computer to display the other makeups. The rest was the Blue species except for two other items. Both were Sasquatch—feeding and strength. *How will I explain this to a pediatrician? She already has five teeth in two weeks.* He asked if humans would be able to bond with her. The computer displayed yes. Morgan was relieved. He asked the computer to display the reproductive cycle. It showed it as monthly; however, its functionality was that of the Blue. Morgan stepped back. He was shocked and did not know how he would handle this, especially having gone through it with Ciril. He asked at what year she would first become fertile. The computer displayed, "Currently." *OMG, NO.* Morgan now knew what he did. The physician walked over to Morgan and told him he should find this out without another person trying to explain and that they would now attempt to reverse this. The physician was not sure if that was possible;

however, he was aware that Ciril was on the other cargo ship and wanted to bring her over to see if she had a suggestion.

Morgan looked at him and sternly said, "No. You can FaceTime her." The physician looked puzzled and told him he was unfamiliar with that technology. Morgan rephrased his request. "Is it possible to talk ship-to-ship in a visual format?"

"Of course."

"I do not want her to know this is my child, and I definitely do not want her here with my wife and family on board."

The physician nodded his head and said, "We will do it your way."

Morgan asked about Aggie continuing to nurse the babies. He told Morgan that was fine as she had plenty of milk for five babies. He advised Morgan to start talking to Aggie about Marsha and her loving the babies and that she could still hold them and love on them. It would be telling her in a nice way that Marsha was their mommy and would soon resume taking care of them. He told Morgan most in her species sleep 24 hours and up 48. He adjusted her medication to reflect the sleep cycle for 24 hours. However, after 18 hours they should reevaluate her vitals and her progress on elimination of mold spores. At that time, we make the call if she needs longer. Morgan then asked about nursing.

"The only issue will be with Caci. We can allow her to latch and nurse for one hour and then off for four hours. He suspected that the sleep setting would also affect her, and she may only be able to nurse for half that time. "If that is the case, we will just adjust Caci to sleep longer periods." The doctor excused himself so he could do more work on the reproductive system and how to reverse what had been done. He put his hand on Morgan's shoulder and said, "I am sure you have already considered this, as I have. She may need to have her reproduction system removed." Morgan nodded, acknowledging that he understood. He walked back to Marsha and sat next to her and cried. If it had to be removed, he would have to do an egg collection first and ask Tig to fertilize them. It would have to be done while they were here because they would not have the technology to do that on Earth. She would have to be told later that her sister was really her child. *OMG, please God in heaven do not let that happen.* The empath of the ship came by and put her hand on Morgan and began to sing:

*When peace like a river, attendeth my way,*

*When sorrows like sea billows roll;*

*Whatever my lot, Thou hast taught me to know*

*It is well, it is well, with my soul.*

She sang it through twice and then leaned over and sang it into Marsha's ear. She turned and left. Morgan thanked God for that wonderful confirmation and blessing.

Tig came running and turned on the news feed. It showed the ground forces had captured General Campbell trying to escape and the forces overtaking him and his upper-level troops. The entire world was rejoicing that this tyrannical monster had been stopped. They were leading him away when he reached into his coat pocket and popped something into his mouth and collapsed almost instantly. The other four men and one woman did the same thing at almost the same time. The ground troops called for immediate medical assistance. Because they were just engaged in a huge battle with the 20-30 foot Nightcrawlers, most medics were tied up. It took 15 minutes to get to them. They were pronounced dead at the scene. There were celebrations everywhere—Times Square, Dubai, Hong Kong, Las Vegas—millions of people celebrating.

The broadcaster interrupted with an official directive for everyone to return to their designated hiding places for the next 24 hours in order to complete the elimination process of all types of microbial alien parasites. "An all-clear will be given at the time it is safe. All acid clean-up, as well as nuclear clean-up, must occur. The projected time frame is 73 hours. Troops will be deployed to check on those displaying a red item affixed to the door or entrance to their safe place. All attempts will be made to provide for those who are in need of medical, food, communication with loved ones, or anything else needed while waiting for this quarantine period to end."

Morgan was so excited for the world but, more importantly, his world, his community. Marsha, Bev, Bitty, and Aggie should all be up and back to normal. They hopefully will have implemented a solution for Caci. They will face challenges raising these three children compared to Dorothy and Morgan. He couldn't wait for Marsha to wake so she could meet her babies. He reached for Marsha's hand and told her it would just be a little longer. He told her she was getting stronger every minute and began to sing to her. He didn't care how loud he was. He sang out.

*When peace like a river, attendeth my way,*

*When sorrows like sea billows roll;*

*Whatever my lot, Thou hast taught me to know*

*It is well, it is well, with my soul.*

*It is well, it is well,*

*With my soul, with my soul*

*It is well, it is well, with my soul.*

Soon those that could sang with Morgan. It was a touching scene. Soon after, a surge of burn victims came in and all doctors jumped into action including Morgan and Jim. They all practiced the same protocol to correct any damage to tissue, using the same meds which were pre-loaded into the med guns. It only took about an hour to see and address all issues of the 14 new patients. Six patients were admitted to the sprawling medical bay. Two of the patients were critical. As they were working on the six that needed more attention, a roar shook the bay. Morgan ran to Aggie. She was looking for Caci and had tried to stand, but the bed locked her in place. One of the physicians yelled to get her under control. Jim ran over to help quiet her and then got Caci and put her in the sling. Panicked, Morgan knew had to get Caci back in the incubator immediately. He dosed Aggie and looked at Jim, who told him to double it. He did and she and Caci were out almost instantly. Morgan returned the baby to the incubator, pulled up the display, and pressed the button to continue therapy. He asked Jim to keep an eye on Aggie to make sure she stayed asleep and secured to the bed. The other physician divulged that they had the capability to erect a force field around her bed so she would not endanger the other patients.

Most Earthlings had only heard tales of Bigfoot and were anxious to see one in person. Morgan asked the physician if they had some type of privacy device and explained that most humans had never seen this species before.

"Computer medical bay, provide a privacy barrier for table 8," the doctor requested. In a snap, the privacy barriers appeared around her bed.

Tig had taken to bottle feeding Caci for all but two feedings. It took him nearly an hour. Morgan took a mid-morning turn. He looked down at her as she fed and thought, *What a fierce warrior personality you have.* He hoped that the aggressive way she nursed would be the way she attacked her studies. Morgan laid her back in the incubator and looked in at the other two. They looked so peaceful as they slept. Jim noticed Morgan from a distance and came to stand by him to offer moral support. He put his arm on Morgan's shoulder and told him that they looked like little angels. Morgan smiled and shook his head yes. Jim told him he could not wait to meet his little angel.

Caci's incubator alarm went off and the project diagnostic screen came up. The other physician ran to the incubator, as did Jim and Morgan. The computer advised them that birth was imminent for fertilized eggs. Morgan said loudly, "FERTILIZED?" The physician asked if either had held her.

"Yes, once, but Tig had been feeding her all day." He shook his head and told them that was how it happened. She was pressed against him. We must remove her uterus immediately. He told Jim to get him a receptacle to deliver the eggs. He ran to the equipment bay and pulled a receptacle off the shelf and ran it to the incubator, handing it to the physician. He told Jim how to position her legs and placed the receptacle which automatically sealed to her. Caci cried as she delivered the eggs. There were only about 50 of them. The doctor directed Morgan to put them in the receptacle incubator. He was afraid for his baby. Jim pulled the surgical unit over to the incubator. Morgan was trying to work up the courage to go to her during this procedure. He approached as the surgical procedure went forward. It took less than 10 minutes to complete.

Jim finished the surgery while the physician turned to speak with Morgan. "You have 50 fertile viable eggs. Actually, it is 52 viable eggs. They can stay in stasis for 25 years." Morgan looked at him with tears in his eyes asking how it would work since they did not have that type of technology. He told Morgan they would accelerate one of the eggs to full gestation. It would take just three days. It would be Caci's, but she would be like a sister. With Caci having had a hysterectomy she could never have children of her own. This affords her a child. "The remainder will be put in stasis; and when Caci reaches maturation, we will bring the eggs for her to select from. You will have told her of these events by that time." Morgan agreed to the terms and asked for the egg to be expedited. If it is a boy child, we shall name him Tig after his father.

Jim assured him she would be okay, she was strong and would heal nicely. "She will accept this when the time comes. In the interim, you have another baby. Congrats. Can't wait to see Marsha's face when you tell her it's four babies." Jim lowered his head and laughed. "You now have a daycare center. You should apply for federal funding." They both laughed. "Well, Aggie should be awake in about five hours. You better have Caci in that sling and nursing prior to that time. She will rip this bay apart looking for her if she is not there where she can see and touch her."

Tig saw Jim and Morgan at the incubator and walked over to get an update on the babies. Jim looked at him and said, "Congratulations, you are a dad!" Tig looked surprised and shocked. It appears all the times you were feeding Caci, she was fertile; and, well, you have 52 fertilized eggs over there calling you dad!" Morgan thanked him for being so delicate in the way he made his announcement of Tig being a father. Tig was still standing there speechless. Morgan looked over to him and asked him if he was okay. Tig nodded, signaling he was okay. He apologized to Morgan, explaining that he had no idea this could happen to a newborn. He knew this was how the Blue species fertilized, but never had he known that a young infant could produce by just being held and fed.

It was time to wake Aggie. They put Caci in the sling, then pulled the projection monitor off the bed and released the restraints. It only took a minute for her to wake up. She immediately grabbed for Caci. Aggie sat up and then stood. She walked over to the other babies. No one stood in her way. In addition, no one spoke. They waited for her to ask questions. She stopped in front of Tig and told him he didn't know this would happen by feeding her and that Caci would be fine with what happened. She told Tig she looked forward to meeting his and Caci's child in the next few days.

Many gathered around the news screen. They watched the cleaning effort while they waited for the President of the United States to speak in the Rose Garden. Everyone looked forward to her remarks. It had been an awful three weeks. Over one million across the planet killed and another three million injured.

"Ladies and Gentleman, the president of the United States of America, President Charlotte Kennedy." She waved and stepped to the microphone.

"People of the United States and the world, I come to you today with a grateful heart. We have the Galactic Federation to thank for the gift of life. Life to all on this planet. True warriors of the Galactic Federation freed us from the microbial alien parasites that have now been irradiated by the catastrophically crippled nuclear power plants of Fukushima, Three Mile Island, and Chernobyl. The Galactic Federation knew that the future of the universe was in peril from this scourge on track to destroy this planet and then advance with the military traitors vying for supremacy throughout the universe. With time running out, several brave American citizens acted with the courage of a lion to save Earth from total annihilation. Their courage shines like the brightest stars In the heavens. It is a beacon of light amongst this darkness and despair. I see our future. We stand on the brink of the greatest leap of humanity. Their indomitable will and determination will spur others to strive for their own greatness in all that they do in order to raise society to the next level of mankind's effort to secure peace and unity in the farthest reaches of the universe. This herculean task will require immense strength in doing what needs to be done to rebuild our planet. As we restore our great nation, our hopes and prayers will guide future generations along a bright and illuminated path to reach for the stars, to learn, and to become not just an American citizen but a Galactic citizen. For now, our future is unwritten; but I have seen your potential. We can be luminaries for the world and beyond. My heart belongs to this nation and its people. We will write our story. Each day it will become clearer. I believe we find our way by choosing to walk forward together. Our resilience as a nation is unshakable. We stand shoulder to shoulder in this pivotal moment. Our hero, Dr. Morgan King, reminded me of the words of a beautiful hymn during our brief conversation, and I would like to close with this.

*When peace, like a river, attendeth my way,*

*When sorrows like sea billows roll;*

*Whatever my lot, Thou hast taught me to say,*

*It is well, it is well with my soul.*

*It is well with my soul,*

*It is well, it is well with my soul.*

# Chapter Twelve

# A NEW WAY FORWARD

Rebuilding was something that all Earthlings would be focused on for the next year, at least. Kron and Virg decided that they would stay on with the Galactic Federation. She would use her skills as a physician and Virg would become a structural engineer. They had a lot to learn but felt it was their calling. Kron was such a natural healer, and medicine came easy for her. She had obvious empathic qualities, as well as the ability to calm a patient down. Morgan thought their choice to stay on to further Kron's knowledge would be best for the both of them. In addition, both Jim and Morgan thought Virg had exceptional aptitude for building things and would be a loyal federation officer in the engineering department. Morgan met with them before he left the science cargo ship. He told them he would miss them terribly; however, after their four-year commitment with the Federation, he would expect them to return to the Cuyahoga Valley. By then, humanity would be working together with other species and aliens as part of the Federation.

After meeting with Kron and Virg, he left the meeting room and walked down the hall to his ready room. He was shocked when the airlock opened and found Ciril standing against the wall in the kitchen. She walked forward and took his hand, telling him how happy she was to see him, and asked if they could sit down and talk. Morgan sat across from her. He was searching for the right words to explain how he felt; however, he was struggling to tell her in a diplomatic way instead of lashing out angrily. He truly wasn't sure if it was just anger or if it was hate. Either one was not healthy, but he knew he had to come to terms and forgive her. They had been sitting for a few minutes and had not said anything to each other. Ciril spoke first by asking him to forgive her. She attempted to explain that once the fertile period occurs, she is no longer in control and the urge takes over her whole being. She looked into his eyes and could see the struggle between hate and forgiveness. She broke down in tears and buried her head in her arms on the kitchen table. Morgan realized she had read what was in his mind and left her to her thoughts for a few minutes. He walked to the kitchen counter and made tea for her and a hot vanilla latte for himself. He returned to the table and placed the mug of tea down in front of her and then sat, sipping his drink. Morgan finally spoke and told Ciril that his heart said to forgive but it was still a struggle for his head to fall in line with his heart. He touched her hand and she sat up. He smiled and told her to have the wonderful tea he made her. Ciril picked up the mug and took a sip. She told him it was perfect then smiled and thanked him. She told him he was a kind man and that Marsha was lucky to have found him. Morgan replied that they were lucky to have found each other and that they had five children to bring completeness and happiness to their lives.

Ciril glanced at him and said, "You mean six children to keep you busy and full of happiness." Shocked, Morgan asked if the child was ready. She told him that he would be ready and full-term later that day.

"How many children will be brought forth from this when all is said and done?"

"There will be 501. These children will provide a much-needed infusion of DNA into our civilization. In addition, what Tig and you left for the other females of our species will also help to give our people a fighting chance for survival."

Ciril asked if she could be there when he picked up the baby. He was quick to agree to her request. He confided in her his concerns of having to explain all of this to Caci when she was mature enough to handle it. It would be a tough day for the entire family. Sometime in the future, he wanted them to meet again so Caci could understand what other species go through. Morgan told her that his hope was for Caci to have an understanding heart like Ciril. That made her feel so much better. She thanked Morgan for his kindness and thoughtfulness in handling this situation. Ciril made one final statement before she stood to leave. She admitted that she was disappointed in having her uterus removed so that other attempts to assist her people would not happen in that fashion. She hoped other opportunities to help would arise. She revealed that she planned on raising one boy and one girl and that she would be hanging up her flight wings for the foreseeable future. Morgan told her how happy that made him feel. He knew she had so much to give, both in love and knowledge. She stood, smiled, and walked out of the room.

Morgan sat back down and finished his latte before they called for him to bring Marsha and the babies to their ready room. It would be at least 24 maybe 48 hours before any of the Earthlings on this ship could set foot on the planet. There was still a massive clean-up going on.

Jim was with Bev in the medical bay. They wanted her to remain there for another nine hours to assure the stability of her pregnancy. Aggie had just been in to see her with baby El. As she took her from the sling, they could see baby Caci on the other side, latched on as usual. El was happy to see her mom and Bev lovingly held her for an hour. Jim, however, could see she was tired. He thought to himself, *She will need help when they get home. She's not strong enough to take care of the farm and El while being pregnant.* Jim wondered how much of the farm had been destroyed during this disaster. He hoped not much. He wanted to shelter Bev from as much as possible with a delicate pregnancy hanging on by a thread. He asked Bev if he could hold El for just a while. She kissed her baby's forehead and Jim took her from Bev's arms. He kissed her as well and told her how loved she was and that she was the biggest blessing besides her mommy in his life. Bev smiled and could see the love between them. He sat down with her. She stared at him as he stroked her hair. She started to fuss and Aggie walked over and plucked her from Jim and put her in the sling to nurse. Jim laughed; however, Bev looked shocked. Aggie turned and left with both babies.

"It will be tough when she has to give up all the babies nursing from her."

Jim laughed and said they could always hire Aggie as a wet nurse. Bev shot him a withering look. Jim knew he was in hot water for saying that so he decided to change the subject.

"So, what are we going to name our new one cooking in your oven?"

Bev laughed, then rolled her eyes. "Well, I think one baby with your name is plenty. I kind of like the name Kit."

Jim asked if the middle name would be Carson.

Bev laughed. "Guess that is a no. Okay, how about the name Dallas."

Jim sat for a minute, clearly thinking about it. He looked at Bev and said, "I love it."

"Dallas it is."

Jim watched as Bev sat back in bed. She looked exhausted. He pulled up the projection screen to check the vitals of her and the baby. Everything looked good. He asked the projection for suggestions. It recommended an eight-hour sleep period and medication. The drug dispenser arrived almost instantaneously. Jim took the recommended medication and immediately injected Bev. He told her to get some rest and he would see her in the morning. No sooner had he gotten those words out when she was asleep. He asked the computer projection to provide audible updates throughout the night.

The medical bay was receiving a steady stream of acid burn patients coming in for treatment, nearly 15 an hour. So far, none were difficult cases and none had to spend more than an hour in the unit.

Jim ran into Kron and Virg while on his way to get some much-needed sleep. He congratulated them on their assignment within the Federation. He told them it was an incredible offer for them and their family. They said their good-byes as they were hurrying to board a shuttle to another ship and still had to pick up Mottice and Grissom. He shook both of their hands and wished them luck then continued on to his ready room.

The airlock to his room opened and he found Ciril waiting for him. He was surprised to see her and inquired how she got in. She held up a white security card. Jim laughed. He asked her what she needed. She stood looking at him, and Jim felt like she was staring straight into the depths of his soul. She stepped forward and asked him if he would consider taking a boy child that was created by her and Tig. She knew Bev and he would provide him with a loving and stable home environment, something he would never have in the regimented environment of their planet. The rest of the 501 children would be going; however, she was keeping a boy and a girl and Morgan and Marsha would be taking a male child. She wanted another of her children to go to a loving home, not a sterile, non-loving facility. Jim thoughtfully considered her request and said he would have to ask Bev. "Three babies all under the age of one year is a lot to ask."

She started to plead with him to take the little boy and was just short of begging. Jim asked what special gifts this child may have that would concern any parent. She revealed, "He could be an empath and have the ability to read minds. He would have greater strength than most humans. He will have a natural gift of math and science. Other than that, he will in every way look, talk, and act like a human child."

"Hope the kid likes sports, like football and baseball."

She laughed and said, "Of course! When will you let me know?"

"What would happen if we said no?"

"He would go to a facility, like a children's home. It is school all day, every day. No play, only study. No love, only structure and rigid mind lessons. Not a nice environment to promote love and a family unit."

"Will he be ready to go when they receive the all-clear that the planet is safe to return home?"

She told him he would be ready in eight hours. Jim asked if there were strings attached or if she would come back and get him when the whim hit her. She agreed that there would be no strings attached. She wanted at least two of her children to know what it means to love and to grow up with a family unit that loves each other. It was very important for her child to learn what true love is—how to receive it and, more importantly, how to give it.

"The highest honor would be for you to take a child of mine and accept him as your own and show him love beyond anything I have ever known."

Jim told her they would be in the medical bay later that evening to meet this little boy. At that time, they would decide if they could take him and provide the love he needed within their family.

It was just about time for Marsha to be brought out of sedation. As Morgan walked to the medical bay, he could not help but smile. He was so excited to talk to her. He didn't know what he would say first. Maybe oops, Marsha, you have four babies. I know you can handle it. Morgan entered and approached two physicians standing by the bed looking at the projection panels. He asked what they thought about the vitals and waking her up. Both agreed that she could be brought out of the medically-induced coma. It was hard for Morgan to stand and watch. He was so excited to hold her and tell her he loved her. They took it slowly in increments to make sure she tolerated each step. Finally, they pulled the breathing tube and decided to let her rest for a bit. The doctors told Morgan they would keep her at this step for an hour to make sure her oxygen levels maintained saturation.

Morgan sat next to the head of the bed and could not help but stare at her. She looked so peaceful. He checked her vitals, and she was doing great. He took her hand and put it to his cheek, then kissed it as he cried. Morgan longed to hold her and talk to her. He sat with Marsha for half an hour. The lead physician approached and looked over the panel projection display. He told Morgan she did very well and would wake her now. Morgan let go of her hand and the physician pushed all sorts of displays. His last step was to administer an injection. He removed the med gun from his lab coat pocket and injected her. He turned to Morgan and told him to call her name. Morgan took her hand again. It was hard for him to speak through his tears of joy. He called her name softly. He leaned in close to her face and called her name again.

She stirred and said, "Go away. I'm tired."

Morgan responded, "Okay, sleepyhead, time to get up. You have babies to feed." She opened her eyes and gazed at Morgan and both held each other as they cried.

Jim walked into the medical bay and saw that Bev was still asleep. Morgan and Marsha were embracing each other so he decided he would visit with them. As Jim approached, he exclaimed, "Marsha, about time you're awake!" Marsha looked up at him. Jim told Morgan to move over, he had the rest of his life to hug and kiss her. He sat down and gave her a hug. He told Marsha that he was so happy she was awake. She tried to speak but could only manage a whisper. Jim told her not to talk, her voice would come back once her vocal cords settled down. He informed her that the babies were doing fine, and good luck getting them away from Aggie and Bitty. As though perfectly timed, through the door came Aggie wearing two baby slings. Marsha struggled to sit up. Jim and Morgan helped her. Aggie approached the bedside and knelt down. She pulled Liam from the sling, and Morgan nestled him in her arms. Marsha began to cry. Aggie then pulled Zoey out and Morgan gently placed her in Marsha's arms, as well. She hugged and kissed them both. Aggie pulled Caci away from nursing her and Morgan took back Liam and laid Caci in her arms. She broke down crying again. Suddenly, the bed alarms began to ring loudly. She was experiencing an arrhythmia issue. Morgan and Jim took the babies and stepped aside as Marsha closed her eyes. They returned the babies to their slings and Aggie left. Jim walked over to the other side of the bed and stood with Morgan as the physicians continued to work on her. They put a device on her chest that readjusted her pacemaker. The medical bay projector directed that two additional medications be added to her protocol. They administered both drugs, and Marsha opened her eyes and immediately began to cry. Morgan sat beside her on the bed and pulled her to him. He held her while they both cried. Jim stood by and monitored the vitals. They looked fine. Jim was concerned about this arrhythmia situation. They would have to have help when they got back. Six children would be too much for her to handle. For now, Aggie could be there until they found someone that could help full-time.

Jim decided to leave them alone and walked over to Bev. The physician asked if he was ready to bring her out of sleep. Jim nodded his head yes. He pulled his medication gun and gave her an injection in her neck. Jim smiled and thanked him. He sat down on the bed beside her as Bev opened her eyes. When she saw Jim sitting next to her, she sat up and threw her arms around him, leaning in for a kiss. She had a big smile and asked how he was doing. He told her he was just fine and that the little one that was growing inside her was fine, as well.

Ciril walked in and approached them. Jim stood and introduced her to Bev. Bev looked confused. Ciril knelt beside the bed next to them. She began, "You and Jim are good people. You're kind, warm, compassionate, loving, and you know sacrifice. On my planet, children are raised in a sterile environment. You are never encouraged to embrace either kindness or love. I have a problem that I need you and Jim to consider. After spending time with humans, I have learned a bit about love and sacrifice. I cannot provide my baby with a stable upbringing. I want him to learn to love and experience the love of a family unit. I want him to have brothers and sisters. I want him to have both of you. Please give him a chance to escape the austere life he would have on my planet and, instead, have a happy future with you as his parents on your planet Earth. Please say you will take him as your own. Please!"

Bev had tears in her eyes as she looked at Jim and said, "Every child deserves love and a home, a mom and a dad. Yes, we will raise him as ours. Right, Jim?"

He laughed and said, "Exactly what I thought you would say. Yes. I want to go right now and see this little tiger."

Bev swung her feet on the side of the bed. Jim warned her, "Not so fast."

She pushed him aside and said, "I am going to see my new baby now with or without you."

Jim picked up Bev and said, "Then I'll carry you." Ciril thought that was very loving.

The incubators were in a separate room. He put her down when they reached the door. The lights came on and she could see the little one. Bev ran to the incubator and asked if he was allowed to come out for a visit. The physician in the room agreed. He reached in and handed the baby to her. Bev's heart was already swelling with love and excitement. She looked to Ciril and asked his name.

"I heard a human talk about beautiful birds. I would like it if you would name him Finch."

Jim laughed and said, "Perfect!"

Bev knew he was being sarcastic and said, "Finch it is." She gave the baby to Jim to hold. Finch had black hair like Jim, so people would automatically see him as Jim's and not an alien. While they were admiring their new baby, Ciril left. The physician approached and handed Jim an envelope containing the baby's paperwork and that he was signed over to their care.

Bev stroked Finch's head. "Your sister will love you. Guess what? You will be baby El's protector."

The physician told Jim and Bev he needed to remain overnight in the incubator to obtain full lung development. Jim gave the baby back to the physician, and they walked back to Bev's bed. As she settled down, she told Jim that she was very happy. She also jokingly remarked that she would be so much happier in Jim's ready room instead of a medical bay. Jim kissed her and said she could leave the medical unit tomorrow as long as her vitals remained stable. He pulled the blanket up and told her to get some rest as her heart rate was elevated and he wanted her to relax. He leaned over and gave her a kiss. The medical projection screen popped up and announced it was time for two injections. Jim told her he was going to leave. He told her to stay in bed and he would see her in the morning.

It was announced that the cleanup effort would be completed tomorrow afternoon. At that time they would be welcoming home the off-planet citizens once the all-clear was given. Everyone was excited and putting plans together to return home and back to some sort of normalcy. Morgan sought out Aggie and asked if it would be possible for her to spend a week or two at his house helping Marsha care for the six babies. Aggie happily agreed. He asked about her babies since Kron and Virg and their babies were staying with the Galactic Federation and told her he would immediately begin looking for a nurse to help her. Aggie told him that Beeze would take care of her babies while she helped out Marsha. Morgan also had to arrange for a cardiologist to care for Marsha and her pacemaker. He was nervous to see if his house had survived and if his lab had sustained any damage.

All those returning home were scheduled to depart at different times. Jim, Bev, El, and Finch were on a shuttlecraft that would land right on the farm. They were leaving in the afternoon. Morgan, Marsha, Dorothy, baby Morgan, Liam, Zoey, Caci, and Tig were leaving in the middle of the night so that Aggie could go with them and care for the children. Bitty would come by to help the following day as she wanted to spend one day with her father Cleg and the tribe first.

There was a lot to do. Marsha could not wait to see her father. She knew he would help with the children. There was so much yet to understand and determine what the toll on the planet would be. Everyone who was off-planet was looking forward to picking up the pieces and discovering how things now fit together.

The group from planet Earth had one last gathering in the medical bay. Everyone survived thanks to the intervention of Blue and their gracious medical hosts. They all hugged and thanked the leaders and the medical team. Kron's last request was for everyone to stand hand in hand, with Bev leading the way by singing her favorite song, one that clearly helped everyone through this deadly challenge. Bev started by telling everyone the story behind her favorite hymn, "It Is Well With My Soul."

"This incredible story of faith belongs to Horatio Gates Spafford (1828-1888). Much like Job, he placed his trust in God during his life's prosperity but also during its calamities. A devout Christian who had immersed himself in Scripture, many years of his life were joyous. He was a prominent Chicago lawyer whose business was thriving. Horatio owned several properties throughout the city. He and his beloved wife had four beautiful daughters and one son. Life was more than good—it was blessed. But faith, no matter how great, does not spare us from adversity. Just a few years later in 1873, Horatio decided to treat his wife and daughters to a much-needed escape from the turmoil. He sent them on a boat trip to Europe, with plans to join them after wrapping up some business in Chicago. Just a few days later, he received a dreadful telegram from his wife, 'Saved alone…' It bore the excruciating news that the family's ship had wrecked and all four of his daughters had perished. In 1873, Horatio was on his way to meet his heartbroken wife, passing over the same sea that had just claimed the lives of his children. It was then that he put his pen to paper and the timeless hymn was born."

Bev started singing, but by the third word, everyone sang.

*When peace, like a river, attendeth my way,*

*When sorrows, like a sea billows roll;*

*Whatever my lot, Thou hast taught me to say,*

*It is well, it is well with my soul.*


*Tho' Satan should buffet, tho' trials should come,*

*Let this blest assurance control,*

*That Christ hath regarded my helpless estate,*

*And hath shed His own blood for my soul.*


*My sin, oh, the bliss of this glorious thought!*

*My sin, not in part but in whole,*

*Is nailed to His cross and I bear it no more,*

*Praise the Lord, praise the Lord, oh, my soul.*

.  .  .

*And Lord, haste the day when the faith shall be sight,*

*The clouds be rolled back as a scroll,*

*The trump shall resound, and the Lord shall descend,*

*"Even so," it is well with my soul.*

As the song ended, Bev walked to the center of the circle and explained, "It's incredible to think such encouraging and uplifting words were born from the depths of such unimaginable sorrow. It's an example of truly inspiring faith and trust in the Lord. And it goes to show the power our God has to overcome even the darkest times of our earthly life. My prayer is that all of us know that it is well in your soul."

Beth Ann Roose was born in Northampton, Ohio. Her ancestors farmed what is now the Cuyahoga Valley National Park. Beth has an appreciation for the beauty and magic within the park boundaries. Her stories embraces much of the folk lore that is still told to this day. Beth takes a "flash" forward approach to her books. Drawing on universal themes, like good versus evil and family, Beth is developing  original content combining folk lore and fiction in her creative projects. In addition, she is an award winning animation writer and director. She continues to expand her creative base, with new avenues in Reality TV shows.

# ALSO BY BETH ROOSE

## FOREST GUARDIANS SERIES

*Forest Guardians Rider Of The Light*

*Forest Guardians And The Hornet Queen*

*Forest Guardians And Bath Masterson*

*Forest Guardians And A Matter Of Humanity*

*Forest Guardians And The Fire Maiden*

*Forest Guardians And Return of Bat Masterson*

*Forest Guardians And The Christmas Gift*

*Forest Guardians In The Fourth Dimension*

*Forest Guardians And The Peninsula Python*

*Forest Guardians And The Lost Child*

*Forest Guardians And The Olympian Women*

*Forest Guardians and The Blue Alien*

*Forest Guardians And The Scenic Railroad Incident.*

*Forest Guardians In Bitty Runs Away*

*Forest Guardians In The Marriage*

*Forest Guardians In Dogman*

## ELF SPARKLE SERIES

*Elf Sparkle And The Christmas Train*

*Elf Sparkle And The Christmas Ribbons*